OUTLAWS FROM AFAR

This Large Print Book carries the
Seal of Approval of N.A.V.H.

Outlaws from Afar

A WESTERN TRIO

Max Brand®

THORNDIKE PRESS
A part of Gale, Cengage Learning

Detroit • New York • San Francisco • New Haven, Conn • Waterville, Maine • London

GALE
CENGAGE Learning®

LIBRARY OF CONGRESS CATALOGING-IN-PUBLICATION DATA

Brand, Max, 1892-1944.
    [Novels. Selections]
    Outlaws from afar : a western trio / by Max Brand.
       pages ; cm. — (Thorndike Press large print western)
    ISBN-13: 978-1-4104-5675-5 (hardcover)
    ISBN-10: 1-4104-5675-7 (hardcover)
    1. Large type books. I. Brand, Max, 1892-1944. Law dodger of Windy
Creek. II. Title.
    PS3511.A87A6 2013
    813'.52—dc23   2012047552

Published in 2013 by arrangement with Golden West Literary Agency

Printed in the United States of America
1 2 3 4 5 6 7 17 16 15 14 13

CONTENTS

■ ■ ■ ■

THE LAW DODGER
OF WINDY CREEK

■ ■ ■ ■

Of the twenty-three short novels and four-teen serials published by Frederick Faust in 1932, all but two appeared in Street & Smith's *Western Story Magazine.* "The Law Dodger at Windy Creek" appeared in the September 24th issue under Faust's most common pseudonym, Max Brand. As in his popular novel, *Destry Rides Again* (Dodd, Mead, 1930) which first appeared as a magazine serial earlier that year entitled "Twelve Peers," this is a tale of revenge by a man, Sam Leader, wrongly accused of murder and sent to prison.

I

He stood out among the convicts of the road gang like a thoroughbred among mustangs, not through size but through quality. Like a flame, Leader drew the eye and held it. There was a harmony in his make-up, for he was big of brow but lean of cheek and jaw, while his body from heavy shoulders sloped away to a sinewy lightness of hips and legs. There was an unfailing harmony in his movements, also, as he swayed the twelve-pound sledge-hammer, and, in his manner, that dignity which seems to give a man possession of the world.

The other men in prison garb worked feebly, with many pauses in which they shrank from the sun, rubbing their shoulders on which the flakes of fire were continually descending. They seemed to shrink from the bigness of the country about them, rarely giving a glance toward the desert floor of the valley beneath them, or the walls of rocks, bright as metal, or the heads of the great mountains, brown and blue, all tremulous with heat.

Of that crew of prisoners, only Leader wore chains, but only Leader seemed free in spite of the irons. He worked eagerly, as though he were breaking ground in his own gold mine instead of breaking worthless rock to surface the road. He seemed to glory in his task, and each time he swung erect, his eye plucked something out of the landscape — a vein of snow in a distant ravine that glinted through the blue of distance, a mountain sheep on a pinnacle across the valley, or a hawk wheeling across the sky.

There were twenty of these prisoners in the hands of two guards; they had been out from the penitentiary for a week and they would continue on the road for another seven days until a new shift relieved them, and they were taken from the hot labor of the days and the long, quiet hours of the night back to the prison echoes and the prison smells. A mile away the chimney of the cook-house stove showed like a black crow above a shoulder of the mountain. A white feather of smoke fluttered on its head and made for the hungry convicts a sign of peace, a promise that would be fulfilled at sunset time.

10

Some of them were drilling the larger boulders, others broke up smaller fragments, and there was a sharp impact of hammers against stone or metal. This continuous noise died away when a rider came around the nearest corner of the road on a horse that stumbled among the roughage; only one hammer continued to *clang*, and that was the sledge that Leader handled, giving such blows that at every second or third stroke the iron cracked the hard stone or crunched through it. The rest of the gang gladly paused. Some of them leaned on their long-hafted sledges, others dropped the tools to sit down, letting their shoulders sag, while their hands fell beneath their knees. Yet Leader continued his toil while the assistant warden rode up and sprang to the ground.

He spoke to the guards first, glanced without interest at the progress of the work, and then shouted: "Leader, stop that damned noise!"

The ponderous sledge-hammer halted at the top of the swing. There it remained poised for a moment, rocking lightly in the hands of the convict before he lowered it and leaned on the handle.

"Any complaints, you men?" asked the assistant warden.

A gray-headed man spat on the ground, and then rubbed his hands together. "I only got one little favor to ask, sir," he said.

"Go on and ask it, then."

"I'd like to kill the cook."

The stiff lines of the assistant warden's face were bent and deformed by a smile. "I hope you do," he said. "I sampled his coffee the last time I was out here. Any other complaints?"

Eager words appeared in the eyes but not on the lips of the gang. The assistant warden regarded them with sardonic interest for a moment, then he stepped on and confronted Leader, measured his distance, and stepped farther back. To make up for this withdrawal, he planted his hands on his hips and scowled.

"Any complaints from you, Leader?" he asked.

One shoulder was shrugged, in answer.

"Go on and talk up," thundered the assistant warden. "I know the kind of poison that's stewing in you, day and night."

But Leader said nothing. His glance, calmly interested, wandered up and down the body of the assistant warden, stopped at his face, examined it in more detail, and then sought the mountains beyond. The assistant warden snarled like a dog.

"Dave, come here!" he called.

The head guard was instantly at hand, his rifle cradled under one arm.

"How's he been acting?" demanded the assistant warden.

"Him?" replied Dave. "Like a cross between a rattlesnake and a deaf mute. Never no sign of noise out of him, never no conversation. Always just like this."

"Solitary is what he needs," answered the assistant warden. "I always said so and I always was right. Solitary is what he needs and what he'd oughta get. It'd break this here silence strike of his."

"He's had plenty of it," answered Dave. "He's been and laid in the dark quite a spell in these three years."

"A three-year strike!" exploded the assistant warden. "That's what it is! And that's mutiny, ain't it? And what's good for mutiny? The whip! That's what. Newfangled ideas are what ruin a prison these days. Give me a whip and I'd make him talk, fast enough."

Dave shook his head. Slowly he lifted his glance up the body of the convict and dwelt on the lean face. He shook his head again. "No, the whip wouldn't make him talk."

"I'd cut him in two, then."

"Maybe, but that wouldn't make him talk.

All leather and bone. There ain't any nerves in him."

"Do his share of work?"

"All day long he never stops. He's more'n four men."

"If he gets a chance, he'll show you that he's six. Mind you, Dave, keep an eye on him day and night. Life's his sentence and dying wouldn't matter to him, if he just had a good, fair chance to lay his hands on a few of us, first."

"He'll have no chance," said Dave. "I keep a finger on his pulse." He tapped the trigger guard of his rifle with an agile forefinger as he spoke, then he went on with the assistant warden to note the progress of the work. Leader lifted up the hammer again and brought it down with all his might. It missed the boulder he had been hammering and beat with full force on the chain that stretched between his spraddled legs, knocking the iron links against another big rock. A faint *jingling* sound followed.

Without looking down, he knew what had happened. All during that week he had repeated the trick over and over again, half a dozen times a day. It was beautiful steel, as strong and hard as science could make it, but on the fourth day he had noticed a crack across one of the links. He had not hoped, however. After three years of silence and of prison, one learns to confine hope to the realm of daydreams. But now, on the very heels of the assistant warden's warning to Dave, the link had snapped under the extra force of that blow.

A sword went through his brain, a burning thrust of joy. After that, he began to plan. The twelve-pound sledge was as a conductor's baton, beating time to the music of his thoughts. Dave and the assistant warden were down the road; there was only that red-headed second guard to master. Then, he would take the man's rifle, spring on the assistant warden's horse, and send it pelting up the way. If he kept it close on the inside of the road, half a dozen jumps would bring it around the next shoulder of the mountain, and then he would be free.

Otherwise, there was the endless length of the life sentence to wear away, and he knew that he would never weaken, never take sickness of heart or body to shorten the term.

Hatred had fed and exercised him during three years since the day when he was accused of murdering Cleve Orping, an unarmed man. Only one mind had known the truth, only one pair of lips could have spoken it; his own mouth had been sealed ever since the jury had found him guilty.

15

Bill Orping could have spoken, but Bill had chosen to keep silence. Therefore, during the three years, in the chain gang, the solitary cell, the prison shops, or on the road, in silence the hatred of Leader had taken root more and more profoundly and grown until it filled the whole horizon of his spirit.

He hated the whole human race. Pretty Meg Hanson had sworn to love him forever, wait for him forever; now she was Bill Orping's wife. No friend had written to him after the first mute year, except for Joe Farnum. His companions in the prison feared him, banded together against him, lied about him to the trusties and the guards. In all the world only one human being looked upon him with sympathy, and against all, except one, he cherished an invincible malice. That one was Joe Farnum, bow-legged, good-natured, fat-sided Joe. He alone had been found faithful where the many had failed.

The sledge-hammer swung as before, in the same rhythm but with mightier blows. With every beat of it, his plan advanced a great stride in his mind. His eye flashed. A numbness came about his lips until he dreaded lest his whole scheme might be discovered in his face. As for the chain that

16

lay broken between his ankles, that was not likely to be noticed while he stood there plying the hammer.

The red-headed guard drew near. He was telling little Tom Wiley, the forger, a story of raccoon hunting in far off Louisiana. The ponderous sledge trembled in the grasp of Leader as the man and his rifle came within range of a stroke. Always Leader had told himself that if murder opened a way to freedom, he would not hesitate. Now, he chose the striking point — the sweat-stained band of the hat that was set jauntily on the head of the guard. Then he found that he could not strike.

Instead, he dropped the heavy tool and sprang in with his hands. As he leaped, Tom Wiley saw him. The mouth of Tom opened and he started to utter a screech over which his throat closed, allowing only a dull squawking sound to come out. That and the pointing of Wiley's hand made the guard whirl about.

It was as though he had planned the maneuver with the utmost nicety, so as to swing his jaw against the piston stroke of Leader's fist. The guard went down. Without stopping in his run, Leader scooped up the fallen rifle.

The horse was his goal. It was a bay with

dark points, a little too heavy in the shoulders and barrel, but with a promise of speed in the reach of the neck and the leanness of the hindquarters. It must be a good horse, or the assistant warden would not be riding it.

Now the flash and rattle of the chains as they flew up around the ankles of Leader, together with the headlong speed of his charge, made the gelding start back, then swerve to the side. Leader caught the pommel with one hand; the next leap of the bay helped to jerk him into the saddle. He fell on it, sprawling, struggling to right himself with all the awkwardness of a man climbing a high board fence.

While he fought to get in place, he noted all that was happening about him. The convicts had come to life, at last; they were running forward to get at him. From down the road came the frightened shout of Dave, then the bellow of the angered assistant warden, who was sprinting ahead with all speed, but Dave balanced the shining length of the rifle barrel at his shoulder, until it became only a bright point, focusing like the glance of an eye on Leader.

He knew what that meant, and with a convulsive twist he flattened his body along the length of the horse.

Then the convicts got at him. All who lent a hand would get good marks for exemplary behavior, privileges in the prison, and a chance at a shortened sentence — perhaps even a parole, for those who took a most active part in the brawl.

Jerry Cope, cattle thief, and Charley Boyd, in for manslaughter, jumped like fighting terriers for Leader's head. Into Boyd's fat, round face, he jabbed the butt of the rifle. The man reeled backward, like a swimmer moving both arms frantically in the air to regain his balance. Cope, with a stranglehold, tried to drag Leader from the saddle and half succeeded. That grip could not be plucked away. Leader found himself sagging toward the ground. His left leg slid off the cantle of the saddle. In a moment he would be down there on the rocks with the swarm settling on him and that meant a solitary cell for weeks, the choking dark, insanity horribly fingering at his brain.

He had to hold onto the mane of the bay gelding with his left hand; his right was encumbered by the unwieldy length of the rifle, but he managed to pull the gun back and send the butt of it *thudding* against the ribs of Cope. The man grunted, tightening his hold, snarling. Blindly Leader struck again and the cattle thief fell to the ground.

His body was twisted; he gasped and bit at the air to get back his breath.

Other hands were gripping Leader, but he managed to fling himself suddenly erect in the saddle. In both hands he swung the length of the rifle and those convicts ducked away from the circle that the gun made. The gelding jumped forward, but staggered in the next stride as Bill Leffingwell, the yegg, leaped up behind the saddle and gripped the body of Leader with both arms.

That was the end. That hold could not be loosened. But at the very instant those powerful arms bound Leader to helplessness, the rifle of Dave spoke. He had fired as soon as he had a clear target, and it was hardly his fault that Leffingwell dived suddenly between, got the bullet through his shoulder, and dropped with a screech.

The bay gelding went off at full gallop with Leader still drawn far back. It was hard to right himself while the horse gathered speed that threatened to tear him out of the saddle.

As he lay flat back, almost falling, a rifle bullet skimmed over him so closely that he felt its breath in his face. Then, managing to get a grip on the pommel, he pulled himself up. Another bullet sang over his shoulder; the bay rounded the next curve, and suddenly there were no more shots, the voices raved and gibbered faintly in the distance, and the thought of prison dwindled into a ghost.

II

No more shots were fired. Later on, he saw the convicts once or twice as they climbed to high spots to take note of his flight, but in a few minutes the bay gelding had carried him beyond the sound or the sight of danger. It was all around him still, as he knew, of course. It was sure to gather closer and he would move inside a smaller and a smaller horizon until at last the law caught him. The law always won. He had before him a year or two, at the most, of liberty. But he thought, as he looked about him, that there was no need of years; every minute, every heartbeat of freedom contained more joy than whole decades of prison misery.

He had two purposes of beautiful clarity. One was to find his friend, Joe Farnum. The other was to find Bill Orping, who with a few words of testimony could have established Leader's innocence at the trial. Perhaps he could force Orping to speak now, but that was not what the mind of

Leader dwelt on, for Orping had to die, and on the manner of his dying Leader had expended long and bitter and futile thoughts.

Orping would come later. The first thing for Leader was to find Joe Farnum. During three years his silence had endured in the prison. Words no longer even formed in his throat. And he vowed to himself that his first utterance should be for the ear of his friend. In the world of suspicion and hatreds in which he had endured for three years, the thought of Farnum gripped his heart-strings and wrung them until tears of affection stood in his eyes. Joe Farnum had become a sacred name.

From the rest of the world, Leader had died away and was as one buried, but Joe remembered, and once a month, during all this time, he had taken the trouble to write a long letter, full of news, full of chatter, full of sympathy and kindness. And the first spoken word from the throat of Leader would be for this man, and for no other.

That resolution did not seem childish to him. A sense of humor is not fostered by the penitentiary.

A scant hundred miles lay between Leader and the ranch of Ollard West near Windy Creek, where Farnum was working, but he did not strike out for the place at once. Instead, he aimed north through the mountains.

Ten miles from the start, he stuck up a cowpuncher who was coming down the trail and made the man change clothes. In the evening, he entered a little crossroads village and made the blacksmith file the ankle irons from his legs. The word went out and, while the file was screeching against the hard steel, the mountain men gathered. Some of them came into the blacksmith shop with their guns, but when they saw how Leader sat with the rifle across his lap and his head high, they merely shuffled here and there, muttered to one another, and stared. Some of them asked him questions, but his face remained uncomprehending, like stone.

When the irons fell away, Leader stood up and smiled at the future, for now, when he died, it would be with free limbs and in free clothes.

None of the villagers tried to stop him as he left the place, but this episode was dignified by the newspapers. He had not fired a shot during his struggle to escape or afterward, but he was termed desperado, man-killer, and gunman in the prints. He saw one of them a few days later. The same journal announced that Clinton Marny, that most famous of manhunters, had taken the trail. That announcement pleased Leader because it surrounded him with a new dignity. His trial for murder had passed with little notice; it was his escape that made him worthy of headlines.

The bay horse went lame in the mountains. By moonlight he roped a good chestnut mare, changed saddles, and went on. He was now doubly a horse thief, but that made little difference to a lifer.

In the dusk of the next evening he crashed against Marny for the first time. Three riders appeared suddenly before him, issuing from a grove of poplars as he journeyed through a mountain pass. He steadied his rifle and fired with care. He was shooting to kill, but the light was bad. He merely got one of the men through the hip and one through the shoulder. Marny he missed completely because the head of Marny's horse got in the path of the bullet. It fell, hurling Marny head over heels, and by the time the manhunter rose to his knees to resume the shooting, Leader was already a fading shape, well up the pass.

The fugitive felt that he had gone far enough in the northerly direction, by this time — far enough to throw pursuers off the trail for the time being. He counted the bullet holes that Marny's posse had left in his clothes, and then turned back south, traveling only by night. On the way, he entered a town in the darkness and found in the general merchandise store what he wanted — ammunition, a good Colt revolver, some underwear and a shirt, a pair of boots, an excellent Stetson.

He now had become, in the eyes of the law, a horse thief, burglar, and murderer. A newspaper that he found snagged on the barbs of a wire fence a few days later called him these names and many more. The whole range, it said, was quaking, wondering where the next blow would fall.

That same morning, from a promontory, he had his first view of Windy Creek. He was among some hills that thrust out from the higher mountains into the rolling lands of the valley. He had turned the mare loose to graze, and, sitting on a fallen tree, he smoked a cigarette while he glanced over the course of Windy Creek. Most of its length he had fished in his childhood. There was hardly a winding that did not speak to him with words and pictures out of the past, until the little river, with the golden brightness of the morning on it, ran into the town itself. He could not pick out houses, at this distance, but with only the slightest effort he could see the main street with its ruts and sun-cracked signs. The houses he could remember one by one, like so many faces, and each of these memories plucked at his heart as though he were in a foreign land.

When he looked away from the town of Windy Creek to the open country, he was still more at home. There were no new ranches. Little naked outlines no larger than the tip of a finger represented whole groups — houses, barns, and sheds, sometimes partially concealed by trees. He knew them all — the Miller place, the Ransom, Tucker, Grove, and Mendel outfits, but his eye went first and last to the woods that lay like scattering puffs of smoke around the ranch of Ollard West, for that was where he should find Joe Farnum.

That thought made him smile, and he was still smiling when he stretched himself in the shadow of a brush covert and fell asleep. When he awoke, it was sunset time. Through the clear fire and beauty of that hour he rode down into the valley, the mare worrying at her bit, dancing, shying at every pretext, for the long rest had freshened her. Sunset darkened into twilight. The trail became dim underfoot, and the eyes of Leader went up to the trembling stars.

Descending into the valley, it seemed to him he had gone straight back into the past. The faint odor of tarweed, the mournful lowing of a cow, the howl of a coyote on its way down some draw — these were all things that he had heard before, and had been intimate with. They spoke to him of this place, and this place spoke to him of them. Then a moon came up, a moon whose full circle was hammered in on one side. The light of it glinted on the wire fences like dew on spider webs. Out of the dimness trees appeared with flat black shadows beside them, and he saw the cattle bedded down in groups against rising ground. The sight of them gave him the old desire for the possession of herds, wealth that breathed and moved, that must be guarded from the dangers of heat and cold, watched against disease, guided to the choicest pasturing grounds. To such labor, Leader felt that he could give his whole energy, but there would be no opportunity for honest work. To dodge the law, that was to be his immediate task, and all his efforts were to that end.

He struck the main road to Windy Creek, turned off again on the lane that connected with the ranch of Ollard West, and so came through the trees near the big corral behind the barn. Beyond the barn, he could see the end of the bunkhouse; the ranch house itself was out of sight, buried in a dense grove. He had one glimpse of these details, then reined his horse suddenly back from view into the covert of the trees, for in the corral were a man, a woman, and two saddled horses. Not till he looked again, peering anxiously through the branches, did he make out that the man was Joe Farnum, a little chunkier in outline, moving with more of a waddle in his step. His whole heart went out to that rather absurd form.

Farnum, a girl, and moonlight! Leader chuckled softly. It was always that way; in the spring of every year Joe Farnum was certain to fall violently in love. This girl was hardly more than twenty. The brim of her hat kept her face in shadow, but she was slim and trim and handled herself like a boy. Considering the time and the place, there was hardly a doubt that she was that same bit of freckles and impudence who Leader had known in the old days as Muriel West.

Of the two horses, one stood patiently by, secured by the mere throwing of the reins, but the other was blindfolded and pulled up to the snubbing post in the center of the corral. It crouched a little, switched its tail impatiently, and steadily leaned its weight back against the head rope. Patently it was

28

about to be ridden, and, strange to say, the girl was to make the attempt. As Sam Leader attended, with an earnestness that made all other sounds draw afar and vanish, he plainly heard Farnum say: "You can ride the mare, Muriel, only I ought to take the edge off her first. Lemme have a whirl at her and then. . . ."

The girl made a gesture with her quirt, at which the mare shrank closer to the earth and looked more than ever like a black panther crouching, slender, beautiful, and dangerous.

"The whole idea is for me to take my chance with her . . . my whole chance," said Muriel West. "After I learn her tricks, I'll show Dad in broad daylight. There isn't much time left, either. A dealer came out here yesterday to look her over. You know what Dad says . . . that she's a man-eater and that he won't have her on the place."

"He's right!" declared Farnum. "That mare has savaged three gents already, and one of 'em is a dead man now. What's eating you about her? You gotta have her just because she's pretty?"

She threw back her head, so that Leader saw the moonlight slip over nose and mouth and chin. She had been pretty in the old days; the three years had given her a definite

29

loveliness.

"Dad has always broken his heart because he has no son," said the girl. "And I want to show him that I can do something that a man, even, would be proud of."

The big hat and the big head of Joe Farnum wagged from side to side. "Suppose that something happens to you?" he suggested.

"We've been all through that. You've promised me, Joe. And that's what's fine about you. Your word is as good as gold."

She went up close to Farnum and laid a hand on his arm. It appeared to Leader that he could see Joe Farnum waver, before he answered: "I'm bein' a fool . . . but I'll stick by what I promised you. Are you ready?"

"I'm ready."

She put her foot in the stirrup and swung into the saddle, with the reins firmly gathered. Farnum mounted the second mustang, gave the head rope of the mare a running hitch around the snubbing post, and then moved off a little distance and halted.

"All set, Muriel?" he called.

"All set!" she answered.

"Jerk off the headstall, then."

It was done. As the eyes of the mare were uncovered, Farnum with a snap of the rope freed it from the snubbing post. The mare shuddered so violently that the moonlight flickered on her polished flank, then she hurled herself into the air.

She came down like a rubber ball, to bounce still higher. The hat, snapping from the head of Muriel West, sailed off over the corral fence; at the same instant a flood of blonde hair flung out on the wind, with the moon gleaming through it.

Around the corral the mare fought her way, dancing, dodging, plunging like a bird that shifts and turns in the air when a hawk is stooping at it from above. Every instant Leader watched to see the rider unseated. She lost a stirrup, regained it. She was hurled forward until the pommel seemed to have been driven through her body. Her head snapped back and forth. But still she kept her place.

The forty-foot rope whose end was in the hands of Joe Farnum undoubtedly helped to save her, for Farnum laid his weight against it time and again at just the moment to stagger the fighting mare, but still there was infinite credit due to the girl herself. If she wanted to prove that she had the fighting spirit of a man, she was proving it now. She was taking a beating, but she took it with set jaw and no outcry. Admiration leaped up in the stern heart of Leader.

Then came the decisive moment. The mare, suddenly whirling about, drove with her full strength against the rope and snatched it from the hands of Farnum. Leader groaned. There was the black mare, freed from all restraint except the slight strength of Muriel West tugging at the reins. What had Joe been thinking of not to secure the rope end with a hitch around the pommel of his saddle?

Inside that corral fence was captivity and pain; beyond the fence lay the wide lands of freedom, and the mare bolted straight for the bars. She rose like a bird. The snaky shadow of the rope flung up against the moonlit sky; the heels of the mare *clicked* lightly against the top rail, and well away she landed in her stride.

Joe Farnum had urged his own mount in pursuit. It refused the jump; Farnum, unseated by the sudden halt, rolled on the ground and came up with a revolver in his hand. But how could he risk a shot at the dodging, veering, leaping form of the mare? He could only slide between the corral bars and run in desperate, useless pursuit.

There was another factor now — Sam Leader had brought his chestnut out of the woods at full gallop. He was soon close, for the black mare was giving more attention to bucking than to flight. Muriel West had lost both stirrups and a plunge to the side half unseated her, as Leader came up. The end of the rope dragged on the ground, twitching, squirming, elusive as a trout in shadowy waters.

One heel hooked on the cantle of the saddle, one hand gripping reins and mane at once, Leader swung low until he could brush the ground. The tips of his fingers touched the rope, lost it, and caught again at a flying film of shadow and secured the lariat in a powerful grip. He clutched it desperately.

As he righted himself in the saddle, he saw the girl shoot sideways, spread-eagle in the air, saw her land in a spinning roll, saw the black mare wheel and lunge for the victim like a tiger with open mouth.

The rope end was already hitched over the horn of Leader's saddle. Now he gave to his chestnut that sign with jerk of reins and sway of body that makes a trained cow pony sit down against a pull, and the horse obeyed. That was why the black mare, coming to the end of her tether, snapped suddenly into the air and spanked the ground with her full length.

Joe Farnum, coming up at full speed, reeling with effort, would take care of the motionless body of the girl; for Leader there was nothing in mind but the savage black beauty that now began to rear herself from the ground.

If she had been a tiger when she charged at the girl, Leader was a tiger in turn as he flung himself from his saddle and onto the back of the other mare. Like a tiger he rode her. The keen rowels of his spurs raked her flanks like claws and roused her from the daze of her fall. The blows of his quirt tortured shoulders, neck, and breast. She fought back for five desperate minutes. After that, as a beaten horse will do, she let her head come up, and surrendered to the strong hand upon the reins. Then she came trotting back, humbly, toward Joe Farnum and Muriel West, who was standing beside him, apparently unhurt.

III

The wind flared the brim of his hat, as he came on, and Muriel West, already on her feet and steadied by the hands of Joe Farnum, cried out: "It's Sam Leader!"

The effect upon Joe Farnum was stranger than words. He actually recoiled and reached as if for a gun. Even Joe Farnum, then, had imbibed too deeply of the newspaper doctrines and reports, building the figure of his friend into a dragon.

It was a profound shock to Leader. He flung himself from the horse, keeping the lead rope in one hand while he extended the other toward Farnum, and cried out: "Joe, what's the matter?"

Farnum recovered himself with a groan and grasped that proffered hand. "I couldn't somehow believe what I seen. The name of you was a shock, though I might've known that nobody but you could teach a horse manners as fast as that. I can't believe it's you, still. You're off there in the prison . . . off there in hell . . . no, you've got loose from there, and you're away up north in the mountains. Sam, I'm kinda stunned, seeing you sudden like this." He poured out the words in a faltering way, still wringing the hand of Leader, still watching him with haunted eyes.

"I almost thought for a minute," Leader said slowly, "that you were making a pass at a gun. And for three years you've been the one thing in the world that I could hitch to and call a friend. Joe, I'm so glad to see you."

He stood close to Farnum and, with a grim affection on his face, he studied the smaller man. A tremor was shaking Farnum in the meantime. His head jerked with the pulse of his blood, and his eyes kept blinking as though he were confronting a miracle.

Leader turned suddenly to the girl. "Get into that saddle," he directed. "Take the little black devil right now, before your nerve's gone."

Without a word, she stepped to the mare and gathered the reins.

"Wait a minute!" exclaimed Farnum. "You're still groggy, Muriel." He began to pant as he talked, as a man does when he argues a lost cause. "Didn't you see the way she was slammed on the ground, Sam? Muriel, she'll throw you and savage you the next time."

"Steady, Joe," interrupted Leader. "She's not an old woman. She's a flash." Turning to the girl, he added: "If you let the idea go cold on you, you'll never be able to sit out that mare. Get into the saddle. Fork that horse and ride her!"

She turned her head toward him for an instant, trying to smile, but it was merely a flash of teeth, and he saw that the pallor of her face was due not altogether to the moonlight. She gave Leader a nod, however, and was instantly in the saddle. Farnum groaned.

The black mare cocked her head. This

feather in the saddle was different from the weight of Leader; her sides were not crushed by the grip of Leader's sinewy legs. For one instant she juggled the bit in her mouth, while Leader deliberately undid the lead rope and turned her loose.

Instantly she skyrocketed. The moonlight flashed on her snapping, dodging body as on a sword. Back and forth she fought, with head stretched out low, back humping. The foam that flew from her mouth gleamed in the moonlight, and the girl was hurled up and down, then from side to side, like a ball in the hand of a juggler.

Joe Farnum began to cry out. He followed the bucking mare with arms stretched wide, as though he were trying to catch the pair. He danced and dodged. One might have thought that he was trying to imitate the antics of the mare. But Sam Leader remained calmly poised, with his arms folded, watching the battle. He knew that he had taken the edge off the mare's devilishness and half broken her spirit.

The girl lost both stirrups early, regained one, lost it, was battered back and forth, but always kept up the contest with a brave face. Sometimes she seemed to Leader like a gloriously gallant creature fit to be a queen over men; sometimes she seemed to him

37

like a small child, tormented for no purpose.

The mare stopped suddenly, as she had with Leader, and stood for a moment with fallen head. The quirt swung, struck against her wet flank, and she was forced to canter in a small circle until the girl stopped her in front of Leader.

Joe Farnum was already beside her, catching at the reins, begging her to get down. "That black devil, she almost had you. She'll kill you one day, Muriel!" he cried. "Look! You're bleeding at the nose!"

She merely laughed, as she slipped to the ground. She was dabbing at her face with a handkerchief while she confronted Leader. Suddenly he saw that she was waiting like a child for commendation or criticism.

"That was a good show," he said. "The nerve is more than the knowing, when it comes to handling a horse. Are you pretty groggy?"

"I'm a little dizzy, that's all."

"You'd better go back to the house. You'll never have any trouble with the mare again."

Joe Farnum bustled in between them and took her arm. "That's right. You go back to the house," urged Joe. "This is a fool business. Couple or three times I thought you were a goner. Look at your blouse . . . all torn to pieces. Your father's going to blame me for this. Come along, Muriel."

She seemed to brush him aside with a gesture. "Will you let me stay a minute more, Sam?" she pleaded. "I want to hear about things. I won't chatter and gossip about it."

"You've seen me here," he answered. "If you say a word, you can bring the whole pack down on my head. I've got to trust you, whether I want to or not." He was sorry, in a way, for the bluntness of these crisp sentences.

She pointed to the black mare. "You stopped Nelly when she was about to put all four feet in my face," said the girl. "That's why you can trust me. I'm not just a curious little fool, Sam. I want to know if I can help."

"Help?" exclaimed Joe Farnum, who was moving uneasily and helplessly on the outer verge of this conversation. "How could you help him?"

"The only hard cash he has is a Colt," she answered. "And I've got some money."

"Twenty or thirty bucks is no good to him," broke in Farnum.

"I've got more than three thousand in the bank. My mother left it to me," she replied. "Sam, you must get out of the country. If you have to pay your way with a gun, you'll be marking out your trail for Marny and the rest to follow. I can give you enough to help you along."

"Three thousand?" muttered Farnum. "Great Scott!"

All the taut nerves in the soul and heart of Leader, which for three years had been tuned higher and tighter, suddenly loosened. A weakness that was like melancholy spread through him.

"I'd take your offer," he said. The quality of his voice had changed. "I'd take it in a minute, but I'm not leaving the country right away. There's a job for me to do before I get out."

She threw back her head so suddenly that the moonlight flashed and rippled over her hair. "You mean Bill Orping," she asked. "Isn't that it?"

He felt the shock of her question as it spread tinglingly through his mind. One feels like that when a fortune-teller probes close to the truth. "What makes you think that?" he asked.

"You swore that you didn't kill Cleve Orping. If that's true, then you could have been cleared if Bill Orping had told what he knew. Bill wouldn't speak to save you. Now you want to murder him."

She set off the word murder by itself; she

spoke it with a low emphasis that took the breath of Leader.

"Suppose that you guessed right, it wouldn't be murder," he argued. "It would be justice."

"Murder," she repeated.

"I wouldn't shoot him in the back. Bill used to be a good hand with a gun."

"If he had ten men around him," answered the girl with a calm conviction, "you could walk through them and get at him. You could kill him with your bare hands."

He raised those hands a little and looked down at them. Labor had built and polished the callous places that covered them.

"You'd better send word to Bill Orping that I'm looking for him, then," he suggested grimly.

"You know that I'll never speak against you," protested the girl. "But if you go after him, it will be horrible . . . a greyhound against a rabbit."

"I ought to leave it to the law, eh?" he asked, and laughed a little through his teeth. Anger darkened his eyes.

"Yes, to the law," she replied.

"The law," he repeated, and laughed again. "You'd better go on to the house."

"Good bye," she said, and held out her hand. It was as though she never expected to see him again.

He took the hand. Her fingers closed over his for a moment while she searched his soul. The torn, dusty clothes of the girl, the sheen of blonde hair, which the wind was tangling behind her head, disappeared for Leader. Only her face remained with the profound pity and trouble in her eyes.

Then she left them. She went rapidly to the corner of the corral fence, where she put a hand on the post, looked back for an instant, and then was gone from sight.

"Whacha think of her?" broke in the voice of Joe Farnum.

An imp of the perverse made Leader answer. "She's one of those sassy youngsters, full of herself," he said.

"That what you think about her?" Joe Farnum sighed, with an obvious relief. "I thought you were kind of sold on her, for a minute, the way you looked at her, but nobody ever could read your mind."

"Orping has the old Carter place, hasn't he?" demanded Leader.

"Yes. She's pretty, though, don't you think, Sam? Muriel, I mean."

"Pretty? She's beautiful! Just to see her is better than to do a fine thing . . . you can carry the thought longer, and it does you more good. Bill is at the Carter place, eh?

Well, I'm going there."

Joe Farnum had fallen into deep thought, as he stared at his friend. "Better than to do a fine thing?" he murmured. "You mean . . . ?" He added aloud: "Wait a minute. At the Carter place? I don't know. I think he was going to town, tonight."

"Where in town?"

"You want to get him, Sam? Is that it?"

"Yes. I'm going to get him."

"I don't blame you. Hold on."

"I'll do it alone. I don't want you to get into this trouble."

"I know you don't," replied Joe. "I'll tell you what. Wait till I've had a chance to spot Bill. Tomorrow night will be time enough. That's it. I'll spot him down for you."

"Will you do that?"

"I'll do it."

"Joe," said Leader, "I can put myself in your hands. I can trust you, and that means more than all the rest of the world to me."

"Sure you can trust me," muttered Farnum. "You're hungry, Sam, I guess?"

"Like a wolf."

"Yes, you're like a wolf," said Joe Farnum, half to himself. "Come along. I'm going to find you a hand-out."

He led the way toward the house, but, although his head was hanging, he stumbled

43

as though he were not seeing the ground over which he walked. Leader felt that it was excess of happiness that overwhelmed the smaller man and made him blind and dumb.

IV

They did not sit up long after Leader finished the meal that Farnum procured from the cook's pantry. As Joe pointed out, he would have a busy day coming, if he were to do his work on the ranch and then ride out to find Bill Orping on the following evening. In fact, Farnum seemed sunk in a sort of stupor and apparently took no interest in anything said to him.

Leader had his own explanation for that. "You're eating your heart out worrying about me, Joe," he said. "But that's all wrong. Don't worry. Whatever comes, I'm ready for it. Five minutes of sitting here with you and hearing the frogs sing down in the pond and the cows bellowing on the hills is better than a hundred years of hell back there in the prison. Whatever comes, it'll be better for me than that. Of that I'm very sure."

Farnum showed him to a safe place. This was in the middle of a grove that topped some high ground north of the barn. There was a natural clearing inside the circle of the trees where the chestnut mare could graze and, wrapped in a pair of old blankets that Farnum had brought from the bunkhouse, Leader closed his eyes, forgot danger because of his nearness to his friend, and slept.

He awoke in the dawn, turned, and slept again. The labor of the long flight had left in him the dregs of a thousand wearinesses. Little by little, these left him. He roused again at noon, led the mare down the slope of the hill, and watered her at a runlet that widened between two rocks into a small pool.

When she had finished drinking and the face of the tiny pond was still again, he regarded his reflection with curiosity. In the three years, he had hardly glanced into a mirror, but now he touched with his fingertips the new modeling wrought by time and pain. He had been a handsome fellow and he had known it; he was a grim sight now, and he felt this the more because he could draw so clearly from his memory the girl of the night before, with the moonlight in her hair and in her eyes. A fire had burned him, and all that remained was hard metal. As for the foolish thoughts that had gone

45

dreaming through his mind, he must put them aside.

That was what he did. Deliberately, as one shifts a burden, he picked the dream and the yearning from his heart and thrust it away. The mare drank again. He led her back to the clearing, saw her begin to graze contentedly again, and once more fell asleep on his blankets. When he awoke, it was because of footfalls coming near, and, as he sat up, he saw the chunky form of Joe Farnum, with Muriel West beside him, coming through the trees.

It was nearly sunset. Where the light slipped through the foliage, it covered the trunks with gold and the leaves with fire. The chestnut mare, thoroughly rested, filled with new strength, arched her neck and tail and whinnied a soft warning as Leader got up to meet the two.

Joe was waving and nodding and laughing a greeting, but the girl came up with a somber face. She said not a word by way of greeting, but pulled out a wallet and laid the mouth of it open over a thick wad of greenbacks.

"Take that!" she commanded.

He took the wallet. Because of the quantity of money inside, he held it awkwardly in both hands.

"What's this for?" he asked her.

"Traveling expenses," she answered. "It's a loan to take you where you'll have another chance."

A puff of wind curled the wide collar of her blouse against a throat as brown as her face, and her face was as brown as her small, strong hands. She had been lovely by moonlight, but that was the beauty of a mere drawing, and this was the painting in full color.

He pressed his thumbs down on the wallet and felt the sheaf of money. "Suppose your father wants to know what became of this money?" he asked.

"I don't care. I know what I'm going to do."

Leader looked at Farnum. "You shouldn't have brought her here," he complained.

"How could I keep from telling her?" argued Farnum. "You don't know, Sam. She always has her way." Joe Farnum was standing a little to the side, so that he could look from one of them to the other, and there was trouble in his face.

"Look," said Leader, holding up the wallet. "This is the sort of thing that I might have dreamed about . . . and I could go on dreaming and sort of hear you say that the reason you're giving the money is because

47

you have a lot of interest in me, and faith in me, and all that. Can you go on and say those things?"

Her mouth and eyes were half grave, half smiling. "I can say all those things," she answered.

"I'll step out and take a look at the dog-gone' sunset," said the coldly restrained voice of Joe Farnum.

They paid no heed to him, and he did not move.

"I know," said the girl, "that you can be the salt of the earth if you try, or else you could be a cruel devil."

"Go on." Leader nodded.

"You've had a hard time. And you think you'll never be able to forget it or forgive other people. But you will, once you can find a chance at happiness."

"Give me your hand," said Leader. He took it, placed the wallet inside the fingers, closed them over it. "I have one job to do," he said, "and you'd call it murder. I can't use your money."

"You'll do what she wants you to do. She's the world champion persuader," said Joe Farnum dryly.

But she was shaking her head. "I won't persuade. I know that I can't," she told Leader. "And I knew that I wouldn't win out, when I came to see you. Only . . . I had to try. God help you, Sam."

"You better stop her," said Joe Farnum as she turned hurriedly away through the trees. "I can see the way it is. About two words out of you, and she'll be inside of your arms, Sam."

Leader held up a hand and with it pushed the suggestion away. He stared until she was gone, then he wheeled on Farnum. "I'm hungry, Joe," he said.

"I've got some chuck for you." He unslung a saddlebag that he was carrying over one shoulder.

"Any news, Joe?"

"Yeah, plenty of news, too." He talked, while Leader sat cross-legged on the ground and ate with a vast appetite. He had spotted the movements of Bill Orping this day, and had learned where he would be for several days to come. Orping would be at home, that night. The next morning, he would leave in the dark and ride for the rodeo at Clearwater, across the mountains. Bill would take a hand in the trick shooting contest; he had won many a prize before this at such competitions. Tonight, therefore, it was very likely that he would go to bed early. Probably he would be found in his bed not very long after dark.

Leader had finished eating and had saddled the mare before all of that tale was ended.

"I'm going with you," suggested Farnum in a half whisper.

Leader put both hands upon the shoulders of his friend. "D'you think that I'd let you ride into trouble on account of me, Joe?" he asked.

"It's my right," urged Farnum. "My place is with you, Sam, if friendship's got any meaning."

"You've spotted the wolf for me . . . I'll do the hunting," replied Leader. "And there's the girl, Joe."

"What about her?" asked Farnum, his forehead wrinkling with pain.

"You like her?"

"She's all right."

"You love her, Joe. Isn't that the straight of it?"

"A mug like me, what chance have I got?" asked Farnum. "I'm not a fool, Sam."

"Wait a minute. You think that she's sort of taken with the convict, the refugee, with me, Joe?"

"I've got eyes in my head. I use 'em. That's all," muttered Farnum.

"Listen to me, Joe," said Leader slowly. "If she were my right hand and my right arm, I'd cut her away from me, if I thought you wanted her. If she were the queen of the world, I'd lock her out of my life, old boy, rather than bother you. D'you believe me?"

A frightful struggle then twisted the face of Joe Farnum. "You mean that," he groaned. "You're trying to mean it, anyway."

Leader was already in the saddle. "I mean it," he insisted. "I'm going now. Wish me luck with that coyote, Joe."

"Wait a minute!" cried Farnum. "You can't mean that she's nothing to you. You. . . ."

"So long, Joe. I'm starting. I've told you the truth, and the whole truth."

"Then," groaned Farnum, "I've done you. . . ."

"What?"

"Nothing," said Farnum. "Only, so long, Sam."

Leader regarded the other for a moment with a curious hardness of eyes, and a certain doubt rested in his mind until he was well away across the darkening hills. But he knew that all men in love are a little unsettled in their wits, and Joe Farnum was merely another one. He had resigned forever all attempt to rival Joe in the mind of the girl.

But what was that, or what was the strange behavior of Farnum, even, compared with the glorious truth that he was drawing near to the most soul-filling moment of all — the slaying of Bill Orping?

He had crossed the main road, taken the side lane, then on through the hollow echoes of the bridge that covered the slough, and so he had come up the slope and through the brush until the house of Orping, the old Carter place, was suddenly before him, like a black hand lifted before his face.

There was no moon. The starlight dripped across one windowpane at the end of the building; fresh white paint made the slender columns of the verandah look like stone; all the house was dark.

He left the chestnut mare in the brush and made a circle of the building to make sure. But nothing stirred. There was no dog to rush up, barking, clamoring with a vast noise in the darkness. There was no sound of a voice within the house.

He went back to the front verandah and paused at the steps. The door was wide open, both panels of it. He could see that much. He closed his eyes and recalled the lay of the land inside, for many a time he had played with young Jack Carter here, in the old days. He could even remember where the old grandfather's clock stood against the wall by the stairs that mounted from the hall. It was a big hall, and it had been opened up to make the dining room larger. Upstairs, to the right down the hall, one came to the big front bedroom, the best in the place. And that was where Bill Orping slept now, no doubt, dreaming of the rodeo and the shooting contest.

Well, there would be a shooting contest of another sort for Bill, and before morning.

He stepped up to the level of the verandah, then felt his way across to the door, putting down his feet with elaborate caution, the outer edge of the foot first, the weight rolling onto the ball of the foot, little by little, so that the boards might not squeak and groan under the pressure.

At the door, he heard a rapid *pattering* of light feet within. He dropped to one knee, revolver in hand, as a cat raced suddenly through the door. Her tail was as big as a club as she spat in his face, then turned aside and was gone.

Leader set his teeth. It had not been a great shock, but it set him wondering, for cats are at home in the dark of their own houses. They do not rush out in terror, every hair on end, unless something pursues them. And what had been frightening this one? Something that lay couched in stillness within the place. It was a small thing, but when a man stands by himself against the world, his brain is moved by the fall of a leaf or the stir of a feather.

So Leader remained there until the ridge of the board beneath him began to hurt his knee. Finally he took out a little square of California sulphur matches, which are split out of a single block of soft wood without being entirely detached, one from the other. They burn with a dull, bluish fire and are deeply impregnated with sulphur at the striking end. Those who wish to save the flavor of tobacco let this impregnated end burn away before they light a cigarette. He took out this block, therefore, scraped not a single match but the whole pack on the floor and, as the entire surface burst into flame, he threw it into the hallway.

By that dull glare, he saw the face of the grandfather's clock beside the stairs and near the clock there was a tall man standing, with a shotgun in his hands. Crouched in the next corner was another who held a rifle at the ready. A third, a fourth, still others were vague forms stationed in the dining room.

As the pack of matches struck on the

floor, bounding along it, leaving behind it small footmarks of glowing phosphorus, a voice roared: "Let him have it!" Then the guns blazed, and the light of the explosions made Leader think that he had come to the mouth of hell.

V

It seemed to Leader that all his muscles went soft and useless, that a weight pulled him back, that he was like an invalid newly risen from a sickbed. As a matter of fact, he was a wildcat bounding from danger. He knew that he had only a split part of a second before the men inside the house would spring through the doorway and open fire so close that they could not miss even by starlight.

There was no time to run around the corner of the building; certainly he could never reach the brush and its heaped shadows of safety. Therefore, he sprang across the verandah, caught one of the bracket arms that joined the low pillars to the roof, and, as a gymnast swings on a bar, so Leader swung himself through a long half-circle and managed to hook a knee over the edge of the eaves. One twist of his body then laid him out along the shingles.

Below, he saw the fighters thunder across the porch and into the open. He waited, with a hardening of muscles that kept him breathless, to see them wheel and begin volleying at him. Instead, they fanned out widely. Some doubled around the house. Some went crashing through the shrubbery.

There were at least a dozen in this hornet's nest that he had roused by throwing the light into the dark of the hallway, and a pair of them remained walking up and down in front of the verandah with guns in their hands. The nearness of that pair kept him lying with a stony quiet.

They needed to do no more than to lift their eyes in order to see the irregular form that was lumped on the edge of the roof. Every moment he could swear that he had been spotted, and yet no bullets came his way. Off in the brush there was a chattering of guns; from behind the house, as though in answer, roared another salvo. But presently the manhunters returned. Those from the rear of the building brought nothing, but those who had invaded the bushes led out the chestnut mare.

She made a focal point of interest that held all eyes. They looked her over as though each man were about to set a price on her. They lighted matches, until Leader could see the crystal shining of her eyes. They were so rapt in their capture that they forgot they were holding up torches by which their hidden enemy might see them and shoot them down, perhaps. Above all, they forgot that Bill Orping was well illumined.

Opening above the verandah roof were two windows and Leader began to maneuver toward the nearest of these, spreading his hands to the full of their width, drawing on his body with rippling and folding efforts, like a caterpillar. Those shingles were dry, and the least crackling noise would draw the glances and then the bullets of the men in front of the house.

In spite of his danger, twice Leader paused and looked over the form of Bill Orping through the sights of his revolver. Orping looked as big as ever, half a head bigger than any other in the group. The three years had not changed him greatly except that he had allowed a short mustache to grow on his upper lip. Otherwise, he was the same as before, handsome, dark as an Indian, with an imperial way of lifting and turning his head.

Of the others, Leader recognized the two Cabot brothers. His schoolboy battle with Tim Cabot at the side of the swimming pool

57

would never fail to send a tingle through him, for the fists of Tim had been as hard as iron. That had been one of the major victories of Leader's youth and perhaps the recollection of the fight was what brought the Cabots here among the others, grim, wide-shouldered, squat men. Leader recognized others — Willie Rawston, big Chuck Lawrence, Garry Maynard. Two out of every three he knew. They had smoked his tobacco, and he had smoked theirs many a time, but now they were willing to lie in ambush against him. It made him feel weak and frightened — more frightened than he had been by the sudden flash of gunfire from the dark hall.

Then he got to the window, slid through feet first, and kneeled in real safety on the floor, for utter darkness walled him away from their eyes.

They were still moving about the mare.

"What he done," announced the voice of Bill Orping with the loudness of conviction, "was to switch around the corner of the house, and then dive for the brush. When we come out, maybe he dropped for the ground, and crawled. I got an idea that he didn't get far, neither. Because I put a slug into him, or I'm a liar."

"So did I," said another.

"I got him through one leg. I put money on it," said Tim Cabot.

The fugitive smiled.

"If he's leaking that much blood," suggested Garry Maynard, "we'd oughta take out some lanterns and look for the trail. It ain't likely that he wiped up the blood as he went along."

With grim passion, Leader stared down at the form of Bill Orping through the sights of his gun. He had only to pull the trigger, and his labors would be at an end. Then he could fade out of this land into a new world where life would begin again. But the mere killing of Bill Orping was not enough. That was not what he had turned, again and again, in his mind during three years of hell, but rather the thought of studying the face of Bill as fear entered it, and doubt — of speaking certain chosen words to the man — and finally of seeing him fall and watching his death struggles. Even brave men may lose their nerve at the last moment and screech for mercy from above, if not from man. In Leader there had been built up for three years a cruel hunger that could not be appeased by a mere mouthful of vengeance.

Some of them went into the house for lanterns. As he moved back cautiously through the upper story of the building, he heard their footfalls beneath him. When all sounds were again outside the building, he slipped down the back stairs. He pulled open the kitchen door and a breath of the night wind cooled his face, for he was covered with perspiration. No one was in sight, the voices were soft with distance and, going to the corner of the house, he saw the swaying lights of three lanterns as the crowd worked through the brush. Leader smiled, as he went toward the barn.

The horses were all there, of course. If he had used half his brain and examined the place carefully before attempting an attack, he would have found them and could have guessed how many men were with Bill Orping. He found a lantern and matches near the door. The lantern he left alone, but he ventured to light a match that he shielded in the double cup of his hands so that only a small shaft of light was thrown before him. Fourteen horses were crowded side-by-side down the length of the barn, and every one of them wore a saddle.

In spite of numbers, it was not hard to choose the best. The gray half-breeds of the Cabot ranch were famous all across the range; it was one of these that he selected, a tall gelding that lifted its fine head to stare at the light.

The stirrups were too short. He lengthened them, took the bridle from the peg on the wall, fitted it over the head of the horse, and led his new mount out the back door of the barn. Now high in the saddle, he made sure that the searchers were still at work in the brush, then he turned the head of the gray and jogged off through the open country. The horse tossed its head and made play against the reins, eager to be going at full speed, but that was not the purpose of Leader for the moment. His trail might be followed.

So he made a wide arc, struck the road to Windy Creek, followed it so that the sign of the gray might be lost in the maze of tracks, turned back a half mile, opened a barbed-wire gate, closed it carefully behind him, and then headed for the West place.

Once under way on the true line, he let the gray use its speed, for an agony of doubt was burning up his mind and that doubt had to be settled.

The moon had come up and made a vast, sprawling shadow gallop beside him all the way to the trees that stood nearest to the bunkhouse. There he dismounted, tethered the gray, and looked to his Colt revolver before he walked toward the bunkhouse.

A cool breeze met him with the smell of

the earth and the sun-dried grass; not a pine tree was in sight, but the resinous odor of them was about him faintly. He took heed of the waves of foliage that rolled against the ranch house and almost covered it, of the weathercock that glinted in the moonlight above the barn. He thought of young Muriel West, as strong-hearted as a boy. But nothing could relieve the trouble that weighed on his heart.

The door of the bunkhouse was open for coolness. He paused outside for a moment, remembering the last dark doorway he had confronted on this night, but through the eastern window of the long room came a slanting tide of moonshine that let him see enough. Only one man was inside; the moonlight fell on the hump of the blankets that covered his feet. So Leader went in, and slipped like a ghost along the wall until he was bending over the sleeper.

Farnum was muttering jumbled words in his sleep. He said — "Look out!" — once or twice, then — "And be damned!" That he repeated, also. It seemed to Leader that there was a terrible significance in these words.

"Joe," he said softly.

Joe Farnum sat bolt upright and brought himself fairly into the shaft of the moonlight, so that he could be studied, and Leader was glad of that. There was no savagery in his heart, only that poisonous and melancholy doubt that had hounded him all the way from the Orping place.

"Hey, Sammy," gasped Farnum. "How was it?"

He reached out a hand; Leader avoided it.

"It was a trap," said Leader. "Orping had a dozen men in his house. They were waiting as though they knew just when to expect me. A dozen of 'em. When I showed a light, it was like touching off a dozen shots of powder. Couple of pounds of lead started for me on the wing, Joe."

"Great Scott!" breathed Farnum. "You ain't hurt, Sam?"

Eagerly Leader stared into that brown face. He wished that it were not so smoothly plumped out. He wished that the features were better fitted for registering emotions with all subtlety. Instead, there was only that wide slit of a mouth and the small, round eyes. But those eyes became round for any reason — mirth, anger, fear.

"How could they know?" asked Leader.

"Dog-gone, but it beats me," said Farnum, wagging his head from side to side. He pushed his feet outside the blankets and sat up. He had gone to bed without taking

63

off his socks. His knees were fat and bent outward. A faint disgust began to master Leader.

"It beats me," repeated Farnum. Then he struck his hands together. "Marny!" he exclaimed.

"What about him?"

"Marny must've found out that you'd doubled back south. First thing he'd do would be to wire ahead and warn Orping."

"Why?"

"Because everybody knows that you've promised to do in Bill. Everybody knows that you hate him. Didn't you stand up there in the courtroom, that last day, and swear that you'd get Bill Orping for a sneaking traitor some time? Of course, it's Marny. He warns Orping, and Bill knows that the first night you're in striking distance, he'll have a call from you. So he simply sets his trap. How in the name of the devil did you manage to get away?"

Leader took in a long breath. "Marny could have done it," he muttered. "Only, there was a bad time for me when I couldn't think who would have been able to tell Orping except . . . well, I was a fool."

Farnum stared at him quietly. "You thought I might have tipped off Orping?" he asked.

"I was a fool . . . ," began Leader.

"It's all right," said Farnum. "I know how it is. When the pinch comes, when a fellow's been through your kind of hell, he starts in doubting everything. It looked pat, too. I knew just when you'd get there . . . and I could have told Orping. I saw him today."

Sam Leader groaned. "Joe, I'm ashamed. I'm so ashamed that I'm sort of sick."

But Farnum patted his shoulder tenderly. "Don't say a word. A fine kind of a friend I'd be if I didn't understand."

"Joe," said Leader, solemnly lifting a hand, "if I ever doubt you again, call me a dog and I'll say you're right."

VI

It was nearly noon of the next day when Joe Farnum sent his mustang loping like a tireless wolf toward Windy Creek. But halfway to the town he turned aside and stopped at the crossroads saloon that was kept by Kelly Dale. Kelly whitewashed his whole place from top to bottom every year. He went over the windmill, the tank house, the barn, the sheds, the saloon, and merchandise store with buckets of wash and a brush a foot broad. By late winter the rains had washed the place pale, but in summer the group of buildings blazed as though they were cut out of solid limestone, and newly cut, at that. There was only a scattering of young trees around the place to break the glare, and people used to pull their hats lower over their eyes when they turned toward Kelly Dale's outfit on a sunny day.

Under the awning, Farnum tethered his horse at the rack. The mustang began to bite contentedly at the crossbar and stamp deeper the hole that had been worn under the rack. Farnum went into the saloon, leaving one panel of the swinging doors vibrating behind him, and stood at the bar for a glass of beer. It was dim and cool in there. Half a dozen men sat at the tables, their voices subdued by the grateful shadow and the sense of the burning sun outdoors. They began to hail him at once.

"Hey, Joe! Seen your friend Leader, lately? Hear what he done at Orping's place? Walked right through the fingers of a dozen of the boys. They bounced a handful of bullets off him, but he's got a tough hide, that fellow has."

A burly fellow with bowed legs stood up and banged his hand on a table. It was Tim Cabot. "I don't care whose friend Leader is!" cried Cabot. "I'm gonna get that horse thief."

"Kind of big for you, ain't he, Tim?" asked another.

"I'll whittle him down to my size!" declared Cabot passionately.

Farnum waved a hand that dismissed all of this chatter in a good-humored way, as a man who will not involve himself in disputes. He was interested in only one of those who sat in the saloon, and that was the hump-shouldered man in the corner, apart from the rest, a fellow with a face as white and as fleshless as the knuckles of a closed fist. For that was Marny, the man-hunter. The message Farnum had received that morning had stated that Marny would be here; it was strange that none of the others seemed to recognize the famous man.

The bartender filled a tall glass from the spigot, whipped off the foam, drove in another shaft of beer, and slid the glass out on the metal grating toward Farnum. The foam was still creaming over at the top and sliding down the sides of the glass. It was cold as frost to the touch. It was colder still against the palate. Farnum drank slowly, hardening his mind against the thing that had to be done.

Then he paid for the beer, went out to his horse, and went on toward Windy Creek at a dog-trot. He had gone a scant mile when a horse pounded up behind him at a gallop, and Marny drew rein at his side. The left hand of Marny was gloved, but the gun hand was blackened by the sun. Farnum thought that the fingers were as long and as bony as the legs of a spider. He noticed the way the knee of Marny fitted close in against the side of the horse he rode; Marny was said to be a matchless rider.

"You're Joe Farnum, are you?" asked Marny.

"That's me. You're Marny, of course?"

"Yes. Orping says that you handed Leader to him on a platter last night. Only, Leader slipped off the dish before the boys could eat him."

"I tipped off Orping that Sam would go there."

"Would you tip me off to the next chance, Farnum?"

"Yeah. I guess so."

"How come that you're off Leader? Used to be great friends, didn't you?"

"Yeah, I guess so."

"You guess so? Ain't it a fact that Leader was fighting your battle the night that he killed Cleve Orping?"

"That's what Leader claimed."

"Ain't it a fact that Cleve Orping, three years ago, had said that he was going to get you and that, when Leader heard about it, he went down to play your game against Cleve? Ain't that the truth?"

"Well, maybe."

"What's turned you against Leader now?"

The questioning irked Joe Farnum. He had taken the rôle of Judas, but still he was capable of shame.

"What's the idea of all the talk?" he demanded bluntly, and for the first time he looked Marny fairly in the eyes. Those eyes were almost as pale as the face of the man-hunter, but they were filled with light.

"The idea is that I'm not stepping into any game till I know what it's all about," said Marny. "If I help set a trap for Leader, I have to know what's working the springs."

Farnum cleared his throat; he had thought out his story long before, in every detail. "Suppose you saw the finest girl in the world losing her head about an ex-convict. Wouldn't you do something to stop it?"

"Maybe I would. Who's the girl?"

"That don't matter," protested Farnum. "I ain't bringing her name into it."

"Yes, you are," insisted the man-catcher. "You want Leader out of the way. You want me to tackle the job. And you'll tell me everything you know. If you hold out, I'll go at the thing by myself. Who's the girl?"

Farnum choked. Then he said: "She's Muriel West. She's the daughter of my boss."

"Belong to you?"

"Who, Muriel? No, she don't belong to me, but the idea of a fine girl like that losing her head about. . . ."

"Has she seen him often? How old is she?"

"Nineteen, twenty, maybe."

"Thick with him before he went to jail?"

"No. She was just a kid, then, and. . . ."

"She's seen him since he got out of jail? Just lately?"

"Yes. She wanted to ride a horse her father had told her to keep off of. But she wouldn't keep off it. She tackled it at night. I was fool enough to help her, but Leader turned up in the middle of the job and kept the mare from savaging Muriel after she was throwed. That's all. Just kind of by accident, he done her a good turn, and she can't forget it. Besides, it's kind of romantic, having an ex-convict around, a man that even Marny couldn't catch." He put a little venom into the last words.

Marny trailed a glance over him and said: "That's all right. Leader's a tough man, but I hope to soften him one of these days. The girl's dizzy about him, and you want him out of the way, eh?"

Farnum shrugged his shoulders.

70

"Does he like the girl?" went on Marny.

"How would I know?" demanded Farnum with sudden irritation. "I don't know what he likes. He don't think nothing of women. Not since the Swede girl turned him down and married Bill Orping."

"Orping is tied into the business with a girl, too, eh?"

"Sam used to travel to dances and things with a pretty Swede girl by name of Hanson. After he was jailed, Orping married Meg Hanson. I guess it made Leader pretty sick."

"Is that why Leader wants to kill Orping?"

"No. That's because Leader says that Orping could have proved in court that Cleve was not shot by Leader. Sam says that Bill Orping was there, and knew that somebody else did the shooting."

"And Bill Orping kept his face shut, because Bill wanted Leader's girl. Is that it?" suggested Marny.

"I dunno," muttered Farnum. "I'm just telling you the way that Leader talks. That's all."

"If he's right," said Marny, after musing for a moment, "I don't blame him for wanting to kill Orping. That's what I'd do. But what Leader says ain't important. My job is catching him. He's made a holy show of me

71

once. But maybe the boys will stop laughing if I put it on him the next time."

"Yeah. They've laughed a little, all right," agreed Farnum. He detested this man, because his own villainy had been so thoroughly exposed by Marny's questions.

"Leader thinks a lot of you, does he?" asked Marny.

"He seems to."

"Does he suspect anything about last night?"

"Well, he come in and stood over me, ready to cut my throat, but I talked him out of it. He swore that he'd never doubt me again."

"Have you got any ideas?" asked Marny.

"He's lying up in the woods near the house. I could show you the place. A patch of woods that you could surround."

"Surrounding a place means a lot of men. A lot of men and horses make noise. And Leader's as keen as a hawk and just about as fast."

Farnum pulled up his horse. The other imitated him a step later and the horses stood head to head, motionless. Now the sun that had been following them caught up and poured its full weight on their backs and shoulders. The last dust that had been raised was blown off by the wind.

"I gotta think," muttered Farnum. "Looks like you don't want to do any of the work. You want me to wrap him and seal him up and hand him to you in a package for the mail. Is that it?"

"After everything's set, and Leader's in place, and we're all ready to knock him over," answered Marny, "there'll still be plenty of work for me to do. Leader will fight till he's dead. And he's not the kind that one bullet will kill. I've seen him work by starlight, and it was quite a show. Got any good ideas as to getting him?"

"I could have him down to the bunk-house."

"How many men in the bunkhouse?"

"Only me. West is a tightwad. He laid off the other man and gave me double duty. I could get Leader down to the bunkhouse tonight, and you could be laid up in there, waiting for him."

"That's not so good. You'd have to come in with him. And when we opened up, we'd be apt to hurt you. If we didn't, Leader would take you."

In spite of the force of the sun, a shudder passed through Farnum. "You could be lying out near the bunkhouse," he suggested. "And then after I got him inside, I could slip off for a minute. Then you'd have him by himself."

"Is the ground clean around the bunk-house?"

"Clean as your hand. A little grass, that's all."

"It sounds to me," declared Marny.

"A fine picture I'm gonna make in the eyes of the girl, after she finds out my share in the job," complained Farnum. "She's gonna think that I'm a hound."

"Well . . . ," began Marny. Then he shrugged his shoulders and added: "Listen to me. She don't have to know what you've done. No reason in the world why she should know. If you want it that way, this is all just an idea of my own. I'm just taking a chance of finding him with you. Understand?"

Farnum grunted. His eyes were brightening.

"What time tonight do you make the move?" he asked.

"After moonrise. Starlight is all right for the guns of Leader, but the rest of us ain't cats to see in the dark."

"The moon comes up pretty late."

"Sure it does. But we've got to have light, or he'll walk through us the way he's done before."

At this Farnum answered, with a sigh:

"Well, I'll find a way to get him down to the bunkhouse, then I'll manage somehow."

"Good man!"

Joe Farnum burst out savagely: "Don't call me that! I know what you got in your mind about me . . . you think I'm a hound. Damn you, Marny, that's what you've got in your mind."

Marny looked at him with a strangely impersonal smile. "Moonrise, old son," he said. "I'll meet you at moonrise, and have the artillery train along with me. So long till then."

VII

All the work that Farnum did on the ranch the rest of that day was performed with a mind half unconscious of the tasks. He wound up finding a steer bogged down on the edge of a water hole, and, after he had tailed the beef out of the mud, he came back toward the ranch house covered with wet clay.

He was a scant half hour ahead of supper time, but he slanted his mustang past the grove that concealed Leader in time to see Muriel West walking in among the trees. The sight of her struck in behind his eyes and numbed his brain through and through. He followed straight behind her, heard her sing out to Leader, and so came to the clearing as she was shaking hands with that outlawed man. The gray gelding of Tim Cabot stood nearby, hobbled and lifting its fine head to watch.

There was one grim satisfaction for Joe Farnum — although the girl was talking, the eye of Leader was not upon her. Instead, he was following every move of Farnum and seemed contented only when his hand was resting on Farnum's shoulder, at last.

"You ought to listen!" complained Muriel West. "It's worth hearing, and I've done some hard scouting to turn up the news."

"I know you have, and I'm listening," said Leader. "But it does me a lot of good to lay an eye on old Joe, here. A fellow's heart can freeze up, you know. It was thinking of Joe that kept mine thawed out for three years. I can't forget it." He added gently — "Old son." — and patted the shoulder of Farnum.

But Farnum was aware not so much of that voice and that hand as he was of the glance of the girl that fell critically upon him. Was she looking at the mud stains on his clothes or was she suspecting those deeper stains that were on his very soul?

She went on hurriedly: "Everyone says that Bill Orping is frightened to death. He's

76

moved with his wife into Windy Creek. Some of his friends are with him, day and night, mounting guard. And everybody else leaves them alone. Nobody wants to be near them, because people seem to think that you're likely to pop up out of the ground or drop down out of the air any minute. The sheriff has sworn in ten of the best men in the county as deputies."

"A couple of those best men have been out here scouting," answered Leader.

Farnum and the girl exclaimed in one voice.

"They worked the ground pretty thoroughly," said Leader, "but they didn't touch this spot. They seemed to think that, if I were around, I'd lie out farther from the house. But tomorrow they may make the search all over again."

"Only two of 'em?" asked Farnum with a strange sensation up his spine.

"Only two," said Leader. "I looked at 'em quite a while down the length of my rifle."

The girl's eyes narrowed. "If they'd started to get into this patch of woods, what would you have done?" she asked.

"Slid out on the far side and made tracks."

"You wouldn't have opened up with a gun?"

"Why," said Leader, "it's Bill Orping that

I want. I'm not out to do murder."

She went on with her budget of news. "The most important thing is Marny. Clinton Marny has showed up. He was seen in Windy Creek, and then he rode out this way. Nobody knows what he did or what his plans are."

"Marny is a tough one." Leader nodded. "I'd rather have any ten other men at my heels than Clint Marny." His words were more serious than his looks, however.

"Are you smiling, Sam?" asked the girl suddenly.

The grin broke plainly on his face at that instant. "I can't help it," said Leader.

"Mind telling me why?" she persisted.

"It's this way," he told her. "Suppose you were on a desert island for years, with no hope and your stomach getting closer to your backbone every day. Then, all at once, suppose the wind changes, the rain comes, the island turns green, and you see sails coming up over the edge of the sea. Well, that's the way with me. There used to be only Joe to think about. Now there's you, besides. And it makes me feel rich. It makes me want to laugh. I don't care how many sheriffs and Marnys in the world are after me. I feel as though I had both hands full of money and plenty of places to spend it."

He laughed softly, as he spoke.

Farnum suspiciously glanced at the girl, and saw that her eyes were shining. The cold hand of jealousy pinched at his heart again.

"Sam," broke out the girl, "you say that Joe and I mean a good deal to you . . . and you know that you mean a lot to us. Suppose we both beg you with all our hearts . . . will you give up the trail of Bill Orping and try to slip out of the country?"

Leader frowned. "He sent me up for life. I might have hanged, for all he cared. He would have liked that better. But he sent me up for life when three words could have saved me."

She was about to speak again, but Farnum could no longer endure the torment of seeing the two of them together, particularly the pain of watching the softening and the brightening of the girl's eyes.

"Come along, Muriel. You can't budge him, so you better come along," he said. "It's close to suppertime. You'll only heat him up, talking about Orping."

He managed to get her away in this manner, and they walked on toward the house together. Still she was reluctant.

"If you put on pressure, you might do something with him, Joe," she declared. "He loves you. If you told him that it was horrible to you, this hunting down of a man, don't you think that he'd listen?" She frowned as she said it; she was plainly accusing him of a lack of effort.

"I've talked when you weren't there to listen," he answered rather shortly. "I can't do anything with Sam. He's all iron."

"He can be as gentle as a child!" exclaimed Muriel West. "He's the finest man I've ever known. There's something big and great and simple about him. See how he trusts you with his whole heart."

"Why shouldn't he?" snapped Farnum.

She stopped at this, and he was forced to turn and confront her. It reminded him of the way he had had to face Marny, but this was even more difficult.

The hills were golden with sunset now and the sky burned gloriously over them as she broke out: "Neither of us is worthy of him, Joe. I lay awake last night and thought it over. He likes us because he's been starved for three years. He's been starved and he's hungry for people. Now he finds you again, and me. He saved my life, Joe, and a great-hearted man is always fond of people he has helped. But neither of us is worthy of him. We're not big enough. We're little people, compared with him."

In the enthusiasm of that renunciation,

she turned and walked on toward the house again, with her head raised, her face stern. And at her side went Joe Farnum, bitterness and fear growing within him.

"You stayed awake to think about that?" he asked.

"Yes . . . almost all night."

He swallowed. "Well, I guess he's fond of you, a little."

"Did he say so?" she asked eagerly.

"He? No . . . you know how he is. He wouldn't waste time talking about a girl. Women, they're nothing to him, since he lost the Swede girl to Bill Orping."

From the corner of his eye he saw her frown, and then saw her smile. "Well," she said, and paused.

"What are you smiling about?" asked Farnum hastily.

"About Sam," she answered. "Because it makes me happy to think about him, and because I think it makes him happy to think about me."

"How do you tell that?" asked Farnum. He felt as cold and as brittle as ice.

At that, she laughed a little and answered: "I can't explain. But I suppose every girl knows when a man is glad to have her around. Something goes back and forth . . . something warms the heart."

81

He said savagely: "I don't suppose I ever warmed your heart much, Muriel?"

She laughed again, on a higher key, and he hated that laughter.

"Good old Joe," she said. "Of course, you warm my heart."

"You're in love with Sam," he said huskily. "That's it. You're in love with him!"

"Haven't I an eye in my head and half a brain there, too?" she demanded briskly. "Wouldn't I be a blithering idiot if I didn't love a man like Sam Leader the instant I clapped eyes on him?"

He groaned; anguish fairly forced the sound between his teeth.

"Why, what's the matter, Joe? You look sick."

"I am, a little. I was thinking about your father. A fine day for him when he knows that you're crazy about a convict, a poor devil that's being hunted down."

"They'll never get him!" she cried. "If they do and if the end comes, well, nobody will ever take his place with me."

Every thought left his brain; only torment filled his body. Then he found himself standing beside the pump, filling the big granite basin with cold water.

Lily, the mongrel hound, came and fawned on him. He kicked her away with a heavy

82

thump in the ribs. She jumped to a little distance and remained there, cowering, trying to make peace, trying to understand and wagging her tail.

It soothed Joe Farnum a little to see her like that. He looked up to the sky, and saw that it was still flaming; he wished that the entire world were caught in the flames and consumed. She loved Sam Leader! All his own days of hope, of careful attentions to her, of politeness, of small talk had been thrown away. He put the basin on the back porch of the house and with a lump of soap lathered his strong hands. It was Leader that she loved. He wished that he could strike Leader dead. He had a desire to tear Sam Leader's heart from his breast. She loved Sam Leader!

The mongrel came up and planted her forepaws on his hip and tried to lick his face. Her tail wagged so violently that her head was moved, also, from side to side, and the mournful, gentle eyes besought his affection. Coldly he stared at those brown eyes. He would like to have Leader like that and an axe in his hand to brain the man. With his elbow he jabbed the dog under the jaw, and Lily fell heavily on her back, writhed, got to her feet, and went off staggering.

"Joe!" gasped a voice.

He looked up and saw the girl at the kitchen door, her face aghast.

"The old fool's always bothering me, just when I'm washing off some of the dirt of this rotten ranch!" exclaimed Farnum. "I never saw such an old fool of a dog."

He began to lather his neck and ears; his hands were trembling. And the girl slowly closed the screen door, disappearing behind it.

That instant, he knew, had closed him away from her by a mighty distance that years of effort would not be able to bridge again.

In his heart he cursed all women.

They don't understand, he said to himself. *They don't understand anything. They're a pack of fools.*

Well, she had been lost to him even before she had sight of his brutal treatment of the dog, and what did this matter, except that he would have to sit at the supper table that night and meet her cold eyes? And Leader was at the bottom of it. Leader was to blame. And at moonrise he would pay heavily for all this pain.

VIII

The moon had risen when Joe Farnum entered the grove of trees and called, softly: "Hey, Sam!"

There was an instant answer in a voice perfectly clear and wide awake. "Hello, Joe." Leader met his visitor on the edge of the clearing.

"I can't sleep, Sam. I want to talk to you. You mind? I've been lying awake thinking, all this time."

"Thinking about what?"

"About you and Muriel."

"Hold on!" said Leader. "About me and Muriel?"

"Come on down to the bunkhouse. We can sit and confab there."

"Why not sit here, Joe?"

"No backs to the seats here. Come on down, Sam."

"It's moonrise," answered Leader. "Look yonder where the old moon is coming up through the trees like a forest fire. It's a bad time for me to be walking about in the open. They may be looking for me."

"Rot!" said Farnum. "This time of night? Who'd be up at this time of night?"

"You are, old man, for one."

"That's because I had you on my mind."

"Plenty others have me on their minds, too. I thought I heard a horse whinny a while back. Somebody may be around."

"One of the horses in the corral likely."

"The noise didn't seem to come from that direction."

"Plenty of loose stock grazing all around."

"Yes, but this whinny stopped in the middle, as though a hand had covered the nostrils of the horse."

"Sam, you're getting scary."

"You bet I am. I'm going to stay that way, too."

"Come on, Sam! Come on down to the bunkhouse. We can sit and yarn a little."

"Well, all right," agreed Leader, after a moment of hesitation. "I'll go along."

They went down through the trees, but at the edge of the grove Leader paused and watched the ripples of wind and moonlight that slanted over the grass.

Farnum chuckled. "What's the matter, Sam? Nerves?"

"Full of nerves and they're all jumping," said Leader. "There's something in the air that I don't like. The barometer's falling for me."

Now, as he stood with his weight on one foot, ready to spring in any direction and that lean face, he looked to Farnum more like a wolf than ever. A shudder went through the smaller man. But he said: "Come on, old son. I want to tell you something that Muriel said to me about you."

"She talked about me? I want to hear that."

Leader glanced uneasily about him once more. Then he stepped out to the side of Farnum and crossed to the bunkhouse door. Here, again, he hesitated, then stepped hastily inside.

"You ain't afraid of the bunkhouse dark, are you?" queried Farnum.

"It's something outside that makes my bones ache," answered Leader. "I don't know what. Something in the air."

"A change of weather coming, maybe. That's a yellow old bird, that moon . . . what's left of her. She's pretty well chewed away."

Leader pulled a chair against the wall and sat down. "I can leave everything to you, Joe."

"Sure you can. I'll sit in the doorway and keep a look-out."

So Farnum sat on the threshold, and built himself a cigarette. It seemed to him that the dark of the bunkhouse was the dark of the grave and that Leader was already more than half dead. Even after the man was gone, however, there was hardly a chance that Muriel would forget him soon; certainly she would not turn to Farnum when she learned how Leader had been betrayed. Aside from that, she had seen him strike the dog, and in that instant she had been able to look too deeply into his soul. Yet, more than ever Farnum wished to see Leader dead. Only then would that weight that had pressed upon his mind for three years be cast off. Now, drifting closer among the trees, Clinton Marny and the sheriff and all the manhunters must be preparing their guns. But how hard it was to blind the eyes of such a man as Leader. The whinnying of a single horse had been enough to set his nerves on edge with suspicion, and only friendship had been able to bait this trap — friendship and the name of the girl. It pleased Farnum to feel that he was now about to flatter Leader and so bring about his death. He would tell the truth, and, while that truth made the heart of Leader rejoice, death would draw nearer every instant.

"What was she saying about me?" demanded Leader.

"Wait a minute. I've got to think of her side of it. She's only a kid, Sammy. Now you open up and tell me . . . does she mean anything to you?"

Instantly Leader replied: "She means so much that I don't dare let myself go. I have to shut the door on the thought of her and turn the key in the lock. Otherwise, I'd be swamped. Understand?"

"Yeah, I understand. She's a pretty thing, Sam."

"Faces don't matter," answered Leader. "You're no Handsome Harry yourself, Joe . . . it's the heart behind your mug that counts with me."

Farnum shifted his place a little and cleared his throat abruptly. "Leave me out!" he requested almost savagely.

"All right, Joe. I won't talk. But I can't leave you out of anything. Tell me about the girl."

"She thinks you're a great man. She talks about the oversize heart that you've got in you. She's all in a tremble when she starts thinking about you. She put on a smile that would have lighted up this whole bunkhouse like a flock of lanterns."

"That's quite enough!" exclaimed Leader.

"What's the matter?"

"I thought that I wanted to hear, but I don't, because I can see how everything happened with her."

"You can see? I can tell you that she's out of her head about you, Sammy."

The voice of Leader was almost a groan as he answered: "I'm the romantic figure, the fellow out of jail, the hunted man. Then I happened to meet her in a pinch, and I had the luck to do her a good turn. That's what makes her so dizzy. I'm sorry that I let you talk about her, because it can't do any good."

No, it would do no good, except to give Leader one more reason for loving life at the very moment when he was about to lose it.

In the shadow of a tree not twenty yards away appeared the dull outline of a man with a rifle in his hands. The heart of Joe Farnum leaped. The fools should not show themselves so rashly. Suppose that Leader, not he, were sitting at this moment in the doorway? At any rate, it was clear that he ought to get away from the bunkhouse at once.

He said: "I've got some more things to tell you."

"It's not right, Joe. She doesn't want you to repeat what she said."

"Wait here a minute, Sam. I'm dry as a bone. I'm going over to the house and pump up some cold water. I'll bring a can of it back."

The front feet of Leader's chair bumped on the floor. "I'll go along with you, Joe."

"No," protested Farnum hastily. "You stay here. This moon is too bright, and somebody might be stirring at the house. Stay back here and let your nerves quiet down. Be back in a minute."

He was already hurrying away. Gooseflesh formed roughly all over his body. Quicksilver tinglings shot up and down his spine. For every step was widening the distance between him and that little island of destruction that held Sam Leader.

As for Leader, from the door of the bunkhouse he watched the hasty steps of Farnum for an instant, saw the chunky form disappear among the trees in the direction of the house, and was about to turn back to his chair, when a rifle spoke out of the shadows close by and the bullet lifted his hat from his head. He leaped back into the blackness of the room. Through the door, then through the windows, he saw little glowworm points of light appear and wink out again in the darkness under the trees. North and east and west of him voices of men shouted on a high key of exultation; the bullets, driving pointblank at the build-

91

ing, clipped through both walls, raking the place from side to side, or burying themselves with heavy, *thumping* blows in the heavier timbers. Twice and again, little invisible fingers plucked at his clothes, and he knew what that meant. Wasps were singing in the dimness of the room. And he had no rifle.

There was the Colt, but nothing else, and the revolver was comparatively useless for work like this. He fell flat on his face. That would diminish by nine-tenths the danger of being struck by a random shot, for most of the shots were being aimed breast-high. To the east, little glimmering eyes appeared along the wall of the bunkhouse, where the bullet holes let the moon look through.

Then someone shouted in loud tones of command; the firing fell away, ceased.

"Leader!" shouted the same strong voice. "Oh, Leader! D'you hear me, man?"

He listened to the rapid, heavy bumping of his heart against the floor. Was it possible that Joe Farnum could have known anything about this? Was it even faintly a chance that he could deliberately have trapped his friend?

That suspicion, Leader put behind him with shame. Better to deny his own soul than to question the pure faith of Joe Farnum. If Farnum was wrong, then the entire world was wrong.

"Leader! Sam Leader! D'you hear me?"

He answered: "Hello! I hear you well enough."

"Leader," said the other, "I'm Clinton Marny. If you'll walk out of that door with your hands over your head, we'll stop firing. I give you my word of honor for that. I'll take you back safe and sound to the pen. That's a fair bargain!"

"It's a bargain I'll never make," replied Leader loudly. "It's easier to die once than to die every day the rest of my life."

"Man," cried Clinton Marny, "we've got you trapped! Nothing in the world can get you out of this hole, and you ought to know it. We'll start at the top and stick a bullet through every inch of it right down to the foundations. If we can't get you that way, we can burn you out. It's better to live than to die there like a sick rat. Think it over and use your brains!"

The huge, bawling voice of Bill Orping — how well Leader remembered it — now rolled thundering from the trees: "Let him take his medicine! He ain't anything but a murdering hound, and his life . . . !"

"Shut your mouth, Orping!" called Marny. "I'm running this party, by the sheriff's permission. And I'll run it to the end. Leader, if you'll say the word, I'll walk up there to the door and escort you out of the bunkhouse so's nobody like Orping can take a crack at you."

"You hear me, Marny?" answered Leader. "I know you mean right, but if you or anybody else shows me a head or a hand, I'm going to put lead through it. You understand? You've got me cornered and I can't get out. I only hope that I'll have the chance to plaster some of you before I finish."

Several angry shouts answered this speech and Leader added: "It's about the last time I'll have a chance to talk. Before I pass on, I'm going to say for the last time what I said in the courtroom the day I was sentenced. I didn't kill Cleve Orping. I didn't kill Cleve Orping and Bill Orping knows that I didn't."

"You lie!" roared Orping.

"Leader," called Marny, "you're a dead game one! I'm sorry that you have to end this way, but I've sworn to get you. Fellows, open up the party. Start from the ground level, and work your way up . . . begin!"

How many rifles were in that party? Twenty? Forty? A hundred? The shock of the bullets in that first volley made the whole bunkhouse tremble. A long splinter, torn from the floor, struck Leader across the face. The next moment, he well knew, lead would begin to plow through his flesh.

Then he heard through the barking of the guns the noise of a horse galloping. Were some of them trying to charge him? Savagely he hoped that they were. He had six bullets in his gun, and, if he used them well, perhaps six lives would pay before his own was taken in exchange.

So he rose to his knees, with the Colt in his hand, and through the open door he saw the rider coming on a hard-running horse that gleamed in a swift streak through the moonlight. It was a small rider that wore wide chaps. No, they were not chaps. It was the fluttering cloth of a woman's skirts, and that was the girl coming to him with all the speed the black mare could muster.

In his excitement he yelled, then stopped suddenly. Marny was shouting; so were the rest. As the rifle fire ended abruptly, Muriel West pulled that wild-headed black mare to a halt and slid to the ground in front of the doorway.

"Muriel!" cried a man's voice in an agony. "Muriel, come back to me. Muriel, do you hear? Sheriff . . . Mister Marny, for heaven's sake don't let a gun be fired!"

Sam Leader stood trembling in the darkness close to the door, and he heard those voices out of a dream-like distance; only the girl was real in this world of illusion.

IX

The long bridle reins were hooked over her shoulder as she came in. Some of that brightness of the moonlight she seemed to bring in with her, a glow about her face and in her hair.

"Sam, are you hurt? Have they killed you? Where . . . ?"

Then she found him, close to her and tall in the darkness. She caught him with all her strength and pulled herself against him so that her head fell back as she looked up at him.

Leader kept his arms at his sides, stiff and straight. "They haven't touched me. I'm all right. But you get out of here," he commanded. "This is my job."

"Being murdered? That's your job? If they kill you, they kill me."

She gripped his arms and shook at them. Out of the distance, her father was calling again, entreating her to come back, but Leader made out only a blur of words. Something was hammering at the secret doors of his brain. In order to keep his arms from her, he had to grip his hands and stiffen his muscles. Speech worked at the roots of his tongue, but he told himself that he was a dog if he uttered a word. Such a woman as this, if she loved and were loved in return, would never forget. And that was what she would have to do. She would have to forget him. She would have to begin to forget him a few minutes hence, after one of the bullets had touched his heart or driven through his skull.

She gripped his rigid arms and shook at them. "Answer me. Say something to me. Tell me you know I won't leave you and that I'm right to stay. Sam, are you trying to shame me? But I'm not ashamed. They're going to kill you, and that gives me the right to love you, first."

"You're a good kid," said Leader. "But don't be silly. Don't make a fool of yourself."

"You don't care for me. Is that what you're trying to say?"

"You're a good, game little kid. But now you're all excited. You're hysterical. Just climb on that horse and go home to your father. He's hollering out there for you."

"I'm a child to you. Is that all I am?"

He swallowed. "You ought to have been a man. You've got plenty of good nerve. But what's the use of pretending, Muriel? I'm in a place where a fellow ought to be honest. You run along home, will you?"

"Be honest. That's all I want you to be. Be honest and tell me why your voice is shaky, and why you're trembling. Is it because you're afraid? No, it's because you don't want me to tie myself to a dead man, but I'm going to die with. . . ." She began to sob; she kept on trying to speak, but the sobbing drowned out the words.

"Quit crying, will you?" said Leader.

"I'm going to quit it," she stammered. "Wait a minute. Don't go away and I'll quit in a minute. I've got to tell you . . . to tell you. . . ."

Something broke in the heart of Leader. His strength crumbled away in his body and then in his brain, as if she were a fire and he were a man of snow that was melting. She had one arm around his neck. As he shuddered and trembled, he began to bend down over her. In his breathing he groaned like a wounded animal.

"If I say a word, I'm a dirty, sneaking dog," he said. "Stand away from me. I don't want you. I'll tell you the truth . . . you're nothing to me. You're just a kid. You're just . . . oh, my God, I love you!"

All the trembling stopped as he took her

in his arms. A great stillness fell between them and spread in a wave that thrust the outer noises farther and farther away. And now it seemed to him that she brightened, that a light struck upward through her translucent flesh, and by this light he was looking at her.

"Now I don't care," she said, sighing. "No matter what happens, I don't care. Nothing else counts. Do you feel that way?"

He said nothing. Words were silly little things, gestures in the dark.

"Even Joe Farnum betraying you . . . that doesn't matter now, does it?"

He straightened under the shock, as brave men do, and stood for a moment like that. As the rain soaks the ground in which a great tree is rooted, and at last the steady hand of a storm bends the giant over, snaps the moorings one by one, and finally sends it sweeping to the earth, so the friendship of Joe Farnum was torn out of Leader's heart and fell away from it forever. The wall of the bunkhouse was just at his back; he let his weight settle against it.

"Didn't you know?" she asked him.

"I was ashamed to know. I wouldn't let myself know. Over at Orping's place, too . . . he framed that, I suppose?"

"I suppose so. Oh, Sam, how you loved

him, and how I pity you."

"Wait a minute," said Leader. "I'm a little sick, but I'll get better."

Suddenly she stepped back from him. The mare at the doorway drew back, also, to the end of the reins.

"Leader!" shouted the voice of Marny.

"I've got to think," said Leader slowly. "I've got you in here with me, and that's not fair. That's not the way to play the game."

"Did you kill Cleve Orping?"

"No."

"Are the rest of 'em playing the game fairly with you? You're not going to play fair with them, either. You're going to get on that horse . . . with me. They won't dare to shoot if I'm with you. You're going to ride straight south into the open. By the time they get on their horses and start after you, you'll be out of close range. I can drop off, and you can go on. The mare will carry you. She's all whalebone and wire. She's too full of meanness to weaken."

He put out his hand, not toward her, but toward her idea. "I get on a horse and let a girl stop the bullets. That sounds pretty," he said.

"Leader!" Marny shouted from the edge of the trees. "It's no good trying to keep her in there with you. It'll harm her, but it won't save you. It'll just blacken your name. It'll make you a sneak and a coward. And if. . . ."

"You're right," Leader said suddenly to the girl. "We're going to ride together. They won't dare to shoot with you in front of me or behind me . . . no one would dare to take a chance, not even Joe. Climb onto the mare!" he commanded harshly.

She was instantly in the saddle. A shout from all those throats went whooping up, roaring and bawling. She was free to leave, and, of course, they thought that she was leaving. Then Leader sprang out of the darkness of the doorway, slid into the saddle as she moved back, and sent the mare flashing toward the south under that double burden.

Half a dozen guns spoke instantly but not a bullet sang near them; it was mere blind excitement that had made trigger fingers contract. Marny and West were thundering commands to stop firing and get to a horse. As they galloped, Leader heard the girl panting at his shoulder: "You're going to win!"

From the trees that had sheltered the men of the posse on three sides of the bunk-house, men ran out, brandishing their guns, yelling in brainless confusion. Hardly a third

101

of them had the wit to run at once for horses, and very few had horses near at hand. So the black mare galloped on through the open ground toward the south until the girl cried: "Slow up a little! I'll drop off here. Then ride for us both. Remember that every danger that comes to you, comes to me!"

He pulled in on the reins, turning in the saddle to take her in his arms for the last time — but she had already slipped to the ground and ran staggering from the momentum of her dismounting, her arms stretched out as she fought for her balance. He could only swing forward in the saddle, bending low over the neck of the mare, and bring the tough little black beauty to full speed.

The bullets began to wing close to him, their brief voices making him duck right and left, although he well knew that the danger was past before he heard the sound of it. In the distance there were men kneeling or lying on the ground, their rifles close to their cheeks, while they strove to judge the distance and hit the target. Those were men who had killed their running deer at 400 yards, but they had no luck with Sam Leader. The mare swept over a hummock, down the farther side, and the gunfire ended; a broad bulwark stretched between the fugitive and those riflemen.

But from right and left came the hammering beat of hoofs as the pursuit started. Those sounds drew together in the wake of Leader. He saw the full flight of half a dozen in the front, of others stringing off toward the rear. Then he took that stanch little mare in hand and asked her for her best.

She gave it with a fine frenzy. He saw her slender forelegs reaching high and far. She stretched her body into a straight line that trembled with effort, and, running with her head turned a trifle, he could see how her ears were flattened, how her nostrils flared, how her eyes shone with an angry, disdainful light as though she were glancing back with scorn at those pursuers and wondering how they dared to match strides with her.

And they fell back! All those men with sharp spurs and laboring quirts fell slowly to the rear. They rode with a desperate rage, for they kept expecting the little black mare to be stopped by the size of her burden, but she did not falter for even a moment.

The open range rose and fell in shining waves that shut out sight of the posse, at last. Then Leader put the black mare down one of the empty draws that opened to his right. A moment later the hoof beats roared past, and he knew that the danger was past.

X

With determined men like Marny and Orping to lead them, it was certain that the posse would not give up the manhunt until they had circled far and wide. In the meantime, Sam Leader took the direction least expected, for he headed straight toward Windy Creek. Near the town, he cached the black mare in a stand of young poplar trees, patted her wet neck for an instant with affectionate gratitude, and then walked straight into the town.

The main street was empty, but there were lights in houses, here and there. He knew what those lamps meant — women and children waiting for the man of the house to return from the battle. In Windy Creek itself most of the posse must have been recruited. Perhaps by this time the chase had been given up and tired men on tired horses were trooping back toward their homes, but he was sure of a sufficient lead for his purposes.

The moonlight showed him the familiar faces of the houses on either side of the street. There was not a single new one. Between the Tucker and the Grant places was still the vacant lot where he had had an historic fist fight with tall Rance Tucker, in the old days. All was so unchanged that it would hardly have surprised him to find his feet bare in the cool dust and short trousers flapping about his knees.

He walked briskly on to the hotel, nodded with relief when he saw that the verandah was empty, and paused outside the door. It was open upon an empty lobby. Not a soul was there except a young fellow behind the reception desk, sound asleep. Lightly he crossed the room and began to mount the stairs. On the desk a gray cat, half asleep, uncurled itself, stared at him with yellow eyes, yawned, and made itself once more into a comfortable round bundle.

One lamp burned in the lobby. When Leader was high enough on the stairs so that his head and shoulders were in shadow, he called out briskly: "Hello, son!"

The young fellow behind the desk jumped hastily to his feet, blinking, stretching. "Hey, who is it?" he asked.

"Rance Tucker," said Leader. "What's the number of Bill Orping's room?"

"Seventeen and eighteen. He's got two rooms. Hey, Rance, I thought you was still clear over in Denver and. . . ."

The fellow came stumbling toward the foot of the stairs as he spoke. Leader turned and mounted, without haste.

"I was in Denver, but I had to make a trip back here."

Then the young fellow called out: "Bill Orping ain't in yet! There's only his wife. I guess she's asleep."

"I've got some news that'll wake her up," said Leader.

As he went down the hall, he listened, and was vastly relieved when no footsteps came up the stairs in pursuit. The door of Number *18* was shrouded in blackness; slits of light set off the door of *17,* and there he knocked.

"Hullo, hullo?" called a woman's voice instantly. Her footfall crossed the room in haste. She jerked the door open, exclaiming: "Any news?"

"Yes. About Leader," he answered.

"Ah," she gasped on an intaken breath, "did they get him? Come in. Did they get him?"

He stepped past her into the light; it was not until he closed the door behind him that she recognized his face and her lips parted as if to scream.

"Don't do that!" he commanded sharply.

The lips closed without uttering the sound. She walked backward from the silent threat of his presence until her shoulders were against the wall. Leader locked the door.

Three years had altered her a great deal. She had been plump and pretty in the days when he took her to dances. Her hair had been a mass of blonde fluff and curls; her eyes were dancing always, with an inexhaustible child-like joy in life. Now she was dim and fat. Three years had altered her as a driving rain fades a bright spring landscape.

"Bill ain't here. You won't find Bill here," she stammered in her terror. "Go on away, Sam. Bill ain't here."

He looked away from her for an instant toward the lamp on the center table. The wick was not trimmed carefully; a thin column of soot was blackening one side of the chimney and filling the air with the stale, choking smell. She had not noticed it. The magazine she had been reading lay face up on the table. Huddled there over a story, she had waited for Orping to return with the tale of how he had hunted her former lover.

When he was able to look back at her again, he answered: "Bill is coming back pretty soon. I'll wait."

Her eyes rolled up in her white face. He thought she was about to faint and took her by the shoulders, steadying her into a chair. There she sat with loosened body, her head fallen forward on her chest. The feel of her flesh had been too liquid-soft under his hands. Physical disgust kept working up from his fingertips through the nerves of his arms.

"Did you know about the scheme?" he asked her. "The trap to catch me?"

She nodded, without looking up. "Bill told me. Walking up and down right where you are now, he told me about it. He kept laughing and telling me. He's always hated you."

"Why? What did I do to him?"

She raised her head, at last. The fear was dying out of her face. Instead of answering his question, she asked: "How do I look?"

"Tired."

"And fat and old and stupid. That's what Bill tells me." She studied his face, a faint hope appearing in her own eyes. That hope gradually died out.

"Don't you get on with Bill?" he asked.

"He hates me, because I found out long ago what a four-flusher he is. He never would've wanted me, except that I was your girl, in the old days. Sam, you're cooked. You're done for. They're going to get you before long, but, if you lifted a finger, I'd follow you out of this room . . . I'd go anywhere."

"Does Bill know that?"

"He guesses it. I got mad this morning and told him if he was a man, he'd never run to cover like this. He'd stay where he belonged and fight it out with you, fair and square. I told him it wasn't murder you wanted, but a fair fight with him. Was I wrong?"

He shook his head. "No. That's what I want, and that's what I'm going to have . . . here."

She started up out of her chair, gasping: "Here? Here? Are you crazy?" Then, as the strength of excitement failed her, she sank slowly back again. "Why should I care? He hates me. He's always hated me since I found him out."

"What did you find out?"

"That he knew you didn't kill his brother Cleve."

"He told you that?"

"I got it out of him."

"How long ago?"

"Two years. More'n two years."

"If you'd told that to the law, it would have set me free, Meg."

Shame puckered her face and made her eyes disappear. "I know. But where would that've left me? Oh, now I wish that I'd done it. But you seemed to be out of the world then. You were like dead, and Bill meant board and keep to me anyway. I know what you think, and you're right. I never lifted a hand to help you when you were in trouble. I never wrote to you when you were in prison. I've been wrong all the time. I was mean and sneaking. I was like a pig that didn't want anything but food and a bed and no trouble." She rocked her head back and forth. "But I've had my trouble. You can go on despising me, but I've had my own hell."

"I don't despise you, Meg."

"That's what you say, but I know what's in your mind."

His voice lowered. "I mean it. I don't despise you, but I'm sorry for what you've been through. You turned at the wrong corner and got onto the wrong street. Whatever you've done, I'm no fit judge for you. If you've ever done me harm, you can make up for it now. Stay quiet when Bill Orping comes back and let the guns do the only talking."

Into the last of that sentence came the noise of many footfalls mounting the stairs. Meg Orping groaned and twisted in her chair. There was a noise of horses jogging down the street; the posse was returning.

Suddenly she jerked her chair about, drew the magazine into place before her, and bent her head over it. "If you're here," she muttered, "I haven't seen you. I don't know anything about you being here. I'm sitting here reading and waiting, and that's my story and I'll stick to it." She turned the page. Her face became perfectly calm, except for the faint smile on her lips. He could see that her eyes were actually working back and forth across the printed page.

No, she was not a good woman, but the very evil in her character was useful to Leader now.

Steps came loudly up the hall. He moved to the door that opened on the adjoining room, Number *18,* and found that it was not locked. That was the best way. Bill Orping could come in freely, and see his fate a second before he met it.

The footfalls paused, gathering at the door of *17.* The handle was jerked noisily.

"Go in the other door!" called Meg.

"Why the other door?" demanded the angry voice of Bill Orping. "Wouldn't budge . . . wouldn't lift a hand. I'm getting sick of her, I can tell you," he added to his companions in the hall.

And the voice of one of them came even more familiarly to the ears of Leader, saying: "Don't be hard on her, brother. It's kind of late, you know."

They were trooping into the next room now. And it had been Joe Farnum who spoke last.

Meg Orping seemed to know that voice perfectly well, also, for she lifted her head for an instant from her magazine and stared at Leader with a white commingling of terror, pity, and sneering satisfaction. Then her head dropped and she was once more lost in her story.

XI

The door of Meg Orping's room that led to the hall was locked. It could be opened and Leader could slip down the hall and away to safety, perhaps, but although there were apparently three men in Number *18,* not for an instant did he think of flight. Not till he heard the third man's voice was he greatly shaken.

A match had been scratched in *18,* and chairs had scraped on the floor. It was Marny's voice that said: "I came up with you fellows because I had something to say."

Marny. That made the job a very different one in every aspect. Bill Orping was a hard fellow to beat, but Marny was a tiger. Joe

112

Farnum, too, might battle like a cornered rat. What had been a hard task for Leader now was turned, suddenly, into an impossibility, it seemed. Yet he could not surrender his hope or his place so quickly. For three years he had waited for his chance at Orping. Now he was willing to die for it. Joe Farnum had done a far more villainous thing, but, for Farnum, Leader felt not so much hatred as a sick disgust.

"The three of us have to handle the thing," said Orping. "Nobody else takes as much interest."

"What I want to tell you is that I'm out of the business," answered Marny.

"Hold on!" cried Farnum. "Out of it? Have you lost your nerve, Marny?"

"A lot of people are going to think that I have, of course. But I'll tell you two the truth. Since I got to Windy Creek, I've talked with a lot of people and I've got the picture of your brother's killing better than I did before, Orping. A whole lot better!"

There was a jarring sound, as though Marny had struck the table with his fist.

"Go on," snarled Bill Orping.

"I'll go on, right enough," continued Marny. "I'm giving up the hunt for Leader because I'm convinced that he didn't kill Cleve Orping."

Leader, amazed, looked wildly around at Meg Orping. But she continued to read her magazine with the same pale smile of interest on her face, never lifting her head to listen to the voices in the next room.

"You say Leader didn't kill Cleve? Who did, then?" demanded Farnum in high excitement.

"You did!" answered Marny.

Out of the breathless silence that followed, Bill Orping grunted: "You're a fool, Marny."

"Farnum killed your brother and, what's more, you knew it, Bill. I'm as sure as though I saw the whole thing. Cleve Orping had threatened to get Farnum. Leader like a good friend went to fight Farnum's battle against Cleve. And Farnum, unknown to Leader, sneaked along to see what happened. He was outside the back window of that saloon when Leader faced you two Orping brothers. Leader told you what he thought of the pair of you, I suppose. He probably dared you to fill your hands, and you were afraid to take the chance with him. It seemed as though everything were going to wind up in mere words, when Farnum decided that he'd make his own hand count. So he fired through the window and killed Cleve. That brought guns into your hands and Leader's. Probably you both fired at the window. At any rate, that's the way I see the story.

"Leader was too good-natured and honest to suspect his friend Farnum of being such a dog. But you had your guess, Bill. Why didn't you go after Farnum, when he'd murdered your brother? Because it wasn't Farnum that you wanted out of the way. It was Leader that you wanted to see in prison. It was Leader who had bluffed you out. It was Leader whose girl you wanted. You and Farnum patched up a dirty truce."

"You're a raving fool," said Bill Orping. "Shut up, or people are gonna hear you talk."

"They'll hear me talk anyway. I'm going to spread my opinion around. I don't suppose it'll save Leader. I can't offer any proofs. But I'm going to let the world hear what I have to say. Now I'm getting out of here. I'm watching the pair of you close. Be careful what you do with your hands till I get through that door."

His footfall retreated; the door slammed; he was gone. Then the low mutter of Bill Orping said: "How in the name of the devil could he guess it? Don't sit there like a fat-faced fool! We've got to do something or we'll be run out of the country. The whole world is gonna know that you killed Cleve, and everybody's gonna call me a hound for not having your blood long ago. Long ago? I dunno why I shouldn't have it here and now."

A chair scraped as though one of them were rising.

"Hold on, Bill! You ain't crazy, are you?" panted Farnum. "We been friends for a long time, ain't we? You wouldn't turn on poor old Joe now, would you, when I need a friend? Bill, don't talk loud and put up that gun."

"I'm gonna clean my hands!" shouted Orping with a sudden thunder that made the room vibrate. "I'm gonna have your blood, you murdering coyote. You killed my brother Cleve and here's what makes us quits!"

Leader tore open the door as Farnum screeched: "Wait, Bill, don't do it . . . don't!"

When Leader could see, the gun was leveled in the hands of Bill Orping. He stood close to the window, just opposite the door that Leader had flung wide. At the farther end of the room, shrinking against the wall, one hand before his face as though that frail shield of flesh and bone could turn the blows of half-inch chunks of lead, was Joe Farnum, pulling his own Colt.

Three spurts of flame jerked from the

116

muzzle of Orping's revolver. The first spun Farnum to the side and brought a scream out of his throat; the second hammered him down to a sitting posture in the corner, shooting blindly all the while; at the third, he collapsed in a loose heap. His head fell sprawling forward between his legs.

"Now, Orping, it's my turn," said Leader.

The brutal joy flashed out of the face of the killer. He had lowered his weapon as he drove the last fatal bullet home. Now, swinging toward Leader, he jerked the gun up again. Actually he fired first, but fear had blinded him like a mask of snow, and the bullet *whirred* vainly past Leader, whose own slug hit the body of Orping and jarred him back against the wall. The gun fell from Orping's hand, slithered down his leg, bumped on the floor. Orping caught at the wound with both hands. It seemed as though the sight of the red blood was fatal to him, rather than the leaden slug that had struck home. For as he looked down at the hole in his coat, his knees gave, he wavered, and fell flat with his arms still doubled under him.

Leader stepped back into Meg's room. Footfalls were thundering through the hotel; voices were shouting. But Meg Orping remained in her chair, still reading, with that small, white smile of interest on her lips.

"You'd better start screaming, now," said Leader, and, sliding through the window, dropped to the roof of the verandah below. As he struck it, he heard the shriek of Meg Orping rise like a frightful siren across the night.

XII

The father of Muriel West was one of those big men who can be broken by time so that their own bulk becomes an unwieldy burden. He still looked young and imposing when he was sitting down, but when he rose and walked, his step was short, his shoulders were bent forward too much, and it seemed in short that the fifty years of his life had all been long ones.

That was true. Without help and without favor he had fought his way into the ownership of a prosperous ranch. Fight was always the right word for him. He fought everything and he fought everyone. He could have been far richer except that he would never join hands with neighbors or bankers. His own way suited him best, and he preferred ten mistakes to one triumph planned by another. He was a man of explosions. The powder never failed in him. And it was always dry.

He was exploding on this evening as he sat on the verandah of his home and talked to his daughter. She, seated on the top step of the verandah, her head dropped back against one of the narrow wooden pillars, smiled blindly at the beauty of the west and at the shadows that were sifting through the trees.

"Shooting down officers of the law . . . is that the act of a law-abiding citizen?" he shouted at the girl.

"No, Father," she said.

"Or stealing horses . . . is that the work of an honorable man?" roared West.

"No, Father," she said.

"As for turning him loose, as for granting him a pardon, I never heard of such nonsense in my life. Did you?"

"No, Father," she said.

"Pardon him for what?" cried West. "What if that rat Farnum did kill Cleve Orping, and what if Bill Orping knew it, as his rascal of a wife now confesses . . . what has that to do with the crimes Leader committed after he escaped from the prison gang? He's blazed his way across the mountains, back and forth, like a damned pestilence, a regular forest fire! Men like that oughtn't to be at large, should they?"

"No, Father," she said.

"Muriel," he roared, even louder than before, "have you heard what I've been saying?"

"No, Father," she said.

He jumped up from his chair and stamped violently. Then, with equal suddenness, he sat down again. "A horse thief and a gunman," muttered West. "Come here, Muriel."

She rose and went to him.

"Stand here in front of me where I can see you. Now get that fool smile off your face. This is no time for smiling."

"Yes, Father," she said.

"Stop smiling, and listen to me. The man's a rascal. You know that. His record proves it. If Farnum hadn't killed Bill Orping, this fellow Leader would have."

"Would you blame him?" she asked.

"Would I what? Don't interrupt me. I say, I want you to get this fellow out of your mind. You might as well. He's finished his business in Windy Creek . . . a pretty lot of business it was, too. And he's away from here with his pardon in his pocket. Off somewhere, holding up a stage, perhaps, by way of making a new start in the world. You've seen the last of him, so get him out of your mind. Will you do that?"

120

"He'll be here before dark," she said.

"Before dark? How do you know? Have you had a message from him?"

"No."

"How do you know that he'll be here, then?"

"I know. That's all."

"Exactly the sort of rot your mother used to talk about . . . well . . . Muriel. Is that Leader? It can't be!"

A rider on a rather small black horse swept over the brow of the southern hill, disappeared behind trees, came into view again close to the house. He carried himself with a reckless ease that made a picture for the mind as well as for the eye.

"That's Leader," groaned West. "I've never seen him, but I know that's the man. He looks like trouble as far as the eye can follow him." Then he added: "What's the matter with you, Muriel? Hurry along and meet him, or he'll think there's no welcome for him here."

She waited one instant longer, until she saw the smile of contentment growing on his face. Then, as he waved his hand, she hurried down the steps, and so, running, went along the path toward the rider.

The rancher settled forward in his chair and dropped his chin on his clenched fist.

121

"You can tell a man by the way he takes a woman," he said to himself.

But that horseman came on without stopping, merely dropping from a gallop to a trot. When he reached Muriel West, he swayed far to the side and caught her up. Perhaps it was his strength alone. Perhaps she sprang up to help him. But now he came on holding her in both his arms, smiling at her, smiling at the world.

"One of the kind that wants his own way," said West. "I'll be having trouble with him before he's been long around the house." And he grinned a broad and contented grin.

■ ■ ■ ■

TRAIL OF THE EAGLE

■ ■ ■ ■

Through 1937, Frederick Faust's output was still strong, but, beginning in the 'Thirties, his markets were increasingly expanding to include *Detective Fiction Weekly, Dime Western, The American Weekly, Illustrated Love Magazine, West Magazine, Argosy,* and *Adventure* in addition to his primary market, Street & Smith's *Western Story Magazine.* "The Trail of the Eagle" appeared in the July, 1933 issue of *West Magazine* under his Max Brand byline. It was one of thirteen short novels, thirteen serials, and ten book length stories published that year. It features a tougher, more perceptive heroine, Sue Jones, than one might expect.

I

Beyond the pine trees, the trail dipped through a green hollow, and McGregor and Peary took this better going at the full gallop, letting their horses stretch out to the work. Peary, young, dark, handsome, leaned forward to jockey his horse ahead, with the enthusiasm of a boy riding a race for fun or a wager. McGregor, sitting straight in the saddle, seemed to let his horse run of its own unguided will, yet he kept even with his companion, and, looking at the iron of his face, it was easier to realize that murder was the goal he aimed at.

Before them, in the midst of the hollow, they saw an old man jogging along on a mule. The hump of his shoulders and the outstanding ridge of his backbone, showed his years, and, as Peary shot past, he had a glimpse of a long white face, and, under the brows, dark eyes like a death's head. This ancient man waved a greeting to McGregor. His hand was a skeleton's claw.

The two passed on up the farther slope, left the trail, climbed a hill, and drew rein behind a clump of trees through whose trunks they could see the white of a road just beneath.

"Here we are," said McGregor. "Barney Dwyer and the girl ought to be coming along this way before long."

"But look there!" exclaimed Peary. "That old idiot on the mule is coming after us. He'll spoil everything."

"He won't spoil anything," answered McGregor. "That old idiot is Doc Adler."

"Who is he?" asked Peary.

McGregor turned on Peary a dull eye, as one who is not sure that an explanation will be worthwhile. Then he said briefly: "Doc Adler has killed more men than smallpox and made more money than the mint. Now he's retired to private life as a sort of universal uncle to crooks who know enough to ask his advice. And we need it now."

Adler rode his mule over the brow of the hill, at that moment, and came straight on. His smile was a toothless gap of darkness.

"Now, boys! Now, boys," he said as he came up. "What's in the air?"

"A pretty girl and a half-wit," said McGregor. "They ought to be coming up this road, in a few minutes. This fellow is Len Peary, Doc. He wants the girl . . . and I want the man . . . dead!"

"Peary wants the girl because she's got a neat face . . . you want the man dead . . . because he's a half-wit?"

"He's called Barney Dwyer," said McGregor. "Does that mean anything to you? His name is spreading pretty fast through the mountains . . . just about as fast as sound can travel."

"I ain't hard of hearing, but news don't come to me no more," said Doc Adler sadly. "There was a time when every dog-gone' wind blew me as much news as an autumn wind brings to the nose of a grizzly. But times is changed, with me. Nobody wants to talk to the old buzzard on his roost. Who is this Dwyer? If he's a half-wit, why is he worth killing? Got money, Mack?"

"He hasn't a penny," answered McGregor. "When I call him a half-wit, I mean that he doesn't know what tricks and quick thinking mean. He's the kind you read about and never see. A lie would choke him. A ten-year-old boy could make a fool of him. He's such a half-wit that he took from Peary's father the job of coming up to Timberline and getting Len away from bad company . . . and Len Peary is one of my best men."

"Well," said Doc Adler, "maybe I'm gettin' old and feeble in the brain, but how could that poor fool bother a pair like you two?"

"Because there's no fear in him," said McGregor, frowning. "And because he has the strength of a team of mules. He can break iron with his hands. He went after Peary. I stopped him and locked him up. He broke iron to get away from my cellar. He took Peary away from under my nose, so to speak. And everybody in the mountains knows, now, that Barney Dwyer made a fool of me. That's why he has to die, Doc. If I lose my reputation, where am I?"

"Nowhere," agreed Adler. He fixed the dark hollows of his eyes on McGregor and nodded to confirm his judgment. Then he patted the butt of the Winchester that lay in its long, saddle scabbard under his left knee. "This here might speak a word that would put an end to Barney Dwyer, Mack. But if he had Peary, how did Peary get away?"

"The sheriff took Peary for a stage hold-up that he did, and for a killing that he didn't do. This dummy of a Dwyer followed on. He was going to do his job, d'you see? He was going to take Peary back to the home ranch in spite of me, in spite of the law, too, and the sheriff's posse. And he *did* take Peary away from that posse by the damnedest bit of cool work I've ever seen. That was only the other day. I was on hand, watching. And this girl, Sue Jones, was there, too. As soon as Peary was loose, the posse came with a rush. I made Peary take the girl's horse and run for it with me."

"And how did the girl get away?" asked Adler. "How'd she manage without no hoss?"

"Dwyer took her up behind him on his mustang, and managed to get her away, I don't know how. What I *do* know, Doc, is that only half an hour ago I spotted the pair of 'em coming up this road . . . I spotted 'em from the top of that hill, yonder, with my field glasses. They're on the way to Greenborough, just over that ridge. And once in Greenborough, they're gone from us for good."

"What keeps you from taggin' him out with a slug of lead?" asked Adler earnestly.

"Because the girl's with him," answered McGregor. "And Peary wants her more than he wants eyes in his head. If we drop Dwyer out of her hand, so to speak, she won't have to guess about who turned the trick. She's another one with clean hands, Doc. It turned her sick to think of Peary on the road with me . . . and one killing would finish him, as far as she's concerned."

"Birds of a feather oughta flock together," said old Doc Adler to Peary. "You look a bright, upstandin' kid. You oughta know she ain't your breed. It'd be an outcross. Leave her be, boy. Leave her alone. Tag Dwyer with a chunk of lead and let him lie."

Peary looked at the old villain in silence.

"It's no good, Doc," said McGregor. "I'll take care of Barney Dwyer as soon as I get him away from the girl. But I can't take him by force . . . not if there's any other way."

"They're coming!" broke in Peary, pointing through a gap in the trees.

"Get the horses and the mule back from the head of the hill," ordered McGregor, dismounting. "Get off that mule, Doc, and lend me your brains."

Doc Adler got down to the ground with remarkable agility, and, as Peary obediently took the livestock out of view, Adler was smiling. Into the shadows of his eyes came a light. "Gimme that field glass of yours, McGregor," he said. It was handed over to him, and, as he busily focused it through the trees on the advancing pair, he muttered: "The back of the legs, that's where a man gets old first, and then in the small of the back, and then in the shoulders, and

130

then in the eyes, and then in the brain. I'm old clean up to my eyes, Mack, but there's a part of the brain left yet, I guess." He steadied the glass and then murmured: "The man's walkin' and the girl's ridin'. But the way she keeps dippin' and bendin' toward him, you'd think that she'd rather be walkin' on the ground with him than settin' dead comfortable in that saddle."

"I'm glad that Peary isn't seeing it, then," answered McGregor.

"This here boy, this here Peary," said old Doc Adler, "is he the right sort to be useful to you?"

"He's all right, but he hasn't made up his mind, yet," said McGregor. "He wants a free life. He hates work. He hates his father's ranch. He can fight like a tiger. And he's fast with a gun, and straight. But being outside the law is a game with him, so far. It's fun for him, and not a business. He doesn't mind stealing, but he hates stolen money. He'd rather take the money one day and give it back the next. But I think I've got my hands on him now. He loaned a hand in a stage robbery, not long ago, and I fixed it so that the shooting of the driver is laid to him. I did that shooting myself, but so long as the sheriff thinks that Peary turned the trick, it's enough to hang him.

Fear of the rope will make Peary what I want him to be, in the long run."

"You're a bright boy, Mack," said Doc Adler. "You got brains. When I was young, I would've wanted a partner like you." He broke off to say: "That's considerable of a hoss that the girl is riding."

"It's a wild-caught mustang," said McGregor. "Dwyer tamed her, and nobody but Dwyer could ride her, up to a little while ago. But now I see he's let the girl make friends with the mare."

"A wild-caught mustang is like a wild-caught hawk," said Doc Adler. "They fly the best. There's something in that girl, too. She carries her head like there was something inside of it . . . and she's got a pretty face."

"She's as clean as a dog's tooth, and very nearly as sharp," said McGregor. "But get that brain of yours working, Doc, will you? How am I to stop that pair from riding straight on into Greenborough? I mean, without using guns. If the girl gets away, Peary will tag along after her, all over the world. And if Dwyer gets away from me, everybody in the mountains will be laughing at me."

Doc Adler lowered the glasses. He turned to McGregor and rested his hand against the rough bark of a pine tree. "If I stopped 'em, and parted 'em, and sent the man away from the girl, what would I get out of it?" asked Adler.

"Stop them . . . part them . . . send the man away . . . how the devil can you do that, Doc?" asked McGregor.

"By brainwork, son," said Doc Adler. "You can go up ahead, you and Peary, and pretty soon, I'll send Dwyer galloping along on that red mare. You can shoot him off of that hoss and the girl will know nothing except that he never came back to her. But what would I get out of it?"

"What would you want, Doc?" asked McGregor.

"The mare," said Adler suddenly, eagerly.

"The mare?" echoed McGregor. "But what would you do with her? You couldn't ride her."

"Does a charm on a watch chain help a watch to keep time?" asked Adler, snarling. "No, and I want the mare not to ride, but just to have. Understand?"

"I don't understand, but she's yours," said McGregor. "How the devil you can manage these things, I don't know. But I'm going to take your word. I'll ride up the road and wait there with Peary. And if you send Barney Dwyer past us alone, and on the

133

mare, I'll call you a wizard, Adler!"

II

The road was more bumps than level, more rocks than soil, but Barney Dwyer stepped over it with his head high and his eyes fixed on the mountains at which he could look through the double fence of the high, dark pine trees. As the road changed, swerved, twisted snake-like back and forth as mountain trails will do, he had an ever changing viewpoint and an ever changing view. But what he saw of them, blue or brown or shining white, was not what filled his soul and kept him smiling; it was the girl, who rode on the red mare beside him, tilting toward Barney, laughing and chatting. She was not only bright to the eye, but she was sunshine to the spirit of Barney Dwyer. In that sunshine the long, cold winter in his heart had dissolved.

"Even the mare knows you, Sue," said Barney. "And even the mare loves you."

"As long as you're with me," said the girl. "But if you were away, she'd pitch me into the air and step on me when I hit the ground."

"She'd never buck with you, Sue," said Dwyer.

"I can see the side flare in her eyes, and her ears are trembling, and she keeps stretching the reins to make sure that her head belongs to herself," said the girl.

"Jog her ahead," said Barney Dwyer. "You'll see that she's as gentle as a lamb, with you."

"She'll turn me into a skyrocket," said Sue Jones. "But I don't mind trying her." She slapped the shoulder of the red mare that now started instantly off at a long, gliding trot, with head turned to the side as a horse will turn it in order to look back at the home place when a journey begins. But when the mare came to the next bend of the road, rather than round it and pass out of the master's sight, she suddenly bounded into the air and landed on stiff legs and with arched back. The shock slung the girl almost from the saddle, but with knee and hand she clung to it, and, before the red mare leaped again, the shout of Barney Dwyer checked her like a rope. He ran up as the girl straightened herself, gasping, pulled her sombrero level, and looked down at Barney with eyes still great with fear.

"She's a pretty dry stick of dynamite, Barney," she said. "But I told you so."

Barney Dwyer shook his head. He walked on beside the mare, smoothing the silk of

135

her neck with his hand, speaking to her reproachfully.

"You can't blame her," commented Sue Jones. "She was never broke . . . she was just gentled. You can't make her fear you, but you can make her love you."

They rounded that curve that the mare had refused to pass the moment before, and they saw before them a figure huddled face down at the edge of the road. His arms were stretched out before him, and an old black hat lay under one limp hand. The long, silver hair burned in the sunlight and blew like a mist in the wind.

The girl uttered a cry; Barney ran silently forward and leaned by the fallen body.

It was warm. He made sure of that with the first touch of his hand. Gently he turned the old man until he could see a long, deathly white face. The closed eyes seemed to be painted over with black. He pressed his ear to the breast, and, after a moment, he made out the beating of the heart. So Barney straightened up on his knees and shouted to the girl: "He's living!"

"I saw his breast move," she said. She was very calm, leaning above the fallen man.

"He's pegged out on the road," said Barney, making his voice soft, as though for fear that limp body might hear him. "Think of it, Sue. An old man like this . . . and thrown out to die, like . . . well, the way some people let old horses loose to starve on the road."

"That's the way the world is," said the girl. "He has a queer look about him. He's either a saint or a devil, I'd say."

"He's a dying man," said Barney. "Nothing but a doctor or a priest can help him. Let's get him off the road, and into some sort of comfort." He picked up that loose, sagging body, and carried it into the shadow of the nearest pine tree. The girl was already there, kicking together, and then smoothing down a bed of pine needles. On that, Barney Dwyer laid the helpless form.

And almost at once the old man opened his eyes. He said: "It's all right, Harry. I'm wore out. You go on. I'll never be no good no more. You go on." Then, from under frowning brows, he centered his gaze on Barney Dwyer, and was silent.

"Who is Harry?" asked Dwyer.

"It don't matter," said the old fellow.

"It was Harry that left you lying on the ground?" asked the girl suddenly.

It rather shocked Barney Dwyer to see that she stood back from the victim, frowning a little as she looked down at him. She had not expressed the slightest concern, from the beginning.

"Harry had to go on, I needed to rest a mite," said the old man. "I just sat down and took a rest . . . that was all."

"You fell on your face!" exclaimed Barney Dwyer. "You walked till you dropped. What's your name? No, don't answer that. I'll get you some water." He took a canteen from the saddle of the mare, and ran to the nearest sound of flowing water. The mare trotted after him like a dog, and the old man on the bed of pine needles closed his eyes.

"Will you tell me your name?" asked the girl, standing close by and tilting her head to one side, very much like a magpie studying a new sight.

"It's all right, Harry," muttered the other. "You go on first . . . and I'll come slow along. You go on. . . ." His voice died away.

"What day is it?" asked the girl sharply.

He opened his eyes and stared feebly, helplessly toward her. "Monday, ma'am," he said.

"Humph," murmured Sue Jones. "It's Tuesday. You been lying out there in the road for twenty-four hours?"

"I don't know," said the other. "I just seem to remember walkin' along, and then . . . I don't remember nothin' else."

Barney Dwyer came back on the run with

the canteen. He raised the head of the old man gently, and tilted the canteen to his lips. The old fellow took only a swallow and then relaxed to limpness, sliding from the hand of Dwyer until he was flat on the bed of pine needles again.

"Barney," said the girl.

He came hesitantly toward her, his head still turned back to look at the sufferer. "Barney," she went on very quietly at his ear. "This may all be a fake. Every bit of it. He talks as though he'd lain in the road for a day. But last night there was a rain. There are no dust and rain spots, as there ought to be, if he'd lived through all of that weather. There's nothing about his clothes to show that he's been out in the weather."

"Why, he was under the trees when it rained, I suppose," said Barney Dwyer. "What d'you mean, Sue?"

"I mean," she answered, "that he may not be honest."

"Not honest? Not honest?" said Barney. "Sue, what can be in your mind? Why . . . see how white his face is!"

"Age does that sometimes," she replied coldly.

"But he's all thin and worn," Barney protested.

"Age will do that, too."

"He was fainting, when we saw him," said Barney.

"Maybe that's a sham, too," she decided. "You have to remember that McGregor is somewhere in the field against you, Barney. And Peary is against you, too."

"Why should Peary be against me?" asked Dwyer, staring. "Perhaps he'd be in jail except for me, Sue."

"I'm the reason," said the girl, flushing. "You know, Barney, that a girl understands when a man really wants her. And Len Peary wanted me."

"Did you want him?" asked Barney naïvely.

"I didn't know you, then," she answered. "Yes, I would have married him, I think. Except that I knew he was friends with McGregor. That held me back."

Dwyer looked long at her. "Anybody who once hoped to have you would do murders to keep you," he declared. "But how could McGregor or Peary have anything to do with this?"

"I don't know," she answered. "But I know that they're your enemies, and that makes me suspect everything that happens to us until we're out of this part of the country."

Barney took off his hat and began to pass his fingers through his hair. "We've got to

140

do something about the poor old man," said Barney Dwyer. "Suspicion won't put him on his feet."

"Maybe he's well enough to get up and walk . . . if he has to. Maybe he's strong enough to run, as a matter of fact," she replied.

"You feel that way, and I'm sorry," said Barney. "But you know better than I do. What shall we do, then?"

She looked around her furtively toward the trees, as though she half expected danger to leap out from behind them at any moment.

"The thing for us to do," she finally said, "is for me to stay here with him, while you ride on into Greenborough. It won't take you long. In an hour or so you can be back from the town with a doctor in a buckboard. And then, if this old wreck is honest, we can take him away where he'll be properly cared for."

"But leaving you behind me?" he asked. "No, I see the point. If you come with me, the poor old man is helpless and alone. Stay here, Sue, and I'll be back as fast as the red mare can fetch and carry me." He jumped into the saddle on the mare. Still, for an instant, he delayed. "But what could happen to you, Sue, after all?" he asked at last.

"Nothing could happen," she answered. "I'll be all right. You ride on. You'll be back in an hour. Nothing will happen to me."

"You're not afraid?"

"No. I'm not afraid. Hurry along, Barney."

So Dwyer took the red mare up onto the trail and galloped her out of sight, out of hearing before the girl, at last, turned back toward her patient, and found him sitting up on his bed of pine needles, looking at her with the eyes of a death's-head.

III

For a half mile the long, elastic stride of the red mare carried Barney up the road toward Greenborough, twinkling through the tree shadows and the alternate stripes of sunshine. There was a darkness in his mind, because he could not understand what had seemed to him cruelly cold suspicion in the attitude of Sue Jones to the old man they had found. He would not pass a judgment on Sue, but he felt pain as though he himself had done a dishonorable thing. So his thoughts were far ahead of him and his eyes were seeing nothing. For that matter, he did not need to keep a look-out, and he knew it. His eyes were not so keen, all his senses never could be so alert as those of

142

the mare that bore him.

She, with her head high and her ears pricked, studied every breath of wind with suspicious nostrils, and examined every sparkle of the sun on a leaf, every stir and shifting far back among the shadows of the woods.

Now what she suddenly saw as she cantered around a bend of the road was no more than another glint of light very similar to the flash of the sun on a bit of varnished green foliage. Very similar, but slightly different. This luminous streak had a harder brilliance, and the mare halted with such a sudden shock that Barney was flung forward across her neck.

Through the space he would have filled if he had been still erect, whined two rifle bullets. One was as high as his heart, and one was as high as his head. And the double *clang* of the explosions knocked loudly on Barney's ear.

The mare did what she would have done on the open range, if a mountain lion had leaped up beside her path. She waited for no orders but bolted through a clump of poplars and took Barney out on the other side into the midst of bigger trees.

Four more bullets had rattled through the greenery as they fled. Then Barney heard

143

the beat of hoofs; he heard the familiar voice of McGregor, ringing like an iron horn, as it cried: "Drive straight through, Peary! Straight through! We've got to get him! We've got to get him!"

Barney had neither rifle nor revolver, but he had the mare. She took him through the dark of the forest like a jagged streak of red lightning that dodges through the clouds. Her hoofs never slipped. She had eyes in them. When she came out on the farther side of the woods, instead of running straight on, she turned to the right and skimmed along under the edges of the trees, aiming toward a little ridge of ground beyond where they would be shut from view.

Barney, totally bewildered, merely clung to the horn of the saddle with one hand, and with the other grasped the loosely hanging reins. The mare not only ran but did his thinking for him.

Looking back, Barney saw the two riders dash out from the trees into the open. He saw the splendor of their horses; he saw the flash of their long rifles. They reined in their mounts for an instant, looking for the prey. At last they saw it, but only as the mare dipped over the rising ground like a red streak and sank into the hollow beyond as a swallow swings down that open green valley

144

between the hills through the air.

Still she was fending for herself, and it was not to her liking. She knew all about rifles. In those old days when she ran free across the range, many a foolish cowpuncher that had failed to run her down had tried to capture her by creasing. Twice her neck had been slashed by bullets.

So she knew that there was not space for her to get out of range before the two riders behind had topped the hill. So while that barrier still rose behind her, she slanted back into the strip of woods again, and, darting through it to the road, her powerful stride snatched Barney around the curves and over high and low toward Greenborough. He heard behind him the rattling of hoofs on rocks, the pounding of them on softer ground. Once Peary and McGregor had a glimpse of him as he rounded a long curve, and they both fired for the fourth time. But he did not even hear the singing of the bullets, and after that there was pleasant silence down the road behind him.

They were gone, and before him was Greenborough, scattered along one side of Green Creek in the midst of green pasture lands. On the other side of the creek stood the pine forest, dark as a cloud in winter.

Barney called the mare back to a dog-trot.

He had dropped the guns of McGregor and Peary out of striking distance behind him, but the town itself might hold danger enough for him. If Sheriff Elder or any of his posse were there, they would be sure to recognize him, and, since he had taken Peary away from them all, they would be as anxious to get at him as greyhounds are to put their teeth in a fleeing rabbit. Barney and the girl had talked over the danger of this chance, but they had determined to risk it. For the railroad tapped Greenborough with the farthest extension of its line, and they wanted the speed of trains to sweep them away from McGregor's pursuit.

So Barney jogged slowly into Greenborough, praying with all his heart that the sheriff with his men might be out combing the woods, searching through the mountains. A bare-legged boy, brown as a Mexican, came out from a house lugging over his shoulder a heavy, long-barreled rifle as old as the old frontier.

"Can you tell me if there's a doctor in this town?" asked Barney politely.

"*You* got a hoss," said the boy. "What a whale *that* hoss is! I reckon she can move, mister, eh?"

"She's fast," agreed Barney. "Is there a doctor in the town?"

"She's got a neck like a stallion on her, ain't she?" said the boy. "Ridin' her must be pretty nigh to settin' on the back of a dog-gone' eagle, ain't it?"

"Is there a doctor in town?" Barney repeated.

"She must pretty nigh fly like an eagle," repeated the boy with round, delighted eyes. "Yeah. Down there at the other end of town you'll see a white house with a green roof onto it. That's where Doctor Swain hangs out, mostly. How old is she, mister?"

"Six," said Barney, and let the mare gallop down the street that followed the bright windings of the creek. Behind him pealed a voice, thin and high as a silver horn, crying: "Hey, are you Barney Dwyer?"

Barney did not turn to make an answer. For the first time in his life, the sound of his own name went through him like a needle point of pain and fear. Barney Dwyer! Yonder in the lowlands they all knew him as Barney the simpleton, or Barney the half-wit. But up here in the mountains they had new and strange ideas about Barney the breaker of iron, the fearless, the man-queller. And the law wanted him because he had stolen Peary out of its strong hands. The irresistible law was reaching for him.

He would have been overcome by these

147

reflections if he had not reminded himself of the exact mission on which he had ridden into Greenborough. Sue Jones had sent him to get the doctor, and Sue was always right — she never made mistakes. She always knew what was best to do.

In the meantime, that small, sharp voice had pealed accusingly after him. Would the youngster tell his suspicions to others?

Far down the street, rounding a curve, Barney glanced back and saw that the boy was coming, rifle and all, at a scamper.

But here was the end of the town, and a white house with a verandah built across the face of it, and a green roof above. It was just the sort of a place one would expect a doctor to live in. There was an air of neatness and order such as a professional man would demand of his surroundings. There was even a semblance of a garden in front of it, with stubby little rose bushes, and a flowering pink border on either side of the front path.

Barney dismounted and left the mare at the hitching rack where a saddled horse already was standing, a great rough-made brute of a brown gelding that looked fitter for the plow than for roadwork.

Barney passed through the front gate and left it swinging behind him, the iron latch clanking softly as it flicked across the catch. The front steps were painted blue. So was the floor of the verandah. And Barney stood in awe at the door, hat in hand, smoothing his hair a little before he knocked.

In answer to his tap, there loomed down the hallway an immense man, a fitting burden for the huge horse in the street. He was many inches over six feet tall; furthermore, he was built with a craggy solidity. He was a mountain of a man, and his dark beard was like a storm cloud that hangs about a mountain's head. "Well?" he asked, in a heavy voice. "Well, young man?"

"I beg your pardon," said Barney, "I only wanted to ask. . . ."

"Nothing here for beggars. Not even a woodpile. Get along with you," said the giant.

"I only wanted to ask . . . ," said Barney, retreating half a step.

"Get off this place!" roared the big man in a sudden fury. "And get off quick, or I'll throw you off. If you're hungry, there's enough fat on your face to keep you from starving for a week. Away with you, and all the rest of the idle, worthless, lazy loafers in the mountains!"

He cast open the screen door, which crashed with a metallic *jangling* behind him,

149

as he stood towering above Barney. And the blue, mild eyes of Barney opened and rounded with fear and with awe.

"Are you Doctor Swain?" he asked.

"I'm Doctor Swain," said the giant. "And I'll doctor you, young man, if you don't get off. . . ."

"I'm sorry," said Barney. "I don't want to trouble you, but I'm not exactly begging for anything . . . I want you to come to see a sick man, yonder in the woods. . . ."

"Not begging . . . sick man in the woods . . . what's he sick of?" exclaimed the doctor.

The small boy with the rifle was now arrived in a thin cloud of dust. He stood gripping the front fence and staring at the big pair on the verandah.

"I don't know what he's sick of," said Barney. "I just found him. . . ."

"What's his name?"

"I don't know," said Barney gravely.

"D'you know anything at all?" shouted the doctor, his anger blasting its way out again.

"No, sir. I don't know very much," said Barney, sighing.

"I'm a busy man. I've got no time to talk to fools," said the doctor. "Get off this place and stay off!"

"D'you mean that you won't come!"

exclaimed Barney, incredulous.

For doctors were to him among the saints of the world. They were the stayers of pain, the enemies of death, the open-handed friends of the poor. Therefore he could not believe the words that the doctor now roared at him.

"I've told you ten times to get out! Now I'll show you the way to the gate!"

With that, Dr. Swain laid on the arm of Barney a grasp that never yet had been successfully resisted. But now, under the iron tips of his fingers, he felt the arm of Barney turn from soft to rubbery hard that twisted suddenly like a snake, out of the grip.

"If you won't come of your own free will, I'll have to take you," said Barney.

"Take me?" shouted the furious doctor. "Take me?"

He was so angry that he struck suddenly at the face of Barney, not with his fist, but with the back of his hand. There was weight enough in that mere gesture to have floored an ordinary man, but it glanced from Barney like a stinging raindrop. He caught Dr. Swain by both wrists and held him so. The doctor, with a grunt of astonishment, tried to wrench away. His effort merely turned the hold of Barney into bracelets of red hot iron that shrank into the flesh, and ground

151

the tendons against the bones.

"My gosh," murmured the doctor.

What was most amazing, what was most unnerving, was that during this brief moment of the encounter not the slightest fierceness appeared in the eyes of Barney. There was merely a rather sad and curious investigation, as though he were seeing, unwillingly, how much pain the doctor might be able to endure.

"Who are you?" asked the doctor.

It was the boy at the fence who answered with a yell: "You can't get away from him, Doc Swain. He's Barney Dwyer! He's Barney Dwyer for sure!"

That name dissolved the last strength of resistance in Swain. He became suddenly a half frightened and totally submissive child. It was the most amazing instant of Barney's life, and he had to say gently: "There'll be no danger and no harm to you, Doctor Swain, if you'll come along quietly."

"In the middle of broad daylight right out of my house," muttered the doctor. But he shook his great bearded head and went with Barney down the path toward the gate.

"I should have known by the mare," grumbled Swain, chafing his bruised wrists. "The Lord knows there's been enough talk about the red mare and Barney Dwyer.

Young man," he broke out in a fervor, "if you had ten necks, there are nevertheless ten ropes that will hang all of 'em, one of these days."

"I hope I didn't hurt you," Barney said anxiously. "I didn't want to hurt you. But d'you mind hurrying a little? You see people are running out in the street, and they may begin to shoot at me any moment."

The doctor put his foot in the stirrup, but hesitated an instant to stare at Barney's mild face. Then he swung into the saddle with a grunt.

And down the street dodged the screeching voice of the boy with the rifle, crying: "Come look! He's here! Barney Dwyer's in town! Barney Dwyer!"

They were coming to look, too. Men and women and children rushed out of houses and shops, but the big gelding and the red mare were already at a gallop, leaving Greenborough and swinging across the open range.

IV

When Sue Jones, turning from the road, saw the old man sitting up, and felt the skull-like darkness of those eyes fixed on her, she gave back several hurried steps. There was nothing about his age that she could fear, she told herself, but a strange premonition and a sense of evil came over her, cold as the gliding of a snake.

He had sunk back again until his shoulders sagged against the trunk of the pine tree. A squirrel ran down to a lower branch and sat up to scold at the intruder.

"Lie down," said Sue, hurrying back, and filled instantly with shame. "You mustn't sit up. Save your strength and lie down. Do you feel better, now?"

"I was kind of tuckered out," said the man. "I jus' kind of give out, sudden-like. But I guess I'm all right now, once I could get onto my feet again. Will you gimme a help, ma'am?"

"You must lie down. Do as I tell you," said the girl. "There'll be a doctor here in a few minutes. You'll be taken care of. Don't worry about that."

"I'd like to stand up," he said. "Wouldn't you lend me a help, ma'am?"

"It will only show you how weak you are," Sue said, and held out her brown, strong young hand to assist him.

Over her wrist fastened the white claw of the other. She gasped with terror, but her effort to wrench away merely helped to pull him to his feet. She could shake him, but

154

she could not burst away from him, and this she understood at once. On tiptoe, eyes dilated, for an instant she trembled with her terror. But the moment she knew that she was helpless, she stood quietly resigned. She took hold of her fear with the strength of her will, and mastered it.

"That's better," said the old man. "That's a lot better. Jest calm and easy is the trick, my beauty."

She looked at the old devil as a man looks, eye to eye. Even her voice was perfectly steady when she said: "I suspected something. I felt the devil in you from the first."

"I seen you did," said Doc Adler. "There was a coupla times when I was afraid that you would put a finger on my pulse. And I couldn't fool you then no more than I could fool a doctor. You're bright enough. Oh, you're plenty bright enough. And there's enough fire in you to cook many a man, I reckon. Yeah, bake him tender right to the wishbone. But if. . . ."

Here they heard the distant explosions of guns, sounding very much like hammer strokes through the thinness of the mountain air. Four shots the girl counted and at every one of them her body jerked a little, as though the bullets had struck home in her own flesh.

"Barney . . . ," she whispered, and waited, staring at the hollow eyes of Adler.

He favored her with his toothless, evil grin. "That's the end of him," said Adler. "I reckon that McGregor would finish him, all right. McGregor ain't the man to miss four times running."

Curiously Adler watched the bluish tinge come into her face. Her lips parted. She began to breathe spasmodically.

And now, from a greater distance, two rifle shots again. It was Adler's time to start.

"They missed him the first time. They've missed him again. God wouldn't let him die!" cried the girl. The life came back to her, as she spoke.

Old Adler snarled: "Four bullets sunk in him, and the mare carries him a ways, and then he drops out of the saddle, after a while. And McGregor comes up and looks at him lyin' there on the ground, writhin' and wrigglin'. Not dead, but dyin'. So he puts in two more shots, just to make sure. Two more shots, and that turns Barney Dwyer into a soggy lump of nothin'." His lips began to twitch over that gaping grin.

The girl shook her head. "They missed the first four times, and then they missed again. The red mare would have him a lot farther away, by that time. She'd carry him like a stone running downhill, faster and faster, if she ran for her life. He's safe, now. He's safe in Greenborough. I know it!"

"If he is," Adler said with bitter venom, "then there ain't any truth or rightness in McGregor and his guns. And I'll be done with him, and may the devil fly off with him!"

So they remained for a long moment, the hand of Adler frozen onto the wrist of the girl, until the rapid pounding of hoofs beat on their ears, and down the road came McGregor, galloping his horse hard; behind him, on a rope, labored the mule of Doc Adler.

He drew up, throwing the rope end toward Adler. "Here's your mule, Doc," he said. "Climb aboard it. Sue, jump up here behind me."

Adler released her wrist. She looked down for an instant at the white marks that surrounded her arm. Then she walked slowly toward McGregor.

"He got away, Mack," she declared.

"Who?" said McGregor, frowning.

"Barney Dwyer. You missed him. He's safe in Greenborough."

"He's safe in Greenborough till the sheriff picks him up and the crowd strings him up to a tree," answered McGregor. "Jump up here behind me."

"Tell me one thing, please!" she begged.

"Well, what is it?"

"Was Len Peary with you? Were you alone, or was Len Peary with you?"

"Peary?" answered McGregor, looking straight back into her eyes. "If he'd been with me, d'you think that he would have helped against Barney? He owes Dwyer his life, and he's too soft to forget that sort of a thing."

She hesitated, and then nodded. "I think he's soft enough to know what gratitude is, Mack," she agreed. "Where are you going to take me?"

He smiled, but his eyes went savage as he stared down at her. "You know how they catch wild hawks, Sue?" he said. "They tie a pigeon with a string, and, when the hawk flies over, it swoops right down into a net. You'll be the pigeon for me, Sue. That fool of a lucky half-wit will never stop hunting till he finds you, and, when he finds you, he'll find me and my guns. Climb up behind me. It's late . . . and we've a ways to go."

She made no resistance, not even with a word. Talking and struggling would be folly, she knew.

"Go first, Doc," said McGregor. "You know the way to your own house."

"My own house?" shouted Adler in a sudden passion. "Am I gonna show the whole world where I live?"

"Go on, Doc," said McGregor. "You're in this with me, and you're going to stay in with me. I'll tell you the whole idea when we're alone. Start on."

Adler looked at him out of those baleful eyes for a moment, but then, surrendering as quietly as the girl had done, he rode across the trail and went up the slope among the pine trees.

V

That was why Barney Dwyer, riding in among the trees, found empty the place where he had left the old man and the girl. He looked with vague eyes of terror at the doctor. He jumped down from his horse, stared at the untenanted bed of pine needles, and then wandered helplessly in a circle, like an animal tethered to a stake.

Dr. Swain said nothing. During the ride from Greenborough he had not talked a great deal, but he had been able to shake off the sense of fear that had possessed him when he left the town. Secure in the enormity of his bulk and strength, he had been bewildered on finding himself helpless in the grasp of a smaller man. It had seemed to him that the power of a maniac was in the grasp of Barney Dwyer, but all the while there had been nothing but gentle consideration in the face of Barney. He had apologized many times for taking the doctor away by force. He had about him an air of deference that was almost awe. And gradually Swain came to realize that he had met that impossible thing — a man who had no desire for physical supremacy, one who felt no glory in a triumph.

And the doctor's sense of wounded pride vanished. He asked questions. He received gentle and honest answers about the strange way in which Barney Dwyer had undertaken the quest for Leonard Peary, and it was at this point that the two men rode through the trees to the place where Dwyer found nothing but the heaped-up pine needles, and the secret whispering of the wind through the upper branches.

"They've gone," said Barney helplessly. "I don't understand. She couldn't have carried him away."

A sudden suspicion made the doctor exclaim: "Well, could he have carried *her* away?"

"Why," Barney said, always willing to repeat everything patiently, "he was very

160

old, you know, and so weak and sick that he could not move. I had to carry him. His poor head and arms and legs hung down. It was like carrying a dead body."

"Wait a moment," said the doctor. "Tell me what he looks like. I've ridden every inch of this range to my patients, and I know a good many thousand faces."

"Well, he's old and white . . . and he has a white, long face, and his eyes are like the black holes in a skull."

"Adler!" shouted the doctor. "Doc Adler!" He lowered his voice. The violence with which he had shouted seemed to frighten him suddenly. He listened, hushed, to the echoes as they fled away.

"Adler? Who is he?" asked Barney Dwyer.

"Adler is what nobody knows . . . except that he's a devil. Except that he's committed every crime on the calendar, no one knows what he's done. Everything from picking pockets to murder. But nothing ever has been proved against him. He has always known how to cover his trail. Adler? God pity that poor girl!"

"But it was an old, helpless, sick man!" cried Dwyer.

"An old man like that could pretend to be helpless and sick, Dwyer. Don't you realize that?"

Barney stretched out his hands as though to grasp something out of the empty air. He looked down at those hands, then struck them against his forehead.

The doctor was deeply touched by this silent agony, and muttered that he was sorry. There were no tears in the eyes of Barney; there was no tremor in his voice because he felt pain, but no self-pity.

"I'll try to find her again," he said. "Will you tell me where I can get at Adler?"

"It would be easier to tell you where a hawk lives," answered Swain. "Adler has been seen around these mountains, from time to time, the way you see hawks in the sky, but no one knows where he lives."

"You can go back," said Barney. "There's nothing that you can do here. I'm sorry I bothered you." He broke off to groan. "She must have suspected him all the time. That was why she seemed cold . . . that was why she seemed to be thinking of something else all the while."

"I can go back to Greenborough and spread the alarm," said Swain. "But if Adler has turned his hand to kidnapping, no one knows what a close hunt will make him do. I'm going back, Dwyer, and give word to the sheriff. And in the meantime, if there's ever a thing I can do for you, let me know.

Call on me."

Barney Dwyer, still in a trance of misery, watched the huge doctor ride away. The red mare, sniffing at something at the edge of the road, brought him to her, gloomily, his head bent in despair. It was that very dropping of his head that enabled him to see the dim outline of a very small hoof. Only a mule could have left that narrow sign.

He ran straight across the road. On the farther side were many rocks. Among them he searched patiently for nearly an hour until, just beyond the rocks, in a patch where no pine needles lay, he found two more footprints, like the first one. And near them was the tread of a horse.

He fled through the woods along that line. With rattling bit-chains and jouncing stirrups, the mare followed him, until he saw a small glint of white on the tip of the lowest branch of a pine tree. It was a very small segment of white cloth, about the texture of a handkerchief, a woman's handkerchief. He held it gingerly on the tips of his fingers. Was it hers? Had she ripped up the handkerchief and left this spot of white as a mark for a turning point, perhaps, on the trail? He knew there was about Sue always a thin fragrance of lavender. But when he tried to find that perfume on this shred of cloth, all he was aware of was the sweating of the mare close by and the keen, pure odor of the pines.

He went on in the first direction, came to open ground, and found no sign at all. He doubled back to the place where the white shred of cloth had been found, and, searching to the right, he located the hoof prints almost instantly.

That settled it in the mind of Barney Dwyer. It was the trail of the old man and the girl. Helpless as he had seemed, Doc Adler must have had a horse and a mule at close hand, and he had taken the girl away at the very time when McGregor and young Peary were chasing Barney through the trees and over the hills toward Greenborough. But as she was carried off, she had known how to blaze the trail behind her. Indians could do that very deftly. A broken twig, here and there, or a bit of scuffed grass were enough to tell their friends how to follow them.

Here Barney closed his eyes and threw back his head with a silent prayer for more cunning on the trail. Then he started forward again.

He rode the mare, now, in order to cover the way more rapidly, stooping low from the saddle to scan the ground. That was how he happened to find the second little white marker, like a pale dot on the leaves. He scooped it up without dismounting and found, to be sure, that it was of exactly the same texture as the first bit. So he abandoned the straight line of the trails and again cut for sign. And this time he found it to the left, where the riders had passed down a long, close avenue of trees, straight as a gun barrel, with a blazing eye of sun at the farther end.

So Barney rode swiftly down that natural street and into the open day again. The blue sky, the icy tops of the mountains, the flash of a stream in the bottom of the valley, all were like rewards to him, and like promises, also.

Where had they ridden ahead of him? He was on a long, naked sweep of rock, but through a crevice grew up a few bushes. On one of these he saw from a distance the thin gleam of a patch of white. It was another fragment of the same cloth. An exultation mastered Barney Dwyer. Nothing in his life compared with the wordless appeal of those ragged little bits of white.

This one pointed him down into the valley, so he descended at once to the bottom, where the stream ran, bright as polished silver. It was very shallow. The trail crossed

and recrossed it. Through the clear flash of
the water, he thought he could mark how
the rocks had been worn by many tramplings of horses or mules.

It was a beautiful valley, with wild, precipi-
tous sides, sometimes of sheer rock, grooved
and battered by a thousand winters, sometimes with projecting shoulders covered
with trees. On the tops of the cliffs the dark
fringe of the forest began again, with the
pale mountain summits rising behind.

He felt that he could ride almost blindly
down this narrow valley, picking up the sign
of the fugitives only now and again. However many people had ridden the trail
before, the ravine seemed empty now. And
if Adler were likened to a hawk, then he
must have carried Sue off to some aerie in
the higher mountains. So Barney made
good time, swinging the mare along at a full
gallop, hardly ever glancing down to the
ground.

That was how he almost ran into the arms
of danger. For rounding a bend just after he
had forded the stream for the tenth time, he
saw the shadowy forms of riders coming
toward him behind trees.

He jumped the mare into a great, green
bowering of shrubbery that covered them
both like a wave of the sea, and, peering out

166

from this, he saw Sheriff Elder and five other riders come streaming around the bend, six grim men on six strong horses, and every man with a rifle laid across his saddle fork.

They came on softly. The wind covered the noise of their horses and not a one of them spoke until they reached the verge of the water through which Barney had just passed.

Then the sheriff halted them all by the lifting of his hand. Barney could hear him speaking. "Justis," said the sheriff, "take Walker and Harmon and go up along the rimrock. Hunt every crack in the rock to the bottom. Because I've got the feeling in my bones that they're somewhere around here."

"Who d'you want the most, Elder?" asked the man named Justis. He looked like a picture of the old type of frontiersman, with long hair hanging down to his shoulders.

"I've got a private grudge against Barney Dwyer," said the sheriff, "but that's not why I've turned a hundred men loose hunting through the mountains. It isn't what I want to find, but what the law wants to find. And the law wants McGregor, and that murdering young Len Peary."

The party split at once into two parts.

Three men turned sharply to the side and started up the slope toward the valley wall. The sheriff and two more of his crew continued down the valley trail.

But Barney remained, quivering like a hunted deer, long after they were all out of sight. 100 men! Thirty-three parties of three — all armed men — all hunting for scalps through the mountains like so many groups of Indians. And he, Barney Dwyer, had no weapons in his hands. It was as though he were attempting to handle red hot coals without so much as leather gloves to protect his skin.

He went out from his covert again. The valley no longer was, to him, an empty place, but rather it was living and shining and trembling with danger. Out of every shadow he expected a rifle to speak.

That was his frame of mind, and he was on tiptoe with tension when he saw another rider canter from a copse a quarter of a mile ahead of him on a horse darkly polished with sweat. By the fine, upright carriage of the head, by something gallant and adventurous in the bearing, he knew that it was Leonard Peary. The woods beside the creek received Peary and covered him, and Barney was instantly after him.

What person other than Len Peary had a

motive in stealing the girl? Might not that sinister Doc Adler have acted as his agent? Barney rushed the mare in pursuit as rashly as though he could afford to despise rifle bullets.

He came to the very spot where the trees had covered the shining horse of Peary. It was a narrow strip. Through the tree trunks he could see the brightness of the water. So he dismounted and went through as soundlessly as a gliding snake. He came out on the bank. He saw where the prints of the hoofs of a horse had rounded the side of the stream and gone down to the water, but, of horse and of man, all traces had disappeared. Len Peary and his mustang had vanished away like a thought.

Barney lifted his eyes with despair. *For* on the other side of the creek, across which Peary might have passed with his horse, there was nothing but a vast wall of rubble and of solid rock that lifted up to a square-topped mesa. Only one tree grew at the base of the rock, leaning its huge trunk and branches out over the stream, but all the rest of the stone wall was impregnable, incapable of giving refuge. Barney felt a darkness of wonder rush over his brain.

VI

The top of that rocky mesa was several acres in extent and it was as pleasant as a garden. It was a gently hollowed basin with a break in the side toward the creek below. Ancient trees stood on that unspoiled ground, and grass thick as a lawn offered the finest pasturage in the world. A gray mule and a herd of three goats strolled on that grass, and under a dappling of shadow moved some sheep, close together, like a drifting of cirrus clouds.

The mesa rose well above the bottom of the valley, yet a spring leaped in the center of the green hollow, ran down into a spacious pool, and then trickled away over the lip of the cliff toward the creek beneath. Only at the spring it kept up a noise like muted conversation. Otherwise, the small current moved noiselessly, clinging to the face of the outer rock all the way to the bottom. And where the pool widened, stood a small log cabin, very roughly built, with McGregor and Doc Adler and Susan Jones seated in homemade chairs before it. The sun was far enough to the west to throw the shadow of the house over the group, and therefore they were at ease — Adler sucking at a pipe, McGregor with a cigarette, and the girl leaning well back, with both hands cupped under her head. A little woolly, mongrel dog that looked like a very under-grown sheep was curled up between the feet of Adler.

"And trout, too," old Adler was saying. "I've hooked trout out of it, too. You can call me a liar, but dog-gone me if I ain't hooked trout out of that there pool, and cooked them, too, and ate them, too. Though whether them trout come up out of the spring or crawled up the face of the cliff, I dunno. All I know is that they tasted uncommon good."

The small dog wakened from sleep, jumped up, and trotted busily off to the edge of the mesa.

"What's your dog going after?" asked McGregor.

"He's goin' the rounds," said Doc Adler. "He's got nerves, is what he's got. That Sammy dog, he likes to be up here high in the air, but he don't want no guests along with him. He's kind of a snob. He's the kind of a snob that would lick a gentleman's hand and bite a tramp in the pants. So he goes the rounds, now and then, and mostly he watches to see that nobody can be comin' up the trail."

"Who would come up the trail?" asked

171

McGregor.

"Well," said Doc Adler, "the facts is, Mack, that there's a lot of folks interested in my past. There's a lot of folks that would like to collect news about me. There's even a lot that would like to cut my throat to see whether my blood was red or blue or green, maybe. And Sammy seems to know that trouble ain't never so very far away. Him and me, Mack, we set up here like lookouts on a masthead, and we keep peerin' around to see what might come over the edge of the sky."

McGregor turned his dull, calm, thoughtful eyes upon the old man. "It's a lonely life," he said. "I wouldn't like to be leading it at your age."

"You ain't gonna be leading it at my age," answered Adler. "Because you ain't gonna be alive at my age. You got too much enthusiasm in you, Mack, to live this long. But it ain't so lonely for me. I got my memories. I'd rather have a lot of my memories than a whole flock of sons and grandsons around me."

"They'd be spending your money, Doc. Is that it?" asked McGregor.

"Money?" snapped Adler. "And what would I be doin' with money, Mack? You're talkin' like a fool. Money? What would money mean to me, roostin' up here like an old buzzard on a rock?"

McGregor smiled, and turned his eyes away. He said nothing, but it was plain that his mind had not left the subject.

The girl stood up. "Tell me a story about myself," she said.

"I'll tell you a story," said Doc Adler. "It goes like this . . . Susan was a good little girl. She never done nothin' wrong, and she always helped her ma around the house, and she washed and dried the dishes, and she done the pans, too, and she always scoured 'em bright. And she never said no, and she never said that she was tired, and everybody loved Susan. So what d'you think became of this good little girl? Why, she went and got fond of a fat-faced fool of a half-wit, by the name of Barney Dwyer, and she got herself clean mired down in trouble, was what she got herself, till finally she found herself setting up on the top of a mesa and never knowin' how she got there, hardly, and every minute she set there, Barney Dwyer was sure comin' closer and closer until. . . ."

"Stop it, Doc," advised McGregor. "Or you'll drive her crazy. What's the matter with that dog?"

For Sammy the mongrel had turned from

the edge of the mesa and bolted toward the cabin at full speed. His tail was tucked between his legs. It was wonderful to see his fear and to notice his silence, in spite of it.

"He's seen something," declared Adler, jumping to his feet. "There's something coming up the trail. It may be a coyote . . . or it may be a whole dog-gone' posse, for all that I know. I'll go see."

He stretched his long legs to cross the little plateau while Sammy, instead of following, crouched before the feet of McGregor. The latter stretched out his hand toward the girl, and she got up instantly and stood beside him, saying: "I'll follow you. I won't try to bolt or to yell. But don't touch me, Mack."

"I'm poison to you, am I?" he asked her. He seemed to look down at her from a vast altitude of years and wisdom.

"You're poison to the whole world," she told him in answer. She stared evenly back at him. "I'd rather touch a snake than you, Mack."

Before he could answer, they saw old Adler turn suddenly toward them from the edge of the mesa. He ran back with a shambling stride, making a signal for them to retreat.

McGregor caught up two of the chairs and

placed them inside the door of the cabin. "We've got to dip into the tunnel, Sue," he commanded, urging her back from the main room of the little house to the storage shed that opened behind it.

She obeyed, but there was a tremor of excitement in her as she heard a horse whinny not far away.

The whole floor of the house was the clean, dry limestone that composed the mesa. It was scored across by many deep cracks, and, under the edge of one of these crevices, McGregor fitted the tips of his fingers and lifted. A whole slab of the stone gave way a little, commenced to resist the pressure, and then stuck fast. McGregor grunted with effort and with surprise. "It's as if somebody were holding it down!" he exclaimed. He gave a great heave. The stone merely shuddered, and, as he stopped pulling, it settled back in place with a jerk.

It was a face polished with sweat that McGregor turned to the girl. "It's stuck . . . something's wrong with it," he muttered.

The footfall of old Adler entered the front of the cabin.

"Are you safe down, McGregor?" he called in a subdued voice, as though others were near who might overhear him.

"The damned top stone is stuck," said

McGregor, hurrying back into the front room, his hand on the arm of the girl to keep her with him. "What d'you do about that?"

"Stuck?" snarled Doc Adler. "You fool, it can't be stuck . . . it. . . ."

Out the door, Sue Jones saw what seemed to her the most beautiful sight in the world — Sheriff Elder and five men coming straight toward the cabin, on foot, each with a long rifle in his hand.

"The attic?" said McGregor. "Or shall we fight 'em, Doc?"

"Fight 'em? Two ag'in' six? Up that ladder into the attic. Quick!"

"And be trapped? I'll never take a step to the attic!" exclaimed McGregor.

"Then let 'em catch you here," said Adler. "You've bungled everything. I never wanted to take you here. But *they* won't bungle things . . . not when they tie a rope around your neck and hang you up, McGregor. You know what they'll do when they see the girl and learn the yarn she can spin. Get up that ladder . . . and I'll try to keep 'em from follerin'."

McGregor looked wildly, desperately around him for a moment. Then he waved the girl before him. Up she went, scurrying. McGregor followed. As they entered the

176

darkness of the attic, old Adler removed the ladder from the open trap, and laid it against the side of the wall, flat on the limestone floor. McGregor lowered the trap; a redoubled darkness poured over the eyes of the girl.

VII

It was not a total darkness, however, that covered Sue. Small dim slits and eyes of light appeared on the floor of the attic, and, lying flat, she put her eye to the largest gap and found that almost the whole of the main room was instantly in view.

Beside her, the whisper of McGregor sounded. "If you make a sound, if you make a move to attract 'em, Sue . . . if you so much as knock some dust through one of the cracks . . . I'll finish you before they have a chance to finish me. You've been wrecking my whole game for me. You've been pulling Len Peary away from me. It's on account of you that Dwyer is on my trail. And now you'll pay for it, woman or no woman, if they corner me with you here."

The whisper ended. And she knew perfectly that he meant what he said. He had merely laid one finger on her arm, but it was like the touch of steel — hard, relentless, heavy.

So she lay still, waiting, watching. One cry from her and the six men who were approaching the cabin would tear it to shreds to find her. But they would only find her dead body. Her prayer must be that her friends would fail in their search.

Old Doc Adler had gone to the door of the cabin, and he could be seen waving toward the strangers. "Hello, boys," said Adler. "Hello, Sheriff. Mighty glad to see you, Elder. Got anything framed up on me today?"

"I've found out your hiding place, have I?" said Sheriff Elder. "And I think I'll be taking you out of this, Adler. I think it's jail for you, now."

"All right," said Adler. "There's plenty of things that I could be stuck in jail for. What have you run down at last, Elder?" He backed away from the door, inviting the others to enter.

Elder came striding in with the long-haired frontiersman, Justis, behind him. Two more of the men entered. Then the sheriff commanded: "Start hunting, boys. Hunt every inch of the mesa and the cabin. I'll stay here and talk to this old toothless mountain lion while you're working the ground over. Sit down, Adler. Wait a minute.

I'll see if you have any guns around you."

The posse men scattered as Adler answered: "No guns, Elder. No, sir, I ain't much good with guns, no more."

"Why not?" asked the sheriff. "Your hands are steady enough."

"My hands are steady, but my eyes ain't no good, no more. I've got a knife on me, and that's all."

"Let me have it, then. Never mind. I'll find it." The dexterous and familiar hands of the sheriff hunted through the clothes of Adler and produced from them, in fact, only one long, murderously sharp Bowie knife. Elder felt the edge of it, and nodded. "That would cut a throat, eh?" he said.

"And maybe it has, Sheriff," answered Adler. "You can't tell. Maybe it *has* cut a throat or two. You take a look, and you'll see that it's been sharpened and sharpened, and wore down and wore down. Not all by skinnin' rabbits and coyotes, neither!"

He sat down facing the sheriff and began to rub his claws together, laughing. With all her heart the girl wondered at that evil old face, for she felt that Doc Adler was almost welcoming the danger of that search.

"We've had word out of Greenborough that may wipe the grin off your face," said the sheriff. "What's become of the girl,

Adler? Answer me that!"

"What girl?" asked Adler.

The sheriff looked coldly at him for a long moment. "Lying won't help you a lot," he said finally. "The girl you were with today. Sue Jones is her name."

"Her that give me the hand when I was down and out?" said Adler. "Is that the one you mean?"

"Go on," said the sheriff curtly.

"Why," said the old villain, "she's back yonder in the pine trees, waitin' for Barney Dwyer, unless he's come and fetched her along to Greenborough by this time."

"What happened?" asked the sheriff.

"I'm gettin' old," answered Adler, "and the way of it was that as I was riding my old gray mule along the Greenborough road, I got dizzy. And I climbed off that mule and started to walk, waitin' for my head to clear. But it didn't clear. No, sir, it just got more clouded over, and the first thing I knew, somebody had picked me up off of the ground, where I must've fainted, maybe. It was Barney Dwyer and the girl. I was considerable weak. Dwyer went off to fetch a doctor from Greenborough, but, after a few minutes, I felt better by a whole pile, and so I just told the girl that I could fend for myself, now, and I went off and found the mule in the trees, and rode back home. That's all."

"And the girl?" said the sheriff, snapping out the words.

"She tried to keep me from goin' off," said Adler. "There's a lot of kindness and goodness in that girl, Sheriff. She wanted me to stay till a doctor came. But bein' my age, I don't want no doctor listening to see is there a leak in my heart, or is my liver goin' back on me. No, sir, I don't want to start dyin' of fear before I'm dyin' in fact. Y'understand?"

"Adler," the sheriff said gravely, "that girl was gone when Dwyer brought the doctor back."

"Hold on!" exclaimed Adler. "What would've happened to her, then?"

The sheriff raised a forefinger, as he continued: "How many murders and robberies you've chalked up to your credit, Adler, I don't know. But if you've had a hand in making that girl disappear, I'm going to make you sweat in hell for it. That is, unless you can turn her up for us. You hear me? Find the girl for us, and no harm done to her, and we'll call the deal square and forget bygones."

"Wait a minute," said Adler, frowning. "Who would've laid a finger on her? Who would've wanted to? Folks don't bother women. Not in this part of the world, they don't, and you know it. Any girl could ride from one end of the Rockies to the other, and no harm ever come to her. You know that, too!"

The sheriff leaned forward, peering earnestly into that long, chalky, evil face. But Adler was wearing an expression of the most open candor.

He even added: "I'll tell you what, Sheriff. If anything's happened to that girl, I'm gonna stir my stumps to find out who bothered her. But it ain't likely that nobody bothered her. She just got tired of waitin' for Dwyer, and she went to meet him on the way back, after I rode off. That's what happened, sure."

"I think you're lying, Adler," said the sheriff, "and God help you if there's any proof of it."

Justis appeared in the doorway. "We've gone over the whole dog-gone' mesa," he said. "We don't find no sign of her. We've found some sheep and goats and a mule. That's all."

"What you find in the shed?" asked the sheriff.

"All kinds of groceries and provisions. Adler has enough chuck in there to feed him for a couple years," said Justis.

"Nothing else?"

"Yeah. Some furs and pelts. And some old traps. And some saddles and. . . ."

"I don't care about that stuff," said the sheriff. "But I want to know a lot of other things. I want to know why that trail up the face of the mesa isn't worn more. Adler's been here a long time, but it took a microscope, almost, to find any sign of a trail over the rocks. We were only guessing, when we left the horses down below and climbed up to the top of the rock."

"The trail ain't wore deep," said Adler, "because it ain't often that I leave here and take a ride. I'm an old man, Sheriff, and, when a gent gets old, he likes to set quiet and smell the wind, and feel the sun, and let the days go by. There ain't much exciting that happens to me. Only wondering if the next winter is gonna carry me off. That's all." He shook his head slowly from side to side, as he spoke.

"Have you looked everywhere?" asked the sheriff.

Justis raised his head and stared at the trap door in the ceiling, then glanced down toward the ladder that was laid along the wall.

But before the deputy could speak, Adler

183

himself had said: "You ain't had a peek into the attic, yet. Better see if anything's up there."

At that, Sue's whole body trembled violently. And McGregor gripped her arm. She felt that she would stifle. Breathing became a studied labor. It seemed that the air had lost all its oxygen.

"That's true," said the sheriff. "Lay the ladder against the hole up there, Justis. What's in the attic, Adler?"

"Dust," said Adler.

Justis raised the length of the clumsy ladder, and fitted it in place on the floor.

"Nothing up there at all, eh?" repeated the sheriff.

"Not that I know of," said Adler. "But maybe I'm wrong. There might be a whole string of bats up there . . . there might be a mountain lion, for all I know, and a whole litter of cubs. I ain't been up there for years. I dunno what you'll find." He chuckled a little, and made a gesture with the palm of his hand turned up, as though offering them free inspection of all of his possessions.

"Climb up there and move the trap door," said the sheriff to Justis. "Be ready to shoot, too."

Justis climbed up the ladder and pressed with one hand at the trap door, and at the same time McGregor softly scraped a quantity of dust over the crack just above the face of the deputy.

It sifted through and fell into Justis's eyes and nose. He clung to the ladder, shaking it with a fit of coughing. Then he retreated slowly, still gasping and snorting. "Dust!" he said. "There ain't nothing but dust up there . . . and old Adler told the truth for once."

"Better open that trap," said the sheriff. "I'll do it myself. We've got to make sure."

"Ain't we made sure already?" asked Justis with irritation, "or maybe I've just gone and blinded myself for nothin'. If there was anything up there . . . if that trap door had been lifted any time recent, would there be such a pile of dust on it? Look there, how it's still falling since I shook that trap door?"

The sheriff screened his eyes and stared up. It seemed to Sue Jones that he was looking straight into her face, that he must see her clearly, so perfectly could she survey him. But then he shook his head. "You're right, Justis," he said. "We'll keep on searching a while, anyway. And if we can't take anything else away from this place, we can take Adler and let him smell the inside of a jail once more."

VIII

Barney, when he reached the bank of the stream and found no sign of Peary before him, but only that blank wall of limestone, with the one big tree lodged in it close above the water, continued to stare for a long time in simple inability to understand the nature of the miracle that could have snatched Peary away.

For Len Peary could not have ridden up the bank or down it without making a loud sound of crashing through the underbrush. He must have advanced into the stream, then — but could a man and a horse simply dissolve there? And how could they be carried away by a rush of water that was hardly more than two feet deep at the deepest?

He was so interested in the problem that he kept on staring long after he had the slightest real expectation of solving the mystery. And it was this length of idle examination that at last showed him a little eye of white on one of the outer leaves of the tree across the creek.

Ordinarily it would have meant nothing to him, but he had been seeing too many similar little white patches on this trail, and therefore, on glimpse of this new one, he pressed straight on into the current until he came to the tree. It stood out in the strength of the sweeping water. There was a deeper pool here, with only a swirling eddy in it. And on an outer leaf he picked off just such a wisp of cloth as he had found before.

His amazement increased. At last, pushing back the branch of the tree that was nearest to him, he looked under it and saw the green reflections deep in the water, with the slow whirl of the eddy ruffling them.

He could see how the tree was moored to the shore now. For at the very base of the limestone cliff there was a small apron of detritus that spilled out into the stream, and in and over this skirting of soil arose the great roots of the tree. It was lifting like a spider on eight immense legs.

Between the branches and the water there was a low, cool green cavern, into which the mare advanced cautiously, snuffing at the air and plainly ill at ease. Then, pausing, she shook her head in positive fear. She began to back up, eyeing the dark arch that extended under one of the largest roots. So Barney idly leaned from the saddle, and, to his amazement, he was able to look a considerable distance under that root into what seemed a tunnel sunk in the vitals of the stone.

He came closer. If he leaned flat forward

in the saddle, it was possible for him to pass under the height of the arching root without any difficulty, and, in a moment, he stood with the mare in a long, narrow cavern.

It was an amazing place to Barney. When he turned and glanced back, he could see the green shimmering of the shadow of the tree that the strength of the sun cast brightly upon the face of the creek. But that was not the only illumination of the tunnel. For at the top of it extended an irregular crevice, one of those many cracks that he had noted from the opposite bank of the stream. Through that narrow opening, he made sure of the nearer details of the cave.

It had evidently been eaten out, ages ago, by the slow action of a stream of water. For water works strongly on even the limestone of the densest grain. In this place it had chiseled a tunnel in some places ragged, in some places with hand-smoothed walls and polished ceilings. Sometimes it was an almost perfect arch that closed the roof across; sometimes it was a sharp angle.

This shaft led at a steep rate not directly up the face of the cliff, but sloping far to the right to a point where it disappeared around an elbow-bend.

But what set the heart of Barney Dwyer beating so fast was that he had seen the prints of the hoofs not of one horse, but of many, on the stone of the cave floor. And this was the perfect explanation of the manner in which Peary had disappeared.

Since he could not guess what lay before him, he abandoned the mare at the entrance to the tunnel, tethering her to a massive fragment that had fallen from the roof to the floor. When he left her, she whinnied after him, but no louder than a whisper, and when he turned back to her in an agony of apprehension and made gestures, she seemed to know at once what he meant. She remained silent, her ears straining forward, the quivering green reflection from the surface of the creek playing over her in rapid vibrations.

Suppose that another man should enter the cave and find her there? Well, such things were not to be thought of. They only stole the strength from his heart before the contest and the real danger began. For if Leonard Peary were somewhere in this underground retreat, then to be sure he would have other men with him — the great McGregor for instance.

He went on gradually and cautiously, ready to leap like a cat at the first sound. But what he heard was the stamp of a horse and a low snuffling sound as when a horse snorts while its muzzle is buried in forage. Then he came on an excellent stable that the work of the water had quarried out of the rock just beyond that elbow bend in the tunnel. Here the underground currents had drilled out a wide passage, and along one side of it, where the rock floor was perfectly level, half a dozen horses were stabled. A meager trickle of water — all that remained, perhaps, of the current that originally had done all this rock sculpting — gathered in a shallow trough that had been scooped in the floor, filled it, trickled over the side until it reached a crevice, and disappeared down this.

Above the stalled horses, through a widening of the crack as through a skylight, sun and fresh air entered. It was as perfect a stable as any liveryman could have wished to establish — this one in the heart of the limestone cliff. Barney could have stopped to admire it at any other time. But as it was, he dropped on his hands and knees like a soundless ghost. For there was Leonard Peary, stripping the saddle and bridle from the back of a sweating horse.

He passed out of the shadow across the strong yellow ray of light, and Barney could see his face perfectly. The dark and smiling beauty of it oppressed him. How could Sue have given up a man like this in order to ride away with such a simple fellow as himself? And that was not all. Someday Peary would again find Sue, and, when he stood beside her, Barney thought a force of natural magic would be sufficient to make her forget Barney Dwyer entirely, except as a subject for laughter.

Len Peary, having finished his work with the horse, stood in the full beam of the sunlight while he rolled a cigarette that he lit, and that sent upward a white cloud that left water-markings of shadow upon the handsome face of Peary.

Barney, slinking low and close to the wall, came up behind the fine fellow little by little. Then one of the horses snorted and stamped with a violence that made Peary jerk about to see what might be wrong. That was how he happened to confront Barney when Dwyer was hardly a stride away.

The cigarette dashed against the wall and knocked out a shower of brilliant sparks in the shadow. The hand that had held it flashed out a revolver, while Peary leaped back and to the side to escape Barney's rush.

But he was much too close. Barney caught the revolver with his left hand and turned the muzzle away from his body. He wanted to beat the iron weight of his other fist into the face of Peary, but he felt that it would be like striking some beautiful vase that would crumble to dust with the stroke. Instead, he grasped Peary by the hair of the head and jerked him to his knees.

By chance, the yellow of the sunlight gilded the face of Peary, showed the flare of the nostrils, the maniac fear in the eyes. That picture sickened Barney and robbed him of his anger. He remembered, too, that Peary had not cried out, had not uttered a sound. Terror seemed to have gagged him from the first instant.

Both of Barney's hands relaxed their grasp, but in one of them he took away the revolver from Peary's fingers. He stepped back. Peary did not offer to rise. He merely slumped sideways against the wall of the tunnel and dropped his head on his chest. It was as though a bullet already had crashed through his body and the life were running out of him.

"I'm not going to harm you . . . I guess," said Barney, and his breath was hot in his throat. "Stand up, Len."

Peary got slowly to his feet. He kept one hand on the wall for support, and his head still drooped. It was clear that shame was the bullet that had struck him.

"Len," said Barney, "you and McGregor chased me and shot at me. I expected it of him. I didn't think you'd do such a thing."

"No," said the faint voice of Peary, "you wouldn't expect that."

Barney waited. But not an excuse was offered.

"You tried to kill me, Len," he repeated.

"Yes," said Peary. "I tried to."

"Why?" asked Barney. "What have I done to you, Len, except to try to help you?"

"Nothing. You've done nothing to me," answered Peary. "But I had to have you out of the way."

Barney made a vague gesture to the side. "It was Sue. Is that it?" he asked.

Peary nodded.

And it was Barney who said: "I'm sorry about that. But she'll see further through me, one of these days. And then she'll forget me, and likely she'll remember you then."

"She's seen all the way through you already," answered Peary, lifting his head suddenly at last. "And she knows that you're better stuff . . . than the rest of us. A lot better."

"Do you know where she is now?" asked Barney, feeling that he could not answer those last words.

"Yes. I know," said Peary. He closed his

193

eyes, opened them again, and then jerked a thumb over his shoulder. "She's here," he said.

"Where? Farther up the tunnel?"

"Clear at the top of it," said Peary. "In a cabin on top of the rock."

A groan of relief came from the throat of Barney. "Anyone with her?" he asked.

"Yes. Adler and McGregor."

"The old man . . . he was Adler?"

"Yes. He was Doc Adler."

"And the whole thing was a scheme to get me away from Sue?"

Peary said nothing. His silence was a sufficient answer.

"And what do they want to happen?" asked Barney.

Finally Peary broke out: "I'll tell you. You've given me my life before. I suppose you'll give it to me again. I've been a cur. Maybe I'm a worse cur to go on talking now. But I'll tell you." He gathered himself with a great effort. "They know that you'll never leave these mountains till you've found Sue. So they wait on the rock like old eagles, until they get a chance to drop on you. And once you're out of the way, then I appear, Barney. I'm to rescue Sue from 'em, d'you see. No one is to know what's become of you. She'll begin to forget you, after a

194

time, and she'll begin to be grateful to me. That's the whole way of it. McGregor evens his score against you . . . and I have my chance with Sue. That was the plan. And . . . if I were you, I'd use that gun you've got in your hand. It shoots straight."

In the pause that followed, there was no sound except the heavy breathing of Barney Dwyer. Then he said tersely: "Maybe I could trust you now, Len. But I'd be afraid to leave you behind me. Walk over there behind the horses, will you? I'm going to leave you tied up so you can't manage any harm while I'm gone."

Peary marched ahead and stood by the saddles and bridles that hung against the wall of the tunnel. With bridle reins, Barney tied him securely, hand and foot, and hand to foot. He took off Peary's bandanna, wadded it into a tight ball, and wedged it in behind his teeth. "Is that going to choke you, Len?" he asked with a strange concern, leaning close above his captive.

Peary shook his head, and slumped back against the wall. Barney, after staring at him a moment, went on up the angling slope of the tunnel until it grew steeper and steeper, and ended against a flat slab of stone. He tried the weight of it. It lifted a little easily enough and let in on his ears the sound of voices and of hurrying steps.

IX

He still had his grip on a rough ledge of the
stone that closed the trap when a strong
pull from above almost tore the rock away
from him. Instinctively he resisted, and
heard the voice of McGregor immediately
above him, exclaiming in fear and astonishment.

McGregor, who could shoot as though a
wizard were controlling the guns. A second
pull came, but this time the iron strength of
Barney secured the stone slab as firmly as
mortar.

After that, he waited for a fresh attempt.
He wondered if he should retreat down the
passage. He wondered if he should suddenly
strive to force his way through into the
cabin, which, according to Peary, stood
above?

Twice, at considerable intervals, he pushed
up the stone a mere trifle. The first time, he
heard the familiar voice of Sheriff Elder
speaking not far away. Then tramplings
came above him. Some small particles of
stone showered down into his face. But that
was all. No one again attempted to lift the
stone, until at last, eaten with impatience,

he pushed it up once more. There was no sound for the moment. Then he heard retreating footfalls, retreating voices. Were they leaving, the girl and the two men?

He lifted the stone still farther, and crawled out into a small storage shed surrounded with shelves and bins, and all the shelves heaped full of tinned goods, and every manner of supply. The earthy smell of potatoes he made out, and the sharpness of onions.

And now he heard a voice that was hardly out of his ears, it was so recent a memory — it was the sound of Doc Adler's speech, as the old man said, "All right, Mack. It's all clear. They've gone over the edge of the mesa, the sheriff and all of 'em."

Hinges creaked in the upper part of the next room.

"Sure he won't come back?" asked McGregor.

"I dunno," said Adler. "Not today, I guess. Him findin' me here, it's spoiled things for me. I've gotta move, after this, and where'll I find as snug a hole as this to lie up in? But I dunno. It was pretty nigh worth a move . . . hoodwinkin' the sheriff like that!"

"He might have taken you with him," said McGregor, his voice descending. "Come on, Sue. Come on down, will you?"

197

"I'm comin'," said the voice for which Barney waited most of all. And he set his teeth, hearing it now. For he wanted to rush blindly in on them all, no matter who might be there, and rush off with Sue. He had to fight against that insane impulse.

"How'd the dust come into the face of that fellow, Justis?" asked Adler.

"I poured some through a crack right over his head," said McGregor.

Adler laughed heartily. "You got brains, is what you got, Mack," he said.

Barney leveled his revolver at the open door between the shed and the main body of the cabin, and then he crept closer.

"Come along, Sue," said McGregor.

"I'll stay in here, Mack," she said. "I'm sick of the faces of you two."

"You'll have a change of scene when the half-wit comes along," sneered McGregor. "He'll brighten things up a good deal for you, Sue."

She made no answer.

Adler's voice sounded from the distance. "Comin', Mack?"

"Come along, Sue!" exclaimed McGregor. "D'you think that I'll leave you alone here?"

"I might slip away down the trap and

198

through the tunnel, eh?" she said. "Well, all right."

Then Barney stepped into the open doorway, and saw McGregor, squarely facing him in the outer door. Those two hands of Big Mack started for guns but paused in mid-gesture.

"Don't move, McGregor!" said Barney. "Be like a stone. Don't move!"

And McGregor did not move. He was admirable in the crisis. Not a muscle of his face stirred to betray fear; not a touch of pallor turned his swarthy skin pale. "All right, Barney, all right, my lad," he said. "You have a handful of aces, again. It's your turn, Barney."

Barney dared not glance aside at the girl, although all his soul was urging him to look at her. She was a presence that he felt, not one that he saw.

She was coming toward him. She had not cried out. She had not uttered a sound.

"What'll I do with him?" asked Barney.

She answered, rapidly: "You can't do murder, Barney. Make him step back inside."

"Oh, Mack! Mack!" called the voice of old Adler from the distance. "I want to you to see. . . ."

The rest of those words Barney did not hear.

"Come in," said Barney to McGregor.

McGregor stepped through the doorway. The girl was instantly behind him, and pulled the door shut. Then her rapid hands filched his two guns.

"Can we take him with us?" she asked.

"Where, Sue?" asked Barney, frowning with doubt. "What could we do with him? Where could we take him?"

"To a sheriff," said the girl. "There's a crime to charge against him now. I've heard him talk here of a good many things, Barney. They only want a ghost of an excuse to put him in prison until his head is white, and we have plenty of charges against him now."

"But if we take him," argued Barney, "you know that the sheriff wants me, also?"

"What's against you compared with what's against McGregor?" said the girl. "Why, they'll worship you, Barney, if you can bring him in. Quick! Here's twine . . . it's better than rope to hold his hands. I'll do it. Never mind. Only watch him."

McGregor made no resistance. He let himself be tied like a sheep. Neither did he speak a word, but his eyes burned like an acid into the face of Barney Dwyer.

The situation might be reversed again,

and, if the time came, Barney could guess how short would be his shrift. There would be no nonsense on the part of McGregor about murder or no murder.

When those formidable hands were tied, Barney could look for the first time at the girl, and she at him. They spared one golden second for that glance, and then they herded the prisoner into the storage room.

"Mack!" yelled the angry voice of old Adler, drawing nearer. "What's the idea of the closed door?"

Barney lifted the stone trap. Into the aperture, McGregor got down at once. The girl followed, weighted down by the burden of the two big Colts. Barney was last. He closed the trap behind him, and so they hurried down the passage to the subterranean stables.

They were almost at the place when they heard a noise behind them, and then the piercing voice of Adler, shouting: "Mack!"

"Here!" thundered McGregor in answer. "Here, and caught by Dwyer!"

X

It was as though there had been loosed after them a river of fire to rush down the tunnel; it was as though all the path they might

201

follow outside of the cave were sown with explosives. Barney Dwyer caught big McGregor by the shoulder and jerked him against the wall. The shock of the meeting between flesh and rock made the eyes stagger in the head of McGregor, but he merely sneered at Barney.

"Now your brains against Adler's brains," he said. "And see who wins through to Greenborough!"

That was it. Their brains against the brains of that lean, devilish old wolf, Adler.

There were six horses there in the underground stables. They hustled saddles onto five of them. The one that had just been brought back by Len Peary seemed too spent to be of much use to friend or to enemy as it stood hanging its head, refusing to eat. Five saddles were more than they needed for their party of four, to be sure, and there was the red mare waiting for her master at the side of the river. But in case they might need to change horses on the way, they might not have time to change saddles at the same time.

With the saddled horses, they went on, McGregor and Len Peary herded in front, and the horses following.

Up to that time, there had not been many words exchanged. The girl had simply said to Peary: "Well, this is the way of it, is it? You were in the whole game from the first, were you? You're not a traitor. You're not even a man."

Peary had no answer to make to that. From the moment when Barney had mastered him, in fact, there had seemed little or no life in him. He went on like a dead thing. He looked down at his feet, never at the girl. And Barney had said to her: "Easy, Sue. Don't be too hard on him. You don't know. . . ."

"I don't know what?" she asked savagely.

"You don't know how much he loves you," said Barney.

She gave Barney such a bitter glance that he was afraid her wrath would descend even upon *his* devoted head, after that, but she said not a word more.

They got down to the mouth of the tunnel, and there they saw the quivering green reflection from the surface of the stream outside. They saw the mare standing there, made trembling and unreal in the strange light.

Peary said a thing that never died out of the mind of Barney in time to come. He said to McGregor: "You see how it is, Mack. Even horses . . . even the dumb beasts . . . are more faithful to honest men."

Mack answered with his dark sneer: "Dumb beasts understand dumb fools better. That's all."

At the entrance to the long tunnel, Barney made McGregor and Peary mount. He tied their horses bit to bit by a length of rope the end of which was fastened to the saddle of the red mare.

Then he said: "McGregor and Len, you see how things are. It happens that I have guns, and you haven't. Also, your hands are tied. If you try to get away . . . if you try any tricks, I wouldn't like to shoot, but I'd have to. Now ride out into the water, please. Don't shout. Don't call out. We must go across silently, because Doc Adler might be watching for us from the top of the rock."

That was the fear, of course. And from the top of the mesa a rifleman might have done terrible execution as they rushed the horses across the narrow little creek. But there was no firing above them. They got peaceably across and into the brush on the farther side. When they looked back, it seemed to Barney that it was no longer a blank wall of stone but a great, evil fortress that stood there in the middle of the valley. It had been merely a huge rock; now it had character, like a face.

But no rifles were fired after them; they

escaped into the cloud of green. When they were shut in by the woods, Barney said: "What shall we do now, Sue?"

"We'll head back for Greenborough, of course," she said. "We've got a double cargo to deliver there."

She looked at Peary when she spoke about the double cargo. Barney wondered at her more than a little. For she seemed entirely at ease, entirely pleased with the situation. Barney would have said, seeing the calm and the brightness of her, that she was on a jolly outing with dear friends, not with the terrible danger of all McGregor's men between her and safety.

"The straight way is down the valley," said Barney. "But if we go that way, won't Adler be able to signal to some of the men of McGregor's party? They're still out in the mountains, Sue . . . don't you think so? They're still searching for their chief, don't you imagine? And perhaps Adler may know where to find them?"

Sue regarded him as one might look at a page of writing in an unknown language, and big McGregor said: "Yes, you can all see that there's a brain in that head, after all."

Barney flushed. He looked guiltily at the girl, expecting contempt, or a reproof, but she merely answered: "Yes, Barney. I suppose there's still some danger ahead of us. At least we're not exactly the same as at home. I wasn't thinking of taking the shortest cut back to Greenborough, but I thought that we'd go back over the hills to the south. Does that suit you?"

He answered hastily, humbly: "Of course, Sue. Whatever you say will be for the best."

"Then we'll head down the valley and throw a loop around the mesa, and then cut to the south down one of the other ravines. Start along, Barney."

He had the horses of the prisoners anchored to the saddle of the red mare. Sue had the two spare lead horses tied to her mount, which was a long, low, powerfully built gray gelding. It was a curious color — black spots on a rather yellowish field. Barney got the leading trio in motion at a canter. At an easy lope they passed down the ravine, until they were well below the mesa. Then they turned to the left into the throat of a narrow gorge.

McGregor said: "It would be easy, Dwyer. One good man with a rifle could pick off all four of us. One good man could lie up in the rocks and cut us all down before we found any sign of cover."

Barney answered him gently: "I know how

you feel, Mack. I'm sorry about you in a way, too. You've tried to do some pretty bad things to me and to Sue, too. But I wouldn't take you to the law. I wouldn't, except that we'd be afraid to let you remain loose."

The girl was well behind by this time, urging her laggard troop along, for horses with empty saddles are apt to go more negligently and carelessly ahead than horses with human burdens. Of Barney's trio, Leonard Peary was the laggard. He had the sick face of a man who is nauseated. His face shone with sweat and there was a streak of white curving down past the mouth. He leaned over the horn of the saddle, and gave himself up to the darkness of his thoughts. So Barney was left practically alone with McGregor who did his part in keeping his brown horse up with the mare. He had a pair of spurs with sharp steel rowels, and a touch of them now and then would make the brown dance, till it was admirable to see the manner in which McGregor kept his seat, though with hands tied behind him. He was a master horseman.

Barney, full of that admiration, burst out finally: "McGregor, what made you do it?"

"Do what?" asked McGregor calmly.

"Go crooked," said Barney. "You could be anything that you want. You have a good mind. People would follow you. You could be rich and happy. You could be anything. What made you go in for crime?"

McGregor's eyes turned dull and dark in his head. Then he said: "If you wanted to catch fish, would you stay ashore or go to sea in a boat?"

"I'd go in a boat," said Barney, opening his round, blue, child-like eyes.

"If you wanted to find gold, would you hunt for pebbles or dig in the rocks?"

"I'd dig in the rocks," said Barney.

"And if you wanted to find a criminal," said McGregor, "would you stay among honest men, doing honest work, or would you mix around with the crooks?"

"Are you trying to find someone?" asked Barney.

"My brother," said McGregor tersely. And he looked away and threw back his head with a slight gesture of revolt and of defiance.

"Your brother?" Barney Dwyer sighed. "I never had a brother, McGregor. And you've lost yours? Will you tell me about him?"

"There's nothing to tell," said McGregor, "except that I loved him, and, while I was still a youngster, he went wrong. He disappeared. He'd killed a man, Barney." With a lowered voice McGregor told of this, and

208

added: "I made up my mind that, when I got out in the world, I'd hunt for him, and keep on hunting till I found him or died in the trying to find him. So when I was able, I followed right out into his own world, and that was the world of crime, d'you see?"

"I see," Barney said, crushed with awe. "It's a great thing that you've tried to do, Mack."

McGregor shrugged his shoulders and frowned as a man who would be pleased to shut off a conversation.

"Have you ever seen him, Mack?" asked Barney eagerly.

"Three times," said McGregor. "Once behind the bars, and once through a window as he ran past, and once in a crowd."

"And what happened every time?" asked Barney.

"I managed to set levers working that got him out of the jail . . . he was about to be sentenced to death. But he disappeared before I could see him. So he did in the crowd, and when he ran past the window."

"But, Mack, does he know that you're looking for him?"

"He does," said McGregor, "but he's a stern man. He'd rather be by himself. He feels no pull of blood, as I feel it. It'll be nothing to him when he hears that they've strung me up by the nape of the neck."

"They won't string you up!" cried out Barney.

"No? And what'll stop 'em, Dwyer?"

"*I'll* stop them," exclaimed Barney, "because I won't let them! I won't take you in. I'm going to turn you loose, McGregor, now, and I'll be your friend. I'll help you all I can to find your brother again."

He checked the horses. A fire of enthusiasm was in his face as the girl came up on them.

"What's the matter, Barney?" she asked.

"It's about McGregor," said Barney. "We've been terribly wrong about him, and now he's told me the truth."

"He couldn't," said the girl. "For one thing, because the truth would burn through the leather of his own tongue, and for another because the truth about him would keep him talking for a year."

"Ah, that's what I thought, but we didn't understand," Barney said, his honest eyes flaming with devotion. "The truth is that he's gone into a criminal life just in order to try to find a brother who went crooked when Mack was a boy. That's the only reason, Sue."

Sue Jones broke into ringing, cheerful laugher. To the amazement of Barney,

210

McGregor joined that mirth on a deeper key, and even Peary was able to summon up a wan smile.

Barney looked from face to face, totally bewildered.

"I don't understand," he said.

The girl stopped laughing. Her amusement actually had brought moisture into her eyes. "Why, it's all a silly lie, Barney," said Susan Jones. "Don't you even see through that? It's just a lie, Barney, that even a child. . . ." She checked herself sharply.

Barney, with a sigh, turned the head of the red mare up the trail again. Sue had been about to say that even a child could see through more than he was able to understand about people. Now Sue would begin to despise him. Was that the answer?

He looked wistfully back to her as they came out of the narrows of that cañon into a broader valley studded with dark little groups of evergreens and with great boulders, and, as he looked back, the girl waved cheerfully at him.

McGregor cut into his thoughts, saying: "She'll be through with you before long. She's bound to be. Laughter's the thing that kills love the quickest. Kills it at the root. Already she knows that you're nine-tenths a

211

fool. And after a while that'll begin to work on her. She laughs at you today . . . she'll leave you tomorrow."

And all the soul of Barney echoed that statement and called it true.

She could not stay near him without ridiculing him, he felt. She was a dazzling bright diamond that for a moment lay in his hand, but in another moment that brilliance would be snatched away from him.

"Why did you lie to me, McGregor?" he asked.

"Why," said the other, "I knew that you were a fool, but I didn't know how big a fool. I thought that I'd find out . . . and I did. The biggest fool that I've ever found in my life."

Barney sighed, and nodded. "I'm not bright," he admitted. "I don't see through people."

"Bright?" answered the other. "You're the greatest dummy alive. And Sue's beginning to find it out."

A hollow, gloomy voice cut in upon them. It was Peary, who was saying: "You know that you lie, Mack. If he's a fool, how does he happen to have you an' me tied like a pair of pigs going to market? Because there's more heart and soul and nerve in him than in both of us, multiplied by twenty. That's the reason. You know it, too. You're simply talking to hurt him as much as you can. It's a cowardly trick on your part."

"Is it?" exclaimed McGregor. "Are *you* turning into a yellow cur, Peary, and trying to curry favor?"

"I'm currying no favor," said young Peary. "I know what's ahead of me. And I tell you what, Mack . . . I'd rather hang, as I see it now, than to keep on with you."

"Ride! Ride!" shouted the girl suddenly from behind.

And to give a point to her words, a cracking rifle fire broke out to the side of the valley. Bullets began to *hum* about them. Looking back, Barney saw seven riders rushing their horses down the slope.

XI

"Ride! Ride!" the girl was crying, spurring her own horse ahead. "They're McGregor's men! I recognize Pete Waller by his mustang. Ride for your life, Barney!"

Barney was already struggling forward. But as the red mare galloped more and more strongly, the two led horses pulled back and neutralized a significant part of that effort.

Sue turned loose the pair that were on her

lead rope. She rushed on the others, swinging her quirt, and slashed them across the hips until the whole party was suddenly rushing away at full speed, every horse doing his best. The red mare swung easily along in front of the rest, keeping the lead rope always taut. She ran not with full strength but with her head high and her ears pricking, as though she were enjoying a mere pleasure romp. She merely shook those sharp ears of hers and flattened them an instant when the singing of a bullet came too close to them.

But the firing stopped. The seven riders, having missed their first, distant volley, had put their guns back in holsters and were giving their entire attention to the riding.

How had they come to this place? The sight of one among them was the convincing answer. That was a form like a gaunt old ape bowing over the neck of one of the fastest of the horses. And as the wind furled the brim of his hat, Barney saw the flash of his silver hair. It was old Doc Adler again.

He must have guessed their probable course of retreat and, leaving the mesa instantly, sped across country to get to McGregor's distant men. So well had he guessed, that, if Barney had delayed another minute of time on the way, the valley would have been blocked. The volley that began the battle would have ended it. But by the grace of a few seconds, Adler brought up those fighting men only in time to see the prey already slipping through the trap.

They were picked horses that the four were sitting upon. But two of them were riding with hands tied behind their backs, and they could not, even had they been willing, jockey along their mounts, and swing with the stride as the pursuers were doing.

But behind the captives was the girl with her whip. She rode like one possessed. There was a fierceness in her face that amazed Barney.

His heart rose as he glanced back at her. And each time she had a wave of the hand and a shout for him. It would have been easy for him to persuade himself that she enjoyed the danger, for the red flare of battle was in her face.

The valley turned from rolling into broken ground. It narrowed to a chasm again, the walls lifting straight up, almost from the side of the water that flashed down the center of the cañon.

As they galloped, the hoof beats ringing loudly in their ears, Barney saw that McGregor was laughing with a savage exultation. He had the meaning of that laughter explained, in another moment, for, as they came toward the head of the cañon, they found that it pinched away almost to nothing. The water of the runlet streamed down from a spring on the left-hand cliff. And across the head of the gorge there was a thirty-foot gap where a more powerful living stream had cut down through the living rock. A scattering of trees grew on the brink of the chasm on either side. From beneath they heard the mournful, rolling sound of the waters.

Another sound was beating behind them, the frantic, clangoring of the hoofs of the horses of McGregor's men.

And McGregor exclaimed: "Now's the time when the game changes again, Dwyer! Now's the time when I hold the cards. You can try to make terms with me, maybe. I don't know what I'll do with you . . . but you're mine . . . you fat-faced fool! You've ridden yourself into a trap. You should have taken the right-hand turn through that gap back there!"

Barney Dwyer, utterly amazed, dismounted, and stood helplessly at the brink of the chasm, where a fallen tree stretched its naked hulk like a natural barrier put there to guard against the danger of a fall.

"We've got to hold 'em, Barney!" cried

the girl. "They're on us, Barney! Get your rifle. . . ."

She showed the way. She had the shining length of a Winchester out of one of the saddle scabbards, and, as the thundering of hoofs rolled down on them and as Barney saw the stream of the approaching men, the girl kneeled by the wall of the ravine to open fire.

He furnished himself with a gun, in turn, but it seemed a futile gesture. For there were seven of them, and every one a chosen man, or he would not have been selected by McGregor in the beginning. Seven of them, conscious of their victory, yelling like fiends as they shot down through the narrows of the ravine.

The girl fired. The seven came on, and old Doc Adler, snatching out a revolver, aimed pointblank and returned that shot.

Sue Jones dropped her rifle and sank down at the base of the cliff, clutching her shoulder. Barney, standing straight — because he was too bewildered to do anything else — had let drive from his Winchester well over the heads of the charging men. But now he saw the girl drop. From the corner of his eye, he saw it, and still, with the rifle at his shoulder, he ran forward.

Through those narrows at the head of the

ravine, hardly two men could ride, side-by-side, and in the lead was Adler with another of the crew. Straight at them, Barney ran, firing as he came, firing blindly.

They answered, but, as they answered, they were working furiously to turn their horses. Apparently they had come charging with the certainty that the enemy was backed helplessly against a wall. And this madman, this Barney Dwyer who they knew to be capable of strange things, was actually advancing against them on foot, his rifle spouting fire as he came.

He wanted to shoot to kill, now, but there was such a red rage on him that he could not take aim. He did not need to. The big .45-caliber slugs from the Colts were fanning wind into his face, but not a one of that seven had the coolness to pause, halt his horse, and take deliberate aim.

As though the charge of Barney had been the sweep of a river from behind a broken dam, it picked up the cavalcade and hurled it yelling in terror down the narrows of the ravine.

They fled far off. The uproar died away into a distant murmuring. And then Barney, standing still, wondered why it was that his heart was dead in him. He remembered then. It was the fall of the girl that he had seen. He turned toward her, hardly daring to let his eyes see the tragedy that he expected, and, as he turned, he saw her ripping a fragment of white cloth into strips, for a bandage. All her left arm and shoulder were crimson from the wound.

Yet she shouted, in a glory of triumphing: "Oh, Barney, you drove them like a lot of curs! God only made one like you!"

XII

Yes, he had driven them like dogs. They had gone swirling back before him. They had shouted and cursed the men who blocked their way. They had gone shrinking away from him, with frightened yelling, as though every man expected bullets in his back at once. But there was no sense of glory in Barney Dwyer.

He simply ran over to the girl and dropped his rifle on the ground. He held his hands out toward her, a little helplessly. He could not see her very well, nothing but the white skin of her arm and shoulder, and the red of the blood running on it — for she had ripped away her shirt sleeve. He was amazed to see that the golden brown of her was only in the face and the hands and the lower arms. It was as though she had on skin-tight gloves that stretched to just above the elbow, but all above was white. Laced with the red blood, it was incredibly white.

The arm hung down dangling, worthless, useless. That hand that had been so swift and clever had no sense in it now. It turned vaguely here and there as the shoulder moved.

"What have they done to you?" said Barney. "Oh, Sue, what have they done?"

"Hold the end of this . . . no, that other end. Wind it around under the arm. Press hard. Harder. Stop shaking, Barney!" she commanded. "No . . . hold this other end, and I'll do the winding. We have to hurry. We have to hurry and do something. They can climb up to the top of the cliff. They can climb it from behind, and, once they're on top, they'll kill you. Then everything would be finished. We've got to hurry. I'm all right. Stop shaking. I'm not going to die. Hold my arm at the elbow and wrist. Hold it harder. Hold it like a vise. That's better."

He fastened his grip on that arm. All the while he stared into her face, for if he kept watching the blood, he felt that he would faint. She was sweating. Just across her forehead and her upper lip there was a sheen of sweat. But she was not pale with the pain.

"They shot you, Sue," said Barney. "They shot at a woman. They ought to be all burned alive!"

"It was old Adler, and that doesn't count," said the girl. "He's not a man. And why shouldn't they shoot when I was ready to sift a lot of lead into them? When a woman starts shooting, she's not a woman any more. There! Now I can navigate a little better. I've got to have it in a sling, though, I guess. Otherwise the arm will be swinging back and forth, and that will start the bleeding again."

She made the sling. The one useful hand worked with the speed and the skill of two, while Barney stood there like a lump, almost helpless.

He began to hear the great McGregor, who was walking up in a terrible fury.

"Those are men who swore that they'd follow me to hell and back," he said. "Those are fellows who have had thousands of dollars out of me, every one of them. They've had the fat of everything. I did their thinking for them. I hung the money up in a Christmas stocking, you might say. All they had to do was to get up in the morning and rub their eyes open, and take in a few thousand dollars more. And they'd die for me. They all said that, Peary."

221

"Don't talk to me," said Peary. "I don't want to hear your talk."

"Because you're sick. Because you're scared until you're sick. That's the reason that you don't want to talk to me. Bah! What a cur you are. You and the rest . . . curs! One half-wit with one gun. One half-wit and a scared girl . . . and seven men run from 'em! Only Adler had any manhood in him. I'm damned if I ever let another crook come near me. I'm through with gangs. I'll find one man, and work with him. With Adler!"

"You'll do your next work walking on air," said Len Peary.

"So will you!" exclaimed McGregor.

"I know it. I'm glad of it. I'm tired. I'm ready to quit the game."

"Because you're yellow!" snarled McGregor.

"Maybe," said Peary. "But mostly because it's dirty. I used to think it was a sort of sport. Now I see what it really is. It's dirty! You shoot women in this game. That's how dirty it is."

The bandage was finished, and so was the sling. Sue was suffering now, and she was weak. Barney could see that by the whiteness around her mouth, and because her eyes were puckering a little in the corners

222

and the pupils dilating.

"Is it terrible, Sue?" he asked her.

"It's nothing. It's all right. The bandage grips a little, but that's the way it should be. Come on, Barney. We've got to hurry. Come, and we'll see what we can do."

Barney followed her to the edge of the gulley. It was a straight drop of at least seventy feet to the shooting water beneath. The coolness of the running water came up damply against their faces.

"Maybe we can bridge the thing," said the girl. "Suppose that we can upend this fallen tree trunk. Then it would reach clear across to the other side. Try to upend it, Barney, will you?"

"Yes, I'll try," he said.

He put his hands on the trunk of the tree she pointed to, well down toward the narrow tip of the log. It came up with a tearing sound, it had been so soldered against the ground by the growth of fungi and weeds. It was half rotten, he saw, as he walked the trunk higher and higher into the air. The whole belly of the log was white and corrugated like cork by the damp. His hands slipped on the wet face of it.

The strain became great. Even his mighty arms could not support that weight. He had to let the log come down on his shoulder, and, with great thrustings and flexings of his body, he worked the burden higher and higher toward perpendicular. The full strain of it was on him now. Every time his body shrugged at the weight, the tree waggled to the slender tip. Foul white bugs came out of the crevices of the log. And Barney detested crawling things far more than he loathed snakes. Something slimy cold went across his forehead and sickened him. Something dropped from the log and crawled down his back.

That was worse than the strain of the lifting, by far. But now the strain decreased every instant as he pushed the log up past forty-five degrees toward the perpendicular. And, eventually, there it stood like a great mast. He looked up along the flank of it, and was staggered by the knowledge that his own hands had erected that mighty shaft.

"That way . . . straight over to the right. Get behind it here, Barney," commanded the girl. "That's the way. Pray heaven that it will fall straight across. There . . . let go!"

He gave it a guiding thrust and then stepped back. The head of the tree wavered, hesitated, as a whiplash seems to hang an instant in the air before it is jerked forward and downward for the stroke. So the tree hesitated, and then whipped down.

The slender tip of it broke straight off against a tree on the opposite bank. Then the mass landed with a *crash* and with an ominous *creaking* and tearing sound inside. Plainly the half decayed timber was badly damaged by the fall.

"But how can we get them across?" asked Barney. "They've got their hands tied behind them. How can we get them across, or shall we leave them here?"

"We've got to put a guide rope across for them," said the girl. She had the coil of a lariat in her hand, and now she stepped out on the slender bridge.

"Sue!" cried Barney. "Come back! Don't do that! Don't!"

She was already halfway across. She could not use both hands to balance herself, of course, but she held up the weight of the lariat to secure her equilibrium a little. She stepped quickly, decisively. She came to the narrow part of the log. It gave under her, springing slowly up and down beneath her weight.

Barney dropped to his knees and gripped the butt end of the log to steady it, a very vain and foolish effort, for she was already across, and knotting the end of the rope around a small tree.

She gathered the noose end, swung it a

little, and then threw it like a man throwing a lariat. Straight and true, it shot to the feet of Barney. He stared down at it, stupidly.

"Tie it to a tree!" she called in command. "It will be our guide rail, our balustrade, Barney. No, not that tree, but the one in line with . . . that's right!"

He made the rope tight. He pulled hard on it and turned it to a trembling cable; rapidly she came back across the narrow bridge to Barney.

"Now, then," she said, tiptoeing with excitement, "you can get them over, Barney! Take 'em one at a time, and steady 'em before you. Quick! Quick! McGregor's men may get to the top of the hill any moment!"

He took Len Peary over first, holding to the guide rope with one hand and steadying Peary with the other. It was easily done. So it was with McGregor, who cursed steadily, softly, as he stepped over the log.

Then Barney, returning, spread his hands over the face of the red mare. She began to whinny softly, as though she understood that he was about to leave her.

"Hurry, Barney!" said the girl. "You'll have her again, one day. You won't lose her." She stepped out onto the log as she spoke, and Barney came behind her. There was no need to steady her. Her step was lighter, surer, colder than his own, and she kept one hand on the guide rope.

McGregor might have used these few moments to take to his heels, but he apparently realized that a man with hands tied behind his back could not go fast enough to escape from such a pursuer as Barney Dwyer. Therefore, he merely stood fast by the tip of the log, and glowered at the pair as they came.

They were in the very center of the log, when he acted. The tip of the fallen tree rested on a rock securely enough, but the surface of that rock was smooth, and now McGregor, with a sudden yell of savagery, thrust at the tip of the log with his foot.

It gave a foot or more, a ghastly wavering ran down the length of the tree trunk, and the girl screamed with fear.

Barney had time to hear Peary cry out and see him throw himself at McGregor. But if Peary hoped to stop Mack, he was much too late. At another quick thrust by McGregor, the end of the tree trunk was dislodged, and the whole length of the log hurled spear-wise down into the abyss, leaving Barney hanging to the rope.

The hold of the girl was broken by the sudden loss of all footing. At the flare of her dress in the wind, as she fell, Barney caught with his left hand, and by the grace of fortune he made good his grip.

XIII

Another shock almost broke his own iron grip on the rope. The sudden pressure had pulled the rope down the slender trunk of the sapling to which it was fastened on the farther side of the gulf. But he maintained his hold, although his own weight and the weight of the girl depended from one hand!

Yet she seemed to be slipping away. She was a loose weight dangling there beneath him, oscillating slowly back and forth. The force of the fall had jerked the dress up so that it bound her around beneath the arm-pits. Her whole body hung lifelessly. Every instant her arms threatened to slip through the sleeves and let her fall to the white rush of water beneath them.

Vainly Barney shouted at her. She made no answer. She had fainted!

It was a strain even for his might, but he managed to draw up her weight until he could grip a thick fold of her skirt with his teeth. Then he started to go hand over hand, toward the edge of the cliff.

Still danger was not over. The devil that had inspired Mack before worked in him still. The rope had slid down the trunk of the sapling to the ground, and now with the razor sharp rowels of his spurs, McGregor was hacking at the rope to cut the strands.

Peary, screeching with horror, came at the bigger man like a tiger. McGregor dropped flat, let the weight of Peary tumble over him, and made him quiet by deliberately kicking him in the head. Then he turned and struck at the rope with his spurs again.

Barney worked with a desperate speed, hand over hand. But he felt the burden slipping not from the grip of his teeth but from the dress in which it was slung like a loose and lifeless thing. Then, under the grasp of his hands, he felt the parting of a strand of the rope. It was like the bursting of a blood vessel in his brain. But he was close, now, to the end of the peril. His right hand reached for the rock, closed on the edge of it at the very moment that the last strand of the rope parted. And there he hung helplessly, the girl depending on the grip of his teeth, his left hand reaching for a fingerhold on the edge of the rock, when McGregor deliberately stamped on his hands.

Those hands turned numb. In an instant more, McGregor could have kicked them from their meager purchase. But now Peary, who had tried vainly twice before to check

McGregor, rose from the ground and came running in again. Blood streaked the side of his face from the gash that the boot of McGregor had cut. But he came in silently, with a face convulsed. Like a charging linesman in a football game, his shoulder struck McGregor.

That was the breathing space that enabled Barney to clamber over the edge of the rock, and then to draw up the girl after him.

She was as limp as dead flesh. She was as white as death, too, yet she opened her eyes almost instantly. Back from the edge of the rock Barney carried her a step or two, into the shelter of the woods.

The mare was neighing desperately on the farther side of the gulch. But more important than her calling, almost more important than the returning life in the eyes of Sue Jones, was the sound of running feet that dodged away among the trees.

All the soul of Barney Dwyer yearned to be in pursuit of that fugitive. He only paused to slash the leather rein that held the hands of Leonard Peary securely lashed behind his back.

"You're free, Len!" he panted. "God bless you . . . you saved her. Watch over her now!" Then he darted forward after McGregor. He heard a faint outcry behind him. It was the girl's voice, but it had no meaning to him. Nothing in the world had meaning except the pursuit of McGregor.

He leaped a fallen log, heard the crashing of a body through bushes not far away, and then all was silence before him. Had McGregor been able to hide himself?

Like an eager hound that has lost the trail, bending far over, scanning the ground almost as though the sense of smell were to help him, Barney rushed through the bushes, turned this way and that, trampled them madly, wrenched them apart — and finally saw a fleeting shadow that slipped away without noise behind the trunk of a nearby spruce.

He had sight of the prey, and he gave tongue savagely, no words rising from his throat, only a wild cry that came out from the roots of his soul. He rounded the tree. The shadow flicked before him through a screen of tall saplings. Blindly he ran on. A low bough struck him to the ground. He rose and rushed forward through a haze of red. And then, suddenly, with a screech of terror, McGregor stood before him, his shoulders working as he strove to free his hands from the bonds.

"Not the knife, Barney! A bullet, if you want, but not the knife!"

Barney, looking down, saw that the knife with which he had freed Peary was still in his grasp. He used it to set free the hands of McGregor. He took McGregor by the arm. He threw away the knife. He tossed aside his Colt.

"Now there's no advantage on my side, McGregor," he said. "I'm going to kill you, but I'm not killing a helpless man." He looked straight into the eyes of McGregor. He looked so deeply into them that they were like crystal wells and a white shining ghost of fear was at the bottom of the well.

"D'you call it a fair fight, when you've got the strength of a horse in your hands?" asked McGregor.

Barney caught at a low branch and ripped it from the trunk of the tree, leaving a long white gash where bark and wood stripped away with the bough. He snapped the length of it in two. He pulled away the little twigs and side-thrusting branches. It was a stout cudgel that he offered to the hand of McGregor.

"You take this. That'll make us more even," said Barney. "I don't want all the chances on my side. I wouldn't taste the killing of you, that way."

The voice of the girl came piercingly through the woods behind him. Barney stepped back half a pace.

"Begin!" he commanded huskily. "Begin, McGregor . . . you've got a club in your hand now."

The lips of McGregor grinned back from the white of his teeth. His eyes were triangles, like the eyes of a fiend.

"I'm going to smash your skull for you, Dwyer!" he said. "You've been a fool for the last time. . . ."

He struck. He had the skill of a swordsman. The bludgeon took life in the grasp of his hand and Barney, leaping in, barely managed to parry the stroke with an upraised arm.

The weight of the blow ground flesh against bone. Another stroke would break either arm or head. And yet he did not falter. The battle-rage clothed him as if with armor. He went in swaying rapidly from side to side, somewhat like a boxer — but his hands were not closed to fists. They were open, and it was the throat of McGregor that he eyed.

McGregor struck again. A lightning flexion of Barney's body let that blow go by, and then he was in.

It was like stepping through an open door into a garden of delight. He plucked the club from the hand of McGregor as an angry man might tear a toy from the grip of an infant. He hurled it far away. He stood close to the frantic face of McGregor. He saw the fist of McGregor shoot at him. The blow glanced from his jaw like a drop of rain. And now he laid his hands on the body of the man.

There were struggles. But those writhings gave him delight. There were frightful screams that had no ending, no pause for breathing, a fountain of frightful shrieking, and it was delicious music to him.

He could see two things — the body of the girl dangling beneath him, slipping through the clothes that held her limp body — and now this other thing, this white, desperate, glaring face of McGregor, who must die.

And in his hands there was the power to rend flesh like rotten cloth, to break bones like sticks of kindling.

Then another voice burst on his ear. It was not the voice of McGregor, although it was screaming. Another face came close to his. An arm wound around his neck.

Through the thunder of his own blood in his ears, he heard his name called. It grew nearer and nearer. It was the voice of the girl, and this was she, thrusting herself between him and his prey.

"Barney!" she was screaming. "It's murder! Stop! Stop! You're killing him."

Stronger hands pulled at him. He turned his head and saw Peary, white as a ghost, trying to drag him away. He loosed the grip of one hand and with a single blow struck Peary to the ground.

He tried to refasten the hold of that hand on McGregor. Instead, his grip found the arm of the girl.

The iron and the fury went out of him at that touch.

"You're murdering him! Barney!" she screamed again.

He stood up. His legs were weak under him, suddenly. His knees were so weak that they would hardly support his weight. They shook, and kept his whole body shaking.

There lay McGregor on the ground, doubled up on his side. He was limp. He looked like a dead man. Barney was sure that it was death, indeed.

"I wanted to kill him," he said. "It wasn't murder. I gave him a club. It wasn't murder, Sue. What have I done?"

She leaned the weight of her body against him. She clung to him tightly. "Look at McGregor, Len!" she said. "See if he's living. I can't look at his face again. Listen for his heart. He may be living."

"What have I done?" said Barney. "He ought to die, Sue. He tried to kill you. I thought he *had* killed you. I thought that you were going to fall!"

"He's alive," said the voice of Peary, panting heavily. "He's going to live, and I don't think his bones are broken. His legs and arms are not broken, anyway. I don't know why not. I thought iron, even, would have broken."

"Thank God for that," said the girl. Her strength came back into her, that instant. "Sit down, Barney. Sit down here."

"Everything was a wall of flame. I couldn't see clearly through it," muttered Barney. "Sue, have I done something terrible? Look at me. You're afraid of me. Why are you afraid of me? I thought you were going to fall. I thought you were dead. If you'd fallen, I would have killed him, first, and then I would have jumped in after you. Why are you afraid of me, Sue?"

She slumped to the ground. She dropped her head against his knees and began to weep wildly, uncontrollably.

Barney looked from her trembling head up the long, brown trunk of a pine tree to the small patch of blue sky above. Then he stared into the face of Len Peary, who kneeled beside the body of McGregor. And

McGregor was beginning to move his limbs. With every move, he groaned terribly, as though his soul were leaving his body.

"What'll I do, Len?" asked Barney. "You saved her back there. Tell me what to do, now."

Peary stood up. There was a great red welt across the side of his face where the hand of Barney Dwyer had struck him, not many moments before. The footsteps of Peary were unsteady as he came to them and laid his hand on the unwounded shoulder of the girl.

"Quit it, Sue," commanded Peary. "You're the only one who can handle him. What if he did break loose for a minute? He'd been tormented almost to death. It was enough to drive anybody crazy. Pull yourself together. Speak to him. He's in hell because you won't speak to him."

She lifted her head toward Barney. There was love in her eyes, he thought, but there was fear in them, also. It broke his heart to see the fear.

She said nothing. Peary leaned over her, speaking earnestly. "If you'd been with him, it would have been all right," he said. "If you stay with him, he'll never go wild again. You've got to stay with him all your life. God knows, he's worth it. But when a man like Barney catches fire, you can't expect to see a small flame. He's not like the rest of us. We're second growth stuff, and he's the real forest."

The fear went out of her eyes, little by little. "I came in time," she said at last. "And I'm never going to be that far away from you again, Barney. Not while we both live."

McGregor could walk, although he staggered now and then, as they started. And they went on through the end of the day until they saw the lights of Greenborough before them. Peary left them there, for he could not venture into the reach of the law as yet.

"You've done your job with me, Barney," he said. "If ever I'm cleared in the eyes of the law, I'm going back to the ranch and work. I've learned my lesson. There's no easy money in this world."

He left them. They went on down the pass with the lights of the town spreading out before them, to the right and to the left.

"Shall we take him in?" asked Barney. "I've stopped hating him, Sue. I hope that I'll never hate another man. Shall we take McGregor in, or give him another chance, like Len Peary's chance?"

"We have to take him in," answered the

girl. "As long as there's life and freedom for him, he'll never rest till he has another chance to kill you, Barney."

That was why they went on into the town. They could hear an uproar from a distance. Everybody was out in the streets. It was McGregor that was recognized, and the others in the light of his presence, as it were. Fifty shouting men brought Barney and his captive and the girl into the center of the main street, and there, at the jail, they encountered Sheriff Jim Elder with a cavalcade of his riflemen, and many prisoners. Two forms leaped out into the mind of Barney — old Doc Adler, tied into a saddle, and the red mare drawn along on two lead ropes.

They heard the story later, when they were in the house of Dr. Swain. Sue Jones lay on a couch in the sitting room, freshly bandaged, her face pale but happy, and the sheriff told how the noise of gunfire had led him and his posse men as with lights down that narrow ravine, and how the McGregor crew had been scooped up easily, with hardly a shot fired, except by that dangerous old wolf, Adler.

"But what I've done is nothing, Dwyer," said the sheriff. "We've been wanting McGregor and a crime to lodge against him all these years. With the end of him, we'll have peace all through this range. Now, man, tell your own story."

Barney looked toward the girl, helplessly. "I'm no good at talking," he said. "Ask her, and she'll say what needs to be said."

She merely shook her head and smiled faintly, at the ceiling.

"Talking is no good," she said, "when you've known better things than words."

■ ■ ■ ■

OUTLAWS
FROM AFAR

■ ■ ■ ■

Frederick Faust's saga of the hero Speedy
began with "Tramp Magic," a six-part serial
in *Western Story Magazine,* which appeared
in the issues dated November 21, 1931
through December 26, 1932. As most of
Faust's continuing characters, Speedy is a
loner, little more than a youngster, able to
outwit and outmaneuver even the deadliest
of men without the use of a gun. He appeared in a total of nine short stories in addition to the serial. The serial has been
reprinted by Leisure Books under the title
Speedy. The first short novel, "Speedy —

Deputy," can be found in *Jokers Extra Wild* (Five Star Westerns, 2002); "Seven-Day Lawman" can be found in *Flaming Fortune* (Five Star Westerns, 2003); "Speedy's Mare" appears in *Peter Blue* (Five Star Westerns, 2003); "The Crystal Game" is in *The Crystal Game* (Five Star Westerns, 2005); "Red Rock's Secret" in *Red Rock's Secret* (Five Star Westerns, 2006); "Speedy's Bargain" in *Treasure Well* (Five Star Westerns, 2006); and "The Nighthawk Trail" in *Rifle Pass* (Five Star Westerns, 2007). "Outlaws From Afar" originally appeared in the August 20, 1932 issue of Street & Smith's *Western Story Magazine.*

I

From the south came a rider on a long-legged thoroughbred. From the north came a rider on a roach-backed mustang. A splendid fellow was he of the south, a tall man with wide shoulders; his saddle, bridle, golden spurs were all the best that money could buy. A shabby, almost ragged rider was he from the north, but, as they looked at one another across the gully, each knew that he was staring at one of the most formidable men he had ever seen. Only one man had either met more significant, and in each case that exception was the same. It was the force of that unseen third that was bringing them together over a course of many hundreds of miles.

They rode down the banks of the gully to meet in the center of the dry ravine. It was like the naked face of the desert that extended beyond the banks as far as the eye could reach, with only a few greasewood bushes, things that looked like puffs of smoke lying on the ground, rather than substantial vegetation that throws a shadow.

But there is always life in the desert, although it may be hard to find. It is usually deadly or made to flee from death or to pursue it. In the ground the tarantulas excavate their holes and line them daintily. Then they couch their loathsome fat bodies there on legs that are ready to spring, seeking for prey in the dark. Over the pebbles and under the edges of the rocks, likewise, glide lizards, swift as the flicking lash of a whip, dissolving before the eye that watches, but not before the eye of the fierce little roadrunner.

There are many rabbits, too, swifter than any jacks or hares in the world, mere tufts of gray fur with an understringing of light bones and hardy sinews. There are coyotes as well, neighbored by famine that sharpens the wits and steels the patience, and there are the big lobos, the geniuses of the lot, that flourish because their brains are mighty and their souls are great. And always, far above the desert, those small specks and larger ones are floating, the buzzards that wait on the wing for death to arrive.

On an errand of death, likewise, these two riders had come together. The third man had to die; their wits and their hands would devise his destruction.

When they reached the bottom of the shallow draw, the Mexican raised his right hand in a brief salute. "*Señor* Dupray?" he said.

The frog-faced man from the north looked with unsmiling eyes at the Mexican, and then answered in the same tongue: "I'm Dupray. And you're Bardillo."

"If there were shade here," said Bardillo, "we could dismount and sit while we talk."

"It's just as well not to leave any footprints," replied Dupray.

The Mexican smiled a little and glanced toward the distant, naked horizon.

But Dupray added: "The job we're on doesn't admit any chances. We have to look sharp from the start."

"Well," said Bardillo, "I believe in care as much as you. When men hunt Speedy, they take their lives in their hands."

"Yes," said Dupray, "they take their lives in their hands. The minute we begin the hunt, there's no insurance company in the world that would give us a policy. Not a single one."

"True," said Bardillo. His long face grew more and more solemn, and his eyes flashed. "But what are the chances of Speedy, then, if ours are so bad?"

"He has an even chance against the pair of us," said Dupray.

"And we each have only half a chance against him?" said Bardillo.

"We each have half a chance to balance his," Dupray answered with much certainty.

"*Señor* Dupray," broke out Bardillo, "if it comes to that, I can have twenty or thirty tried men on the hunt."

"I could have as many as that," said Dupray. "But numbers are not what count. Once there was a time when every one of my men was more valuable than anything money could buy, but they've fallen off from the old standard."

Bardillo stared at him, asking: "What do you mean by that, *señor?*"

"I mean," said Dupray, "that since Speedy invaded my camp and made a fool of me, my authority is gone. I can still pick up men to follow me, now and then, but, after a job is done, they melt away. They've lost their faith. There was a time when the name Dupray was enough to bring a hard man a thousand miles. But that time has gone. Speedy has done it."

Bardillo flushed and was silent for a moment. Then he added: "Since Speedy walked into my house and took my great horse, the

Nighthawk, away with him and since I hunted him through my own hills and he rode through my lines . . . since that time, my men have fallen away from me, too. I have the remnants, but they are hardly worth keeping together. Once I had men who would ride through the gates of hell and bring out a handful of flames. That was the sort of men I had around me, *señor.*"

"I had the same," said Dupray. "They had wits like coyotes and the craft of foxes, but they won't come back to me until the world knows that Speedy is dead and that I had something to do with his death."

"So!" said Bardillo. "The same is true of me. If I can send out word that I've managed the death of Speedy, then I know that my men will come back . . . perhaps better men than the old ones."

Dupray nodded. "If we can arrange the trap and take Speedy," he said, "then I want you to get the credit, Bardillo."

"Hah?" exclaimed Bardillo. "All the credit for me? Is that what you mean?"

"I mean that," answered Dupray, although he made a wry face in speaking the words.

"But," said the Mexican, "one of your reasons for wanting him dead is that your men may know that you've had a hand in it."

"True," said Dupray. "But my chief reason for wanting him dead is to please myself. My share in it has to be as secret as possible."

Bardillo shrugged his shoulders, as one bewildered.

"I have a nephew, my sole relation in the world and my sole heir," Dupray went on. "He owes everything he is today to Speedy. It was Speedy that saved him from being hanged and brought him out of jail . . . it was Speedy who brought up the stallion from your own house for the sake of Al . . . it's because of Speedy that Al is now a respectable rancher. Even his father-in-law looks up to him a little, simply because Speedy is his friend. If he knew that I'd laid the weight of a finger on Speedy, Al would hunt me down. Now I've told you frankly how the matter goes. If we corner Speedy, you have the credit for it. I give you that as freely as the air you breathe. I insist on it!"

Bardillo jerked up his head with a smile. "It is not difficult to persuade me," he said. "There is no good reason why we should not work together, particularly as you want me to have all the credit."

"Credit?" said Dupray, his fat, round face wrinkling with incredible malice. "I only want to see his blood run and look down into his eyes when they're as blank and empty as the eyes of a dead fish. You understand that, Bardillo?"

"A good hate is more warming to the soul than a long draft of wine," said the Mexican. "My hate for him has made me thin. My ribs stand out like the ribs of a hungry wolf . . . but your hate for him keeps you fat. We shall be able to work together, Dupray. First, we try to find his trail. Do you know where he is now?"

"He may be anywhere," Dupray said gloomily. "He may be singing songs as an entertainer in a Mexican café . . . he may be reading fortunes in a Gypsy crew . . . he may be a juggler in a circus . . . he may be riding the rods of a freight train, or the blind baggage of an express, traveling simply because it makes him nervous to be still for too long at a time. He may be playing cards with as crooked a gambler as himself. Wherever there are men who live by their wits on the stupidity of ordinary men, there you're apt to find Speedy living on the crooks as the crooks live on the honest men."

Bardillo stared, but nodded. "I've heard all of that before," he said. "And I can't understand. Why is it? To punish the criminals and save the honest men?"

"No," shouted Dupray in a burst of emotion, "but simply because there's only one bread, one meat, one drink for him!"

"What is that?" asked Bardillo, frowning with wonder.

"Danger!" cried Dupray. "Danger is what he lives for. Always danger. Is it dangerous to rob a robber? It is. That is why he robbed you . . . that is why he robbed me. Curse him!" He had to stop speaking for a moment, because he was choked by his passion. Then he resumed, while Bardillo was silent, also. "As for finding his trail . . . look." He pointed up. "What do you see, Bardillo?"

"Nothing but a buzzard in the sky."

"Could you trail that buzzard through the clouds, then?"

"Why, no, of course not."

"How could we bring it down to the ground?"

"With a dead bait," Bardillo responded instantly.

"And that's what we'll have to do with Speedy," said Dupray. "But not with a dead bait . . . a living one."

II

Bardillo considered this suggestion for a moment. "A living bait?" he repeated. "Well, and who will be the bait?"

"How can I tell?" Dupray said with irritation. "If I had a perfect scheme and a perfect trap for him, would I have asked you to meet me here?"

Bardillo, offended in turn, was silent, but at length he said: "Well, that is true. We must use our brains together. It is a problem, like the problem of a mathematician. I have a brain which will work, and so have you. We shall accomplish a scheme together."

"Perhaps," muttered Dupray tartly.

"This," said the Mexican, pursing his thick and projecting lower lip, "is the chief thing to remember, as it seems to me. He loves danger more than he loves life. Is that true?"

"That is true," rumbled Dupray, his head hanging thoughtfully to one side, his brow puckered.

"And if there's a criminal to be thwarted, that is the special game of Speedy?"

"Why do you ask?" snapped Dupray. "What has he done to you? What has he done to me? It speaks for itself."

"It speaks for itself," said Bardillo, growing calmer, as the other grew more and more excited.

"Lost causes are what he wants," said the great Charles Dupray. "The more completely lost, the better he likes 'em. There was John Wilson, running amuck as a gunman. He tamed Wilson and made a good rancher out of him. Why? Partly because the man's wife asked him to help, but chiefly because he'd thought of a way of scaring Wilson into good behavior. That way was to ride him up to my camp. Both their necks were inside the noose . . . but still Speedy got them safely away. We have to tempt him, Bardillo. That's the bait."

"What's the greatest temptation he could have?" asked the other.

"The most dangerous task in the world."

"And what would be the most dangerous thing in the world for him?" went on Bardillo. "To come into your camp, or into mine. Is that true?"

Dupray shrugged his shoulders. "Invite him up? Speedy is not a fool," he said. "He's almost a fool, throwing away his life every day, as he does, but he's not as gross a fool as that."

"We'll give him a reason, then, for going up to your camp. A good, sufficient reason."

"What reason is sufficient to make a man commit suicide?" asked the other.

"He has many disguises," suggested Bardillo.

"I know most of his parts, and he knows that I know 'em. He can be a scar-faced peon or a ragged Gypsy or a white-bearded mind-reader and prophet, or half a dozen other things. But I know 'em all. Even if he put on some new disguise, I'd recognize his voice, if I so much as heard him whisper in the dark, and he knows that I'd recognize him, too."

"All the better," said the Mexican. "Then he'll have to go to your camp without trying at a disguise."

"That may be," said the other. "Yes, when the sun sinks at noon and the moon dances jigs with the Great Bear. What sort of nonsense are you talking, Bardillo?"

"It's not nonsense. The greater the danger, the more he'll be tempted, and that I know. Let me tell you what happened in my house. When he appeared before me, one of my men recognized him and warned him that in five minutes he would warn me. Yet Speedy did not use those five minutes in getting as far as possible from the house. Instead, he used up the time in merely stealing the great horse from my men. He stole it, and he rode off while the alarm bell was beating. *Hai,* Dupray, think of the nerves of that man, like steel, enduring the passing of the minutes, while he tried, a man on foot, to capture the stallion, though I had two guards with it."

"How did he manage to take it, then?" asked Dupray, his eyes wide with curiosity.

"Don't ask me," groaned the other. "I go more than half mad, when I think about his name even. Only, once he is challenged to go to your camp, knowing that you would know him even through all of his disguises, I think that the more he pondered on it, the more he would be attracted by the thought. The danger would lure him, like an imp of the perverse. I am sure of it. There remains only the bait to be found. As for that, you still have men with you?"

"Only one worthy of the old days," Dupray said gloomily again.

"Who is that?"

"Bones is his nickname, the only name I have for him."

"What is he like?"

"Bones? Bones is the cruelest fiend north or south of the Río Grande."

"Well, all the better, then. Does Speedy know him?"

"He wanted to cut Speedy's throat when

Speedy was with us in my camp."

"Still, Bones may be the very man for the thing I have in mind, Dupray."

"What is it?"

"We send out word into the world where Speedy lives . . . the world of tramps and yeggs and drifting criminals, eh?"

"Yes, that's his world," agreed Dupray.

"Then, we send out word among those people that Speedy is wanted in a certain town, where a certain man would give a great deal to talk with him. In the meantime, we provide the man. Then. . . ."

"You think that Speedy will be lured on by any such idea as that?" said Dupray, sneering. "I tell you, Bardillo, he might come to look the place over, but he would come like a shadow, with the eyes of a hawk and look over the man and the place with the eyes of a hawk before he let himself be known. You could never set a trap around a bait as clumsy as that."

"Let me finish, Dupray," answered the other. "My idea is simply this . . . we hire a trustworthy man, who will send out word that a reward will be given to the man who brings in Speedy. When Speedy arrives, the hired man speaks to him like this . . . '*Señor* Speedy, we have desperate need of a desperate man. No one but you will do. We need a man who will adventure into the camp of Charles Dupray. We send for you, because we know perfectly well that you have done the thing before.' "

"And Speedy," broke in Dupray, "simply answers that he's not such a great fool as to try a thing like that, eh?"

"Speedy," went on the Mexican, "may be surprised, and may say so, but he's sure to be interested. What is the reason for the errand to the camp of Dupray? Why, the reason is that our agent . . . he should be a lawyer, by the way . . . has word that a client in the East, a very rich man, is casting about for an heir, and finds that all of his next of kin are dead. But he has seen a picture of Bones . . . would that do? Could anyone have been apt to see a picture of Bones in a newspaper, say?"

"His face has been in the papers often enough," growled Charley Dupray. "What of that?"

"Well, then, the rich man has seen a picture of Bones in the newspaper. And he has recognized in it a great likeness to the features of others of his family."

"A pretty family, then," said Dupray, "because Bones earns his nickname. He's an ugly, skinny, buck-toothed devil."

"All the more reason for him to be vain.

Ugly men are always sure to think of their personal appearance a good deal."

"True," said Dupray. "Bardillo, I begin to understand. We hire a lawyer, who gets in touch with Speedy and tells him that the disposal of a very considerable fortune hangs upon getting word at once to Bones. But Bones is wanted by the law. He cannot be advertised for openly. It is a secret messenger who must strive to find him. And that messenger must find him in the camp of the outlaw, Dupray. Then Bones must be persuaded to come down to the town. Is that it? To come down to the town, and then he will be put in the way of getting his hungry hands on his mysterious patrimony, eh?"

"You have the idea," said Bardillo.

Dupray shook his head, but presently he began to frown once more with profound consideration. "I don't know," he said. "It may be the very trick that'll catch him . . . whiskey on an empty stomach . . . the thing that will pull that buzzard down out of the sky."

"I'm sure of it," said Bardillo. "I begin to feel the thing working in my bones, as if I were Speedy."

"To bring good news to Bones, the throat-cutter," murmured Charles Dupray.

"There's a fellow, at least, that I could count on. I tell you that he'd give up ten years of his life for the hope of putting a knife into the heart of Speedy. That's why he's stayed with me . . . because he was with me, he was in the same hut with Speedy and Wilson the night they came." Dupray began to laugh a little, swaying from side to side in his saddle in the excess of his mirth.

Bardillo said in the most business-like manner: "It begins to seem that we have a trap to lay and bait for it, then?"

"Besides," said Dupray, "I know the very lawyer in the very town who will take my money as a bribe and do my work, no matter what it is. I know the man, Bardillo. I know the man."

"Shall we ride on, then, together?" asked Bardillo.

"We'll ride on together," answered Dupray. "Bardillo, we should have met face to face before this. But it took the devil himself walking the earth to bring us together."

They rode up the side of the draw. A strong, hot wind came up from the desert and rained a volley of flying sand in their faces, but they paid no heed to it. Happiness and the hope of a great triumph were shining in their faces.

III

In the office of Raymond & Raymond, lawyers, in the town of Rusty Creek, Mr. Henry Raymond, a member of that firm, leaned back in his chair, on a day, and, resting his heels on the edge of his desk, he stared out through his office window and off into the sky.

When he saw a shadow appear on the outside of the clouded glass of his door, with a long practiced movement he jerked his feet from the desk top, unclasped his hands from behind his head, and swayed forward over his desk. When the door opened, he was in the midst of heaping papers, writing busily.

"One moment, please!" he called in a cheerful voice. Then he turned, still holding his pen, took off his glasses, and peered with a sleek smile at the stranger.

This stranger was a fellow of middle height, slenderly built, and very roughly clad. His skin was as brown as a berry; his eyes were very dark and bright; and what was the distinguishing feature of a most unexciting appearance, otherwise, was a certain electric tingle of physical well-being that was exhaled from the youth and touched Henry Raymond even at a distance.

The stranger had his hat in his hand. He might be twenty-five. Raymond's plump forehead gradually clouded. He reserved his own pleasant facial expressions for creditors and clients who seemed likely to be able to pay a large bill. He did not get many clients in the course of a year. When he did, he knew how to put the screws on them and extract all that was possible.

"Good morning, Mister Raymond," said the stranger.

"Good morning," said Raymond. "Is there anything that I can do for you?"

"No, sir," said the other. "I came because I was sent for, I think."

"Sent for?" said Raymond. "Some mistake, I'm afraid. I haven't sent for you, son. Who said that I did?"

"A fellow by the name of Lank Wallace," said the young fellow.

"Lank Wallace? Lank Wallace?" said the attorney, frowning as he concentrated on the name. "No, I never knew a man by that name. Where did he reach you?"

"In Fort Craven," said the man.

"Fort Craven? Let me see . . . why, the only Fort Craven I know of is fifteen hundred miles from here."

"That's about the distance," said the youth.

"The devil!" exploded Raymond. "You mean to tell me that an unknown person called Lank Wallace called on you in Fort Craven and told you that I, Henry Raymond, wanted to see you? And you came fifteen hundred miles on account of that message?"

"Well," said the other, "it wasn't exactly like that. I was ready to hop off in this direction, anyway."

"Ah, hum," muttered Raymond. "I see. One of the knights of the road. Is that your occupation?"

"You mean . . . am I a tramp?"

"That's a hard word," said Raymond carelessly.

"I'm a tramp most of the time, if you mean by that, a man without any steady occupation," said the young fellow.

"Tell me," said Raymond, "what Lank Wallace looked like? What sort of a man was he? This is one of the strangest stories that I ever heard. Let's have the truth. It will serve you better than any lie, I can assure you."

"Why," said the other, "Lank Wallace was about six feet three. He had ears as big as your hands, and a nose bigger than both his ears put together. His shoulders were stooped a little, and he had the largest hands that I ever saw."

"That's a pretty picture," said the lawyer. "Lank Wallace, eh? Why do you say was when you speak of him?"

"He used to be, but now he's only was," said the stranger. "He was making the trip southwest with me, but on the way he started to play tag with a railroad detective, and the detective won the game."

"You mean . . . ?"

"Tagged him with a Forty-Five-caliber chunk of lead, right between the shoulders. Yes, he won that game."

"By heaven, he murdered Lank, eh?"

"Nobody could murder Lank," replied the stranger slowly. "Wallace was wanted for too many things that meant anything from life to a hangman's rope. But the detective didn't know that. He simply took a chance and happened to be right."

"Ah-ha!" exclaimed Raymond. "Something will happen to that railroad detective one of these days."

"Something did happen to him, just after he killed Lank Wallace," said the stranger.

"What?"

"Why," said the other, looking Raymond steadily in the eye, but speaking very slowly, "why, he had a lot of bad luck all in a bunch. He had about enough bad luck to last him the rest of his life."

A glint of appreciation appeared in the eyes of the lawyer. "What kind of bad luck do you mean?" asked Raymond.

The other looked steadily back at him. "Oh, just bad luck," he said.

Raymond twisted a little in his chair, like one who is close to interesting information that still cannot be fully revealed. All right," he said at last. "You can keep your secrets. I suppose you used a gun on the big cop?"

"I never carry a gun," the youth said mildly.

"Well," muttered Raymond, "let it go. But tell me, what about the message that this late Lank Wallace gave to you from me?"

"Why," said the other, "he said that you wanted to see a fellow named Speedy."

Raymond started. "Speedy?" he exclaimed. "Ah, I see. It's true that I've offered a five-hundred-dollar reward to anybody who'll bring in Speedy. Mind you, though, it doesn't go except to the man who brings him in. That is to say, to the man who marches him into this office."

"Five hundred is a lot of money," said the young fellow. He nodded his head, as though considering the sum.

"If you know anything about where I can get in touch with him," said Raymond, "I'd shell out a few round dollars for that, too . . . or, else, you might be able to go wherever you've heard he may be and bring him in here to me. Though I guess," he added with a laugh, "that it would take a dozen like you to get Speedy."

"Oh, no," said the youth. "I'd be enough."

Raymond stared. Then he laughed again derisively. "You'd be enough? For that man-handler?"

"Yes, I'd be enough. I'm Speedy, you see," said the youth.

Raymond leaped from his chair. "Why don't you say that you're the devil on wheels, while you're about it?" he demanded angrily. Then, suddenly, he began to remember the descriptions of this famous man, as he had heard them — a fellow not over twenty-five, looking perhaps three or four years younger, a face unseamed and unwritten upon by time, of middle height, and of a slenderness that quite belied the sinewy strength he had shown so many times, with features of an almost feminine delicacy and beauty, a very sun-tanned skin, a gentle voice and manner, and eyes very dark, and yet very bright.

As he summed up these remarks, he could see that the ragged young fellow now standing before him answered each particular, and yet he burst out: "It's not possible.

You're not Speedy . . . the Speedy who's wrecked so many gunfighters and who. . . ."

He paused again. The other was shaking his head in a deprecatory manner.

"I'm Speedy," he repeated in the pause.

"You're Speedy?" said the lawyer. "Well, do something to prove it. I mean, I've got to have some proof. This is an important business that I want to talk to you about."

"Well," said Speedy, "I don't know what I can do."

"The real Speedy," said the lawyer, "can do anything with his hands. He's magic. Throws a knife straighter than crack shots throw bullets . . . juggles half a dozen things at once, spins a crystal ball on the tip of one finger without letting it fall off."

"Well," said Speedy, "if that's enough, here's the crystal."

It appeared in his hand at the same moment, although Raymond could not see from what spot it had been produced.

The young fellow balanced it on the tip of a slender forefinger and, with a twist, started it spinning. His somber, long-lashed eyes were lowered, while he considered the spinning ball.

"Go on, now that you've got it going. Read my mind for me, Speedy, because, by thunder, I see that you're the man that I want."

"You cross my palm with silver, first," said the other.

"Here's a dollar," said Raymond, chuckling. "This is rich. Go ahead, Speedy, and let me have a look at the inside of my mind."

"I'm to read your mind . . . your thought at this moment?" asked Speedy.

"Yes," said the lawyer.

There was a pause, while Speedy continued to stare steadily into the flicker of light in the center of the crystal, a shining streak like the glimmer of a little, polished sword blade, trembling to and fro. Then he began to speak in a quiet, monotonous voice. "You are thinking," he said, "that if I'm fool enough to do what you propose to me, it will be a tidy sum of money in your pocket." He caught the ball in the palm of his hand and made the big crystal disappear again into nothingness — not up his sleeve, surely, but where? The magic of that hand was far swifter than the gestures of the swiftest eye.

Raymond's exultation had disappeared as he listened to the answer. He was so taken by surprise that he did not even have wit enough to protest at first. He could only gasp out: "How the devil did you know that . . . ?" Then he paused, agape, realizing

266

that he had committed himself with those few words too far to draw back.

But Speedy looked up at him with a peculiarly quick, flashing smile that had no malice in it. "It's all right, Raymond," he said. "I know that you're not in the deal. I know that somebody else is behind it. What is the main idea, anyway?"

IV

It seemed to Raymond that he was truly trapped between the devil and the deep blue sea. He had before him a man whose formidable qualities were famous all through the West, and he himself had been suddenly tricked, thrown off his guard, and forced into a confession that promised to ruin everything. However, he did not instantly give up the game.

Henry Raymond was one of those liars who weave only a certain percentage of falsehood into their remarks. So skillfully is it done that even the most expert eye is often deceived and it looks as though all is the one true, real, artistic pattern. Now, when he was cornered, this talent came to his aid. He saw, with a flash of genius, that his partial downfall could be turned into his salvation, if what he had heard of this

Speedy were correct.

He burst out, in a tone of hearty relief: "Well, it's a dirty business, and I'm glad that you saw through it, Speedy. I don't think that I could have gone through with the rotten game, anyway."

"Dupray, eh?" Speedy asked gently.

"Sit down," said Raymond, himself rising and striding up and down the room. "Sit down, Speedy. I'm going to show you the whole cursed business. I'm going to make a clean breast of it. It's not the first time that I've soiled my hands for Dupray. But it's going to be the last time."

He stopped and faced Speedy suddenly, as the latter leaned lightly against the desk.

"Speedy," he blurted out in a passion of remorse, as it were, "you'll be thinking that I'm a hound. You'll be about nine parts right, too. But what's important to me, just now, is to do you right in this business. It is Dupray. But how in the devil did you guess it? Or can you really read the mind?"

"I only look in the crystal," said Speedy with the faintest of smiles. "I only look in the crystal and try to understand what I see there . . . and what I see is that Dupray is dreaming night and day about killing me."

"He hates you, Speedy," said Raymond. "I never heard of anybody hating another man the way Dupray hates you. You broke up his gang for him. I think that's the chief reason."

"I didn't break it up, exactly," said Speedy. "I gave it a jolt, though. That's one reason he hates me. The other reason is more important, though."

"What's the other reason?" asked Henry Raymond.

"Well," replied Speedy, "it's the reason that the wolf hates the dog, and the dog hates the wolf. We're different kinds."

Raymond stepped closer, summoned a frown as though he were making a point to a jury of twelve good men and true, and raised his voice and let it ring. "Speedy," he said, "Dupray would sell his soul to the devil to put a knife through your heart."

Speedy nodded. "And just now," he commented, "Dupray will make his big effort, eh?"

"I think he will," said the lawyer.

"The hate has been piling up in him, piling up like water, and the dam is apt to break. But that's all right," said Speedy. "I knew that the crisis would come, sooner or later, and then one of us would have to die. I'm sorry about it, though."

"Sorry? To kill a beast like that, Speedy?" asked Raymond.

"I'll tell you why," said Speedy. "His

nephew, Al Dupray, is a friend of mine. A great friend. And if his uncle's blood is on my hands . . . well, that's the end of things between Al and me, of course."

Raymond sighed and shook his head. "It's a mighty hard one," he admitted.

"Yes, it's hard," replied Speedy. "But I have a feeling that the finish has come at last, for Dupray and me. One of us has to go."

"If that's your feeling," said the other, "then back up out of this job, Speedy. Because Dupray has laid the trap for you."

"What trap, man?"

"Why, there's a sick man back East with a few millions lying around loose and no heir in the world except one of the men in Dupray's gang. You understand? Dupray knows about it. But he won't pass the word to Bones . . . that's the name of the crook who could be the millionaire . . . and no one else can get to Bones to let him know about his good luck. You see? As a matter of fact I've got the whole correspondence here, all the letters and telegrams that Littleton . . . that's the millionaire . . . has sent to me." He reached into a drawer of the desk and tumbled a confused mass of documents onto the face of the varnished wood. "There you are . . . all that!" said the lawyer. "Little-

270

ton sent his own personal counsel out here, all the way. When the man couldn't locate Bones, he turned the business over to me. Well, I've located Bones, easily enough. I thought that my only job was to get word to him, in one way or another. Then, in comes Dupray himself and tells me how I can be worth ten thousand dollars to him."

The glance of Speedy fell upon a line of a telegram that was only partially exposed, saying: *Time remaining short. Hurry. Inquiry following.*

"Ten thousand dollars?" said Speedy. "Is that the price that he pays for me?"

Raymond flushed a little. "He gave me five thousand as a retainer," he said. "And he gave me a promise of five thousand more. Do you despise me, Speedy?"

Speedy shook his head. "It's all in the line of business," he said. "I don't despise you, Raymond. When people have set up a style of business, it's the style that matters to them, not the morality. I knew a fellow who was smuggling Chinamen across the frontier, over the river. Most honorable man you ever met in your life. Scrupulously exact in everything. Nearly shot a man who wanted him to smuggle opium as well as the chinks. And you know, Raymond, if you've been working with crooks like Dupray, you've

271

probably simply decided that the only thing for you to be concerned about is doing your job in the most effective way."

"You put it kindly, but I know what I think of myself," said the lawyer. "However, the point now is, how can I help you, Speedy?"

"Help me?" said Speedy. Then he added, a little coldly: "I haven't paid you any retaining fee, Raymond."

The lawyer flushed again. "Perhaps you'll trust me to give you my best advice, free of charge, Speedy. I'm not quite as bad a hound as you may think."

Speedy waved away the thought of such a condemnatory attitude on his part. He said: "What's exactly the plan of Dupray?"

"Well, his plan is exactly this . . . the fellow back East, Littleton, is lying nearly dead, waiting to get word to his heir out here in the West. That heir is a crook working in Dupray's gang, wanted by the law, or the rope, maybe. Dupray says that the one thing to do is to get hold of Speedy and say to him . . . 'Everybody knows that you got to Dupray's gang before. Well, try the same thing again, and make yourself even more famous. Get to Bones, tell him about his inheritance and do it fast, because there's a dying man back East, waiting from hour to hour and fighting for his breath.' "

A shudder ran through the body of Speedy. He closed his eyes and puckered his brow with pain. "That poor devil Littleton," he muttered.

A single flash of triumph appeared in the face of Raymond, as he saw that one part of his lie, at least, had succeeded.

Then Speedy added: "And the gain of Dupray is that, when I start hunting for Bones, he'll be on the look-out?"

"That's it. He's expecting you now. He's on the look-out every minute. Oh, he's waiting like a cat for a bird."

Speedy nodded. "It's not a bad scheme, take it all in all," he said. "Brains behind it, plenty of brains, and it might have worked, too. However. . . ." He turned toward the door and laid his hand on the knob of it. Bitter disappointment darkened the brow of Henry Raymond.

But, with his hand on the knob of the door, Speedy paused and shook his head. "That Littleton, that poor devil," he murmured. He turned suddenly around. "Look here, Raymond," he said. "How old is Littleton?"

"Forty-three."

"That's young enough. What's the matter with him?"

Raymond made a wry face and laid a hand

273

over his heart; he made the hand flutter like a falling leaf. "Not a bit of good. Heart's no good. Littleton just lies and gasps," he said. "He ought to have been dead weeks ago. But you know how it is. Will of iron. He won't die until he knows that he's found the man who'll get his money. You see?"

Speedy groaned aloud. "I wish that I hadn't heard that," he said.

"It's a bad business." Raymond sighed.

"Because," said Speedy, "it means that I've got to go, whether I want to or not."

"Go where?" asked Raymond innocently.

"To the Dupray camp to find Bones. Any idea where the camp is now?"

"To the Dupray camp? To find Bones? You're not crazy, Speedy, are you? Don't you understand what I said . . . that Dupray will be on the look-out every minute?"

"Oh, I understand," Speedy said almost wearily. "I understand all that, but Littleton, that poor devil of a Littleton." He sighed and shook his head again. "Bones is a cold-blooded cut-throat," he said. "But I've got to try to get the word through to him."

V

High up among the mountains, where the peaks gave back on three sides and on the fourth the hills sloped away toward the plains, set in at the foot of the loftiest peaks, there was a lake. It was as blue a lake as one could find among the mountains. It was as bright a lake as one could find in all the ranges of the Rockies.

It had the appropriate setting of a belt of meadow grass around one side of it, with a mighty array of trees bordering the opposite shore. One could sit beside that lake all the day long and every instant see changes, as clouds blew over, as the water trembled in the wind, or as it smoothed out and lay still as ice.

Charles Dupray, by the side of this lake, sat on the top of a large boulder. But he was not looking at the beauties that mirror revealed. Instead, he was puffing at a pipe and looking down at a letter that he held tightly in his right hand.

It was not a very long letter, but the bandit read and reread it with singular enjoyment, like a poet repeating the lines of his lyric over and over.

"Hey, Bones!" he called at last. There was a lean-to built against the trunk of a giant tree, and out of that lean-to appeared a tall, gaunt form, stooped in the shoulders, narrow of chest, prodigiously long of arm and vast of hand. The outthrust of his upper teeth kept him smiling continually, but his eyes were as steady and bright and evil as the eyes of a snake. "Well?" said Bones.

"Where's Bardillo?" asked the leader.

"I dunno."

"Don't you?"

"No."

"You ought to."

"I ain't a watchdog over no greaser," said Bones.

"Vincente Bardillo's something more than a greaser," suggested the great Dupray, and frowned.

When Bones saw that expression of anger appear on the flat frog face of the leader, he shrugged his shoulders and subsided. "Yeah," he said, "I guess it's all right. Bardillo's a good shot, anyway. So's that Diego Marañon that he's got with him. They were shooting at rocks that they threw up for each other last evening. They can shoot, what I mean. Only, nothing's coming of all this here business."

"You mean that Speedy won't come here?"

"That's what I mean."

The other smiled. "Go get Bardillo for me,

Bones," he said.

"Sure, he's just over the hill, maybe," said Bones. He strode off, lifting himself rapidly along the slope with his gigantic strides; he loomed vast on the top of the hills, then disappeared in two steps. Presently he returned, striding as rapidly as before; behind him came the two Mexicans, Bardillo almost as tall as Bones, but much heavier, and Marañon shorter, older, grayer.

When they came up, Dupray nodded to them. Then he said: "It's all right. Speedy's coming."

"The devil he is!" exclaimed Bones.

Dupray looked at him with a grin. "Listen to this," he said, and read aloud.

Dear Dupray: Speedy arrived. That keen devil saw through the outside layers of the scheme. He knew that something was in the air. I was cornered and had to confess that I was working with you. But I made out that there was a fellow in the East called Littleton, a man dying of heart disease, and fighting off his death until he hears that his heir, Bones, has been located. That picture of the dying man was too much for Speedy. He knows that you're on the look-out for him, but he's made up his mind to try to get past you to Bones, and take Bones East to Littleton. You won't believe it, but it's true.

I've told Speedy just where to find you. He's going ahead slowly, watching every step of the way, because he expects that you'll tackle him almost at any point going up to the camp. I'm sending this letter ahead by the relay that we arranged. It ought to get to you twenty-four hours before Speedy is anywhere near. He's a cool devil and quick as a flash. I hardly dared to let a thought come into my mind, for fear that he'd be able to read it through my forehead, as if the thought were in printed words and my forehead made of plate glass. However, the idea of the dying Littleton was too much for his tender heart, and the fool has gone off on his last adventure. At least, it ought to be his last if you do your part as well as I've done mine.

Another thing. He knows that you're in the deal, but he doesn't dream, so far as I know, that Bardillo and Marañon are also on the reception committee.

Bones ought to be grateful for another chance to cut his throat, and I hope that Bones has his way because, if Speedy comes out of this alive and finds out that, when I pretended to confess, I was only telling a more complicated lie than before, he'll never go off my trail until he's broken me to bits.

Yours hopefully,
Henry Raymond

"What do you think of that?" asked Dupray.

"I think," said Bardillo, "that any lawyer who writes words like that, even in a code, is a fool."

"Raymond is not a fool," said Dupray. "But he's not as bright as he thinks he is. However, that was a useful set of lies that he told. Speedy is comin' . . . Speedy knows that I'm trying to trap him, but Speedy does not know that Bardillo is on the ground with Marañon, and Speedy does not, most of all, realize that the man to whom he's bringing the great news is part of the trap that'll catch him. See that, Bones?"

Bones actually smiled in earnest, his lips stretching, and his upper teeth thrusting out with a white sheen. "I've always kind of had an idea," he said, "that I'd have the carving of that bird before the finish of things. I've always sort of had a hunch that he'd be my meat."

Dupray grinned in turn contentedly.

"Bones," he said, "you're a comfort, is what you are. But let me tell you all, no matter how many advantages we have, Speedy is still something to be handled with care."

Bardillo waved his hand and his long face lengthened still more, his thick lower lip thrust out.

"There's no danger that we'll be overconfident," he said. "Speedy is fire that's burned us all, but this time I've an idea that he's riding to his finish. Eh, Marañon?"

The older man looked up with a start, as though recalling himself out of distant thoughts. Then he remarked: "There's this much for us all to say . . . Speedy is so accomplished a man that the killing of him will bring honor to all four of us. It will be a great day for us all. Bardillo, we ought to hurry forward and meet him on the way."

"Where?" asked Bardillo.

"At the crossroads hotel, down there at Clive's Corner," suggested Dupray. "That's the place to wait for him."

"I don't know the place," said Bardillo.

"I do," said Dupray. "We have plenty of time to get there and explore. I know the people. They know me. I've helped them with hard cash and harder advice. One of their boys wants to join me. I'll take him, too, when he's a little more seasoned. It's a perfect place. And I know every step and inch of it. Bones, rustle up the horses, will you?"

"I'll saddle 'em," said Bones, "just as if I was gonna go to my wedding."

He strode off, and Bardillo smiled upon Dupray.

"Charles," he said, "I think that *Señor* Speedy is riding on his last journey."

"The life he's been leading," said Dupray, "he had to come to the end of the trail sooner or later. What I'm wondering now is . . . which one of us will have the luck to send the right bullet into his heart or between his eyes?"

Marañon muttered something under his breath.

"What is it?" asked Bardillo. "Speak out, Diego."

"Why," said Marañon, "it's simply this. There are four of us, all acting together, all good fighting men, all armed to the teeth, and up the trail is coming one young fellow without even a revolver. Yet I suppose all four of us are more nervous than that young devil knows how to be."

VI

The morning is delayed by the shadows of the mountains, and the night is hurried on; so it was that even before sunset, Speedy found that Clive's Corner was a dreary place. The upper sky and the white tops of the peaks were still gilded with fire, but the ravines that crossed at Clive's Corner were flooded with dimness. Looking up was like looking from the bottom of a well.

There was promise of a stormy night, as well. The wind was beginning to whine on a thin, high note that would have had peculiar meaning to a violinist. And the clouds swept out of the northwest, foamed up around the shoulders of the mountains, and then went on thronging across the sky, taking the rose of the evening above and giving leaden shadow below.

Speedy gave a glance at the unpainted, unkempt shack known as the Clive Hotel. Then he shrugged his shoulders. It looked to him like a proper setting for a murder. Then he went to the rear, found the stable, and, in the murky interior of the barn, a shadowy figure cleaning the stalls with a fork. He came to the door and stood, fork in hand, looking down at Speedy. He was a big young man, but with a head that was hardly more than a handful and red hair that bristled. Small as his face was, it was all mouth and jaw. Nose and eyes and forehead were pinched together, crowding one another.

"Yeah?" he said to Speedy, and hitched at his one suspender.

"I'd like to put up here for the night," said Speedy.

"Would you? I reckon you might put your hoss up in the barn, anyways," said the lout.

Speedy looked at the other again. It was a magnificent body. A heavyweight wrestler might have been proud of that swelling chest and those mighty shoulders.

"Hotel's not crowded?" Speedy suggested politely.

"Crowded? Ain't had a visitor to pay a penny for ten days. Here, I'll take your bronc'." He took the reins and led the mustang into the barn.

Speedy did not follow, but lingered on the threshold to peer into the shadows and make out the lay of the land. It was an old custom that had now become a fixed habit with him. Small details, well imprinted on the mind, had saved his life a score of times. The same sort of information might save him again on this night, for he knew that he had entered into the territory of the enemy.

When he was sure that he had probed the dimness long enough to have made out the main features of the barn, he went to the back door of the hotel and knocked.

A woman's voice called out for him to enter, and he stepped into a kitchen where a brawny woman of middle age or more was rolling out biscuit dough into a thin slab.

"Yeah?" she said, looking up at Speedy through some ragged frontlets of streaming hair.

"I'm looking for a room for the night," said Speedy.

She continued to stare at him for a moment. Then, leaning still on the rolling pin, she called out: "Hey, Pa! Come here!"

A dragging step approached from a front room, and then there appeared a man of fifty years with a dignified carriage and a tobacco-stained beard. He carried a knife in one hand and the stick he had been whittling in the other. He put knife and stick in the fingers of one hand, took off his spectacles, and stared at Speedy.

"Wants a room for the night," she said.

"Ad!" called the man. "Hey, Ad! Where are you? Oh, A-a-a-d!"

The woman had begun to roll the dough once more. The light, which struggled out of the smoked chimney of the lamp, only partially conquered the gloom in the room; the night seemed to be soaking into the place like a dark stain in clear water.

"Ad!" called the man again.

"Comin'!" answered a voice.

A door opened nearby, and let in the sound of the voice and heels scuffing along the floor.

"Comin', Mister Clive!" called the voice again.

"You're always comin', and you ain't never here," said Pa Clive. "Here's a gent that wants to be put up for the night. Go and show him a room, get out the register, sign him up, and do what you had oughta do to make a gentleman comfortable." He turned and addressed his next remarks to Speedy. "You take the way things is today, stranger, it ain't hardly possible to get no good servants. A gentleman, he can't hardly live a decent life, because there ain't no servants. Everything goes to hell, when there ain't servants in the house." He smoothed his yellow-stained beard and looked more dignified than ever.

And Speedy followed Ad out of the room and up the stairs. She was a poor near-sighted drudge with a mouth that was always hanging open and eyes that appeared stunned by all that they beheld.

The room was what he expected to find. There was a washstand with an oval linoleum mat in front of it, the linoleum surfacing long ago worn through and the tough inner fibers showing. There was a cot decorated with two brass knobs at its head, only one knob was off. There was no table of any kind; there was no closet. Nails, hammered into the walls, could serve all purposes for accommodating clothes.

Ad, the hotel drudge, fumbled for and found the lamp, lighted it, regulated the flame, and then shaded her eyes with a fat, greasy, shapeless hand. She stared at Speedy, mouth open, eyes bewildered.

"Might you be wantin' anything, mister?" she asked.

He asked for hot water and was glad to see her out of the room. When she disappeared, he went to the window and looked out. The kitchen was in a penthouse at the rear of the building, and the edge of that sloping roof was about six feet away from the edge of his window. A man might stand on the windowsill and jump for the roof, if he were pressed to leave that room otherwise than by the door. Again, an active man could hang from the windowsill at the length of his arms, and swing himself across the space, if he were very agile. Landing in that way, there would be much less noise. Landing on stockinged feet, he knew how to land; there would be no noise at all, no more than is made by a prowling cat.

When he had finished this survey and noted again the distance and the angle toward the barn, he regarded the dark masses of the pine woods that marched down toward the hotel on all sides. Above there were the vast slopes of the mountains and the shining summits high above the place.

There was something suggestive about this picture, but he did not stop to work out a meaning for it. Ad, the drudge, had just come back carrying some lukewarm water in a pail. She brought a piece of yellow laundry soap, as well, and with this he scrubbed himself thoroughly.

Then he went downstairs and found Mr. Clive waiting for him in the sitting room. Mr. Clive had put on a coat, in the meantime, and combed his beard, but had not washed it. He was revealed sitting close to a lamp on a center table, with a large volume spread out before him on his crossed knees.

He looked up, took off his glasses, located Speedy, put on the glasses again, and resumed his apparent study of the book. He turned two pages together — a fact that the unerring eye of Speedy at once detected — and continued to peruse, as though lost in the contents.

Speedy stood before the darkening window and teetered up and down on his toes.

Presently the volume closed, the pages slipping loudly together.

"That's a bright man that wrote that book," said Mr. Clive. "A mighty bright man, and yet he went and made his mistakes, too."

Speedy glanced toward the book and saw the title in large letters: *The History of Abrams County* by Fletcher Phineas.

"Mistakes, eh?" Speedy murmured.

"Lotta mistakes, too. There's what he says about old man Wheeler. Wheeler didn't kill Traxton with a shotgun. Wheeler, he would've despised to use a shotgun on man-size game. No, sir, I could tell you what I've seen in my time."

"I'd like to know," said Speedy.

The host settled back in his chair, and thrust his thumbs into the armholes of his waistcoat. "Seventy-two ain't young, would you say?" he asked.

"No," said Speedy.

"I've seen old man Wheeler, when he was seventy-two years old, stand out under a tree and take up his old Kentucky rifle, his hands wobbling till he found the bead. Then, him and his old arms and his hands and the gun, all turning into one rock, I've seen him shoot, and I've seen the squirrel fall a hundred feet out of the tree. You go there to the window, will you?"

It was only a half turn of his body for Speedy to look out at the window again.

"See that sugarloaf?"

"Yes," replied Speedy.

"Got a big old bald-faced pine right on a line with the sugarloaf?"

"Yes."

"Well, sir, that's the very tree that I seen old man Wheeler shoot the squirrel out of, just to prove that I ain't no liar." He said this proudly, and then he added: "But you take a man like that Fletcher Phineas, he was young and he was smart. He was educated pretty good, too, as a matter of fact. He was pleasant and he was agreeable, too, but he made mistakes. When he says that old man Wheeler shot Traxton with a shotgun, he was wrong. I didn't see the body, but I know Wheeler."

Speedy nodded absently.

Mr. Clive went on: "But I was sorry for Phineas. He was young, that was mostly the trouble with him. And Bill Cather, I've always said, was dead wrong . . . he was just

289

kind of hasty, when he went and killed Phineas for the writing of this book."

"Why did he kill Phineas, then?"

"Why, it was for something like saying that Bill Cather had a father that had done time, or something like that."

"It wasn't true, eh?"

"Why, it was true, all right, but, as Bill says, he didn't mind his old man being in jail, as long as he didn't get into a book about it. Bill took to brooding on it, and pretty soon he just had to go and kill Phineas. It was too bad. Me, personal, I always spoke up and said that it was too bad."

"Yes?" murmured Speedy.

"A gent losing his temper like that," said the hotelkeeper. "That's what's too bad about it."

Speedy nodded. "What happened to Bill Cather?" he asked.

"To Bill?" said the hotel man.

"Yes."

"Why, I dunno. What should've happened to Cather?"

"I mean to say," asked Speedy, "what happened to him after the killing of young Phineas, who wrote that history of the county?"

"What happened to Cather after that?"

said the other, still somewhat puzzled. "Why, nothing happened to him. What would've happened to him?"

"I thought he might have been run in for murder," suggested Speedy.

"Murder?" exclaimed the host. Then he put his head back and laughed heartily. He finished laughing with moist, bright eyes. "You ain't been in these mountains long, have you?" he asked.

"No," replied Speedy.

"Well," said the host, "it wasn't murder, at all. Nobody ever did claim that it was that. It was just self-defense. Phineas, he must've taken and made a move toward a hip pocket, or something like that. Nope, it was just self-defense, of course, but I've always held that it was mighty hasty self-defense on the part of Bill Cather, because everybody knowed that Fletcher Phineas never carried no gun."

VII

They had their supper in the kitchen. The wind had come up higher and was thrusting and prying through every crack in the battered old house, putting fingers of ice into the rooms. The kitchen, heated by the big stove, was the only comfortable quarters for

291

these reasons, and the host, with apologies, had suggested that they should have the meal in the warmth.

So they sat down as the dark lowered outside the misted window panes.

The big fellow from the stable appeared, Alfred to his mother, Alf to his father, and the three sat down with their guest while the hotel's drudge, Ad, labored back and forth, waiting on the table and setting dishes of food on the table from time to time.

It was a queer meal. It had begun cheerfully enough on the part of all except Alfred, but he sat bolt upright in his chair with fire in his eyes and his jaws gripped hard together. Food he would hardly touch.

"Take and look at Alfred," said his mother. "Will you, Pa?"

"Suppose that I take and look," said Pa Clive. "He's big enough to be seen, I guess, the first shot?"

"Yeah, he's maybe big enough to be seen," said Mrs. Clive. "But don't you notice nothin'?"

"Well, what?"

"He ain't eatin'!"

"Leave me alone, Ma, will you?" demanded Alf.

"Hey, Ad, look at him," said Ma Clive to the serving girl. "Here's Alfred not eatin' nothing, hardly."

"My lands," said Ad. "Ain't you eating nothin', Alf?"

"It ain't no business of yours whether I'm eating or not," said Alf. He glared at his mother. "Why don't you keep your yapping to yourself, Ma?"

"What kind of impression you gonna make on the gentleman, Alf?"

"What the hell do I care what kind of impression I'm makin'?" demanded Alf angrily. All at once, as he spoke, his eyes started from his head, and he looked hastily down at his plate, as though he were afraid of a rebuke in more than mere words.

"Alf," his father said sternly, "I wouldn't sometimes think that you was a gentleman's son. I wouldn't sometimes think the blood what you got running in your veins. That's what I say, and that's what I mean." He had laid down his knife and fork noisily as he made this declaration. Now, as he resumed them, the gentlemanly Alf buried his face in his coffee cup and sipped noisily.

He was heard to mumble, after this, that he wasn't trying to step on the toes of no strangers, nor he didn't mean no offense, neither; only pa and ma sort of nagged him on and made him forget himself.

Speedy waved the need of an apology

aside. He merely said genially: "This is good . . . never tasted better biscuits. Never in my life."

Ma Clive grinned, but she looked to her husband. That worthy rose readily to the mark. He said: "There's some that says Molly Wendell, she makes better sour-milk biscuits than Ma does, but I dunno of any that are any sight better than Ma's." He broke one of the biscuits open, as he spoke. Then, he turned to Speedy and added gravely: "The way it is nowadays, the servants are so dog-gone' poor that a gentleman, he can't set and take his ease in his own livin' room."

Alf took advantage of this stirring bit of conversation to raise his queer face from behind the coffee cup and stare long and profoundly at the stranger. He surveyed him with care, his hands, his shoulders, his wrists, his face. He studied the dimensions of his chest, and then, glancing up toward the ceiling, he drew a long breath.

There was a thought in the mind of Alf, although it might die before it ever saw the light of day.

Dinner came to an end; Speedy declined to remain for a second cup of coffee and withdrew, as he said, to study more of the history of the county.

As he left the table and passed into the next room, Mr. Clive said in a subdued voice, but with the air of a connoisseur: "A right quiet-spoken kind of a young gent. I wouldn't be surprised that he was something or other of a pretty good family. He seemed to kind of have an eye for things."

"He's ate after some good cooking, is what he's done," said Ma Clive. "I'll tell you what . . . he's ate after good cooks."

"He's ate after good cooks," agreed Pa Clive. "You could see . . . like the way that he laid into that venison steak. You see, he knew venison from beef, maybe." He nodded, pleased with himself.

"Alf," said his mother, "are you trying to break your neck or are you just lookin' at the cracks in the ceiling?"

Alf slowly raised his backward fallen head and stared straight before him. "I wouldn't've never thought it," he said.

"I didn't know that you bothered yourself thinkin' none, most of the time," said Pa Clive severely. "But lemme hear what you gotta say."

"Nobody would ever think it," said Alf.

"Think what?" asked his father.

Alf shook his head and sighed.

"Don't play the fool. Nobody would think what?" asked his gentle mother.

"Look!" said Alf. But he was pointing his hand, like a gun, at nothing.

"Look at what?" asked his father.

"You know about Speedy?" said Alf.

"Speedy? What you talkin' about? The man-eater, that they talk about?" asked Mrs. Clive.

Alf raised his great hand and presented the flat of it to her.

"Him!" he said.

"Him?" murmured Clive. "What you hushin' your ma for?"

"Whisper," said Alf.

Pa Clive whispered: "What's it all about?"

From the next room came the sound of a guitar being tuned. An old one had hung many a year from a hook on the living room wall.

"It's about him," said Alf.

"Alf, don't go and make a fool out of yourself," said his father. "What's about him?"

"Speedy!" said Alf.

"Speedy?" gasped his mother. "You mean to say . . . ?"

"Five thousand dollars is what I mean to say," said Alf.

"He's gone out of his head," the father said, his voice dying away to nothing as he leaned across the table.

"I ain't crazy," said Alf. "Do I know Charley Dupray when I see him? I do! And he was here not half an hour ago. He's still here . . . outside."

"Dupray!" Mrs. Clive cried, and rose as though she saw a ghost.

"It's all right, Ma," said Alf. "It ain't us that he'll harm. It's Speedy that he wants. And Speedy is him that's in that room, twiddlin' at a fool guitar."

VIII

Pa Clive laid hold on the sides of the table with both hands and with such force that his arms began to shake. "Who told you that was Speedy?" he asked.

"Who you think?" demanded his son in return.

"Dupray," whispered the father.

"Nobody but him," said Alf.

"Five thousand dollars," murmured the father.

"Dupray'll pay that if we help him to the scalp of Speedy," announced Alf. He passed the tip of his red tongue over his thick lips. His eyes rolled, as though he saw some delicious dish before him on the table.

Ma Clive rose up from her chair. Her voice shook and quavered and grew dim as

297

she murmured: "Pa, you ain't gonna do it. You ain't gonna sell. . . ."

"Shut your face!" hissed Pa. "Five thousand dollars! You said five thousand, Alf?"

"That's what Dupray said. And here's what he paid." He cast one furtive glance toward the door of the living room from which there now issued the first strains of "Ben Bolt", sung in a low, but very true and resonant voice, accompanied by the guitar.

"Five thousand dollars," whispered Pa Clive.

In the meantime, his son suddenly produced a sheaf of bills and, wetting his right thumb, proceeded to count them. "Here's twenty-five hundred dollars," he said. "That's the advance payment."

The long, lean claw of Pa Clive reached for the stack. "I'll take charge of that, my son," he said.

The great fist of Alf closed over the money. A deadly glare shone from his eyes. "That's mine," he said. "That was give to me, not to you."

"Alf," whined the mother as she felt the eye of her husband fall bitterly upon her, "what you talkin' about? What you thinkin' about? Ain't there any proper respect in you?"

"Say, Ma," exclaimed Alf, keeping his

savage eye still fixed upon his father, "who should I be respectin'? An old bum like that, or twenty-five hundred bucks? You can have him, if you want, but I'll have the coin." He grinned vastly, pleased with himself and his clever ideas. Then he stuffed the money back into his coat.

His father had turned gray with rage and hatred. He trembled from head to foot, and said: "You wouldn't think that Alf was no gentleman's son, but looks like he's all your child, Ma. Besides, I dunno that I'd let a thing like this take place in my own house."

His wife stared with haunted eyes at the coat pocket inside which the money had disappeared. Her own scruples had been removed by the sight of the money.

"Five thousand dollars, all in one heap, all in one family," she said, "ain't to be sneezed at. They ain't, is a fact."

"Where's that fool of an Ad?" asked Pa Clive.

"She's outside fetchin' in some wood, is all," said Mrs. Clive. "Pa, don't you go and do nothin' wild."

The host had pushed back his chair, although a rising note of the plaintive ballad that was being sung in the next room drowned out the sound.

"I gotta mind," said Pa Clive, "to go and

tell him, is what I got a mind to do."

His son swayed forward, as though ready to leap to his feet and hurl himself at his father. Instead, he lifted one huge, grimy forefinger, and merely said: "Likely Dupray is listenin' in at the window, right now, and hearin' what you got to say."

"Set down, Pa," said Mrs. Clive, perspiring profusely and wiping her wet face on the sleeve of her dress.

"I won't set down," said Pa Clive. He turned away.

With two enormous strides, his son was before him, towering, with a green devil in his eyes. "You think that you're gonna rob me out of the only decent chance that I've ever had to make a man out of myself, do you?" demanded Alf. "You think that you can rob me out of that, you damned old goat? I'll take and wring your neck for you, if you come between me and my chance!"

"Alf, Alf, for goodness' sake," whispered the mother fiercely. Yet there was a certain glitter in her own eyes as she looked from her son to her husband.

"Stand back outten my way," said the father.

"I won't," said Alf. "I've got a mind. . . ."

"Stand back," repeated the father, his voice weakening, "and lemme get at that

300

stove to fetch some coffee. Gonna try to order me around in my own house?"

Alf, hearing this excuse, stepped back, but still kept himself formidably posted between his father and the door to the living room.

Pa Clive went to the stove, picked up the blackened coffee pot, and carried it back to the table. "I dunno that I want this stuff," he said, poising the nozzle above his cup. "Ain't there no corn likker left in that there jug, Ma?"

"There wasn't no more'n a drop left to moisten my throat with it, after you and Alf took your swigs before lunch," said Ma Clive.

Her husband gave her a bitter glance. "A fine life I lead here," he declared. "A damn' fine life. But there's gonna be an end, there is." He filled his cup and carried the pot back to the stove, without offering any coffee to either of them. "There's gonna be a change, a big change," he said, slamming the pot back into place and returning to the table. His voice changed. "What's the scheme, Alf?" he muttered.

"The scheme?" said the son. "What for should I tell you, and let you blab it?"

"I was only riled a little," said the other. "It ain't for me to take away that luck that comes to my house, is it? Besides, I reckon

301

that I get the other coin, when the job's done?"

"I reckon you get it," said the son unwillingly. "I dunno why, though. A lot of help you're likely to be."

"Your pa's got a brain, when it comes to scheming things up," said his mother. "Don't you go and be too fast and ready with your tongue, Alf."

"Well," said Alf, "maybe he could be useful, if he wouldn't be shootin' off his face all the while. Maybe."

"Where are they?" asked the father, his eyes gleaming as he leered at Alf. He poured off a steaming draft of the coffee, and, poising the cup high, he went on: "Seems like I'm getting warmed up to it. That Speedy . . . if it's him . . . he ain't done nothin' but raise hell all over the map of the world. There ain't any reason why he should keep on livin'. There ain't any reason as good as five thousand dollars, I reckon. Where's Dupray?"

"Him and the rest, they're outside," said Alf. "They're waitin' for me to call 'em. That's all."

"And what's the scheme?"

"It's an easy scheme, and it's a good one. All we gotta do is just to ask him in here, after we got 'em posted. Four of 'em, and all dead shots. And outside will be one. And three inside, with me and Pa. We can do our bit of shootin', too, when the pinch comes."

Mrs. Clive grunted. "The floor will be a terrible mess," she commented.

"Ain't there soap and water and scrubbin' brushes?" demanded her spouse savagely. "Ain't there all of those things, I ask? And don't fresh blood wipe up like nothin' at all?"

She sighed. "Maybe so," she said. "Maybe so. I ain't gonna be here when the shooting comes, though."

"We don't want you," said her son. "Where's that big fool of an Ad to?"

She came in, at that moment, carrying a high-heaped load of wood. Her face was very pale. Her eyes were starting from her head, only her lids were lowered and she was looking at the floor. She put down the wood with a crash beside the stove. All three of the others jumped.

"You clumsy fool!" said Alf.

She dusted her hands, and said nothing. Still her eyes were not raised, and still the others could not see the gleam that was buried in them.

"You go on to bed," said Mrs. Clive. "I'm gonna go to bed, too. The men, they got something to talk over."

"Have they?" muttered the girl with a sneer.

"Yeah, they have, and this here is the only decent, warm room for 'em to talk in. Come on. We'll go up the back way."

The thick, wide shoulders of Ad shrugged as high as her ears, and she shuffled toward the door as the ballad singer in the next room swung into that sentimental old passage:

Oh, don't you remember sweet Alice, Ben
    Bolt,
Sweet Alice with hair. . . .

It seemed to strike the ear of Ad for the first time as she neared the door, walking behind her mistress. She stopped short and her head jerked high. For a moment, she stood there, listening with wonder and awe and a strange doubt in her face.

Mrs. Clive turned back to her. "Gonna stand there all night? Whacha thinkin' about?"

"I was thinkin' was the scraps carried out to the pigs," said Ad.

"Damn the pigs," said Mr. Clive angrily. "G'wan and get out of here."

The two women disappeared, and a moment later the song in the living room ended.

"Well," said Pa Clive, setting his teeth and turning on Alf.

"Yeah, I'm gonna go out and tell 'em that the coast is clear," said Alf. He stepped to the back door, then turned about. "You ain't gonna go and make no fool of yourself, Pa, are you?" he asked, scowling.

"You mean, tell Speedy of the plan? Is he worth five thousand dollars, or the half of what that would do to put this family back where it belongs? No, sir, he ain't. He's gonna get just what he's give to others, many a time before this day."

"Yeah, he's give it, and he's give plenty," said the son. He opened the door, paused an instant with the wind rushing into the room about his bulky figure, then stepped out into the darkness and closed the door behind him.

Pa Clive, with a shudder that might have been caused by the cold, went to the stove and extended his hands over it. He rubbed those hands busily. Then, as the warmth seemed to be penetrating into his chilled body, he lifted his head, listening to the distant roar of the wind through the big pine trees and, afterward, as it caught the house with a strong hand and shook it violently.

Usually it was a pleasure to listen to the howl of the gale, when one sat comfortably in a kitchen, with the fire burning well in the stove. But there was no pleasure of that sort tonight. Instead, it seemed as though the full power of the storm were beating against his face and stirring his heart. He turned from the stove, drew himself up to his full height, and buttoned up his coat to the neck.

He struck an attitude of such gravity as he deemed fitting to a gentleman. He put his left foot forward, with half his weight upon it. He brushed out his beard with his fingers, wiped the moisture of the coffee from his lips, and then folded his arms.

At that moment, the back door opened again, and they came in.

IX

Speedy was no longer in the living room. He had plucked at the rusted strings of the old guitar and sung his songs for a few minutes, and now he went up the stairs to his room, not taking a light with him, but using his memory only to illumine his way through the dark. Twice he had covered those stairs and the twisting hallway, but he had used every faculty, and now he could recall every foot of the way, the very look of the banisters, the width of the landing where the stairs turned, and the very height of the ceiling in the hallway above.

So he came, unerringly, to the door of his room, opened it, and, passing inside, saw the pale outline of the window in the starlight, found and lighted the lamp. Then he sat down and, drawing up the stool close to the window, he looked out at the stormy night. The wind blew from the other direction, just now, so that it did not strike against the window, and, with it open, he felt the tremor of the wind rather than its direct force. He watched the clouds tumbling across the sky. The stars were like flying sparks.

Someone knocked at his door. He called out, and in came the burly servant, Ad. Her eyes were on the floor, a glowering look was on her face as she brought in a pitcher of drinking water, placed it on the washstand, and turned to go.

Speedy stood up, and, even when her back was turned to him, he stopped her with his eye.

At the door she turned back to mutter: "Good night."

"Good night, Ad," he answered cheerfully. She had the door half open, but closed it again, as though compelled by the unexpected kindness in his voice. "A bad night for sleepin', though," said Ad, "what with this wind, I mean . . . and. . . ." She stopped herself, and hastily pushed open the door again, but Speedy was saying: "I can sleep through worse storms than this, when I'm in a house filled with honest people, Ad."

She was half out in the hall, when she turned back with a start and a grunt, like that of a horse when it has been struck by a whip. "What?" she said. "Whacha say?"

"I said honest people make safe nights," said Speedy.

She gaped at him. "Yeah, maybe," said Ad.

"But," said Speedy, "I can see in your face that there's trouble in the air."

"How can you see that in my face?" asked the girl.

"You know, Ad," said Speedy, "if one knows how, one can read thoughts in the eyes." Narrowly he watched her while he said this.

She was startled again and swung the door almost shut, but, changing her mind once more, she took a full pace inside the room and confronted him.

"You're jokin', ain't you?" she asked.

"Joking? No. Why should I be joking?"

"I mean about readin' the mind. That's a

joke, ain't it?"

"Not at all."

"You could read the thoughts in my head?" Ad asked, scowling.

"Well, not every word, Ad," he said. "But I could see pictures and begin to get a very good idea."

"You could, could you?" Ad said defiantly. She closed the door behind her, planted her fists on her wide hips, and faced him with an air of triumphant and surly defiance. "Now you go ahead and tell me what I'm thinkin' about now!" she exclaimed.

He watched the savage, brutal glare of her eyes for an instant. "You're seeing me dead, Ad," he said.

Ad's resolution and defiance were gone instantly. She shrank back against the door, cowering, as though a gun had been pointed at her. "Ah," she gasped, "how did you know that?"

He controlled the disgust and the horror that were rising in him. There was something in the air, and he could guess that she might open the door of the mystery to him.

"I know it," Speedy said gently, "because I could see the workings of the mind behind your eyes."

"I never heard nothin' like it," breathed the poor girl. "Did you read somethin' in the eyes of Alf, too, when you was settin' at the table opposite to him?"

Speedy nodded gravely.

"You did?" gasped the girl. "Whacha see in his eyes, then?" Terror and curiosity kept her gaping at him and hanging on his answer.

"I saw," said Speedy deliberately, "the gun that he was thinking of."

She caught her breath, and he knew that his second guess had reached the center of the target.

"It's spooky," muttered Ad. "I never heard of nothin' like it. Nowhere. I've heard of fortune-tellers, but they all talk about things to come, that don't never come at all. Oh, I know about 'em. But you . . . you seen the gun in the eyes of Alf?"

"Yes," Speedy replied calmly.

"How could you set there so still, then?" she asked, more amazed the longer she thought of it.

He shrugged his shoulders.

"Maybe," she said, "you didn't see who he was gonna use that gun on?"

"On me," said Speedy, stepping out under her own guidance with that stroke of guesswork.

The result was the complete collapse of Ad's nerves. She gripped at her own fat

310

throat with both hands and moaned: "D'you mean that you really know they're gonna murder you?"

His blood may have chilled as he heard her speak the word, but he showed nothing in his face. There was much more to be learned from this creature, if only he could keep on using her in the right way. One wrong guess, and her belief would be at an end.

"I know that they intend to murder me," said Speedy.

"You was talking about the honest men in the house a minute back," she exclaimed, confused and doubting.

"Because," said Speedy, "I wanted to see if you would lie to me about them. But you couldn't lie, Ad. No matter what your tongue was saying, the truth was in your eyes as clearly as in a glass."

"It kind of staggers me," said the girl. "It sure beats everything that ever I heard. But whacha gonna do? You ain't gonna just stay here, are you?"

"Why not?" said Speedy. "Why should I leave?"

"With six bloody murderers ready to kill you . . . six of 'em right here in the house?" exclaimed the girl.

"They've come a long distance to get a

311

chance at me," said Speedy. "And it's only right to let them have a few shots at their target. They'll miss, Ad."

"My land," cried the girl, "are you gonna tell me that you can read the future, too?"

"I can read part of it," said Speedy. "Not so clearly, though . . . everything in the future is dim and misty and dark."

"Yes, and I reckon that it's dark for you, the future that you're seein'," said the girl.

"Dark enough," he murmured.

"Six of 'em down there, and you here so cool and calm. So mighty cool and calm."

"You know, Ad," he said, "that a man can't escape from his fate."

"Well," she said, "I'd take a pretty good chance at it. I'd get on a hoss, if I was you, and I'd try how fast four legs could gallop me away from this here Clive's Corner!"

"Would you?" murmured Speedy. "Well, Ad, the truth is that a man has to meet the dangers that luck has stored up for him. And some of those men are dangerous enough."

"You know who they are?" asked the girl.

He actually shaded his eyes with one hand and concentrated his stare upon her.

"I can see their faces, very dimly in your eyes, Ad," he declared.

"Here? In my eyes can you see it?" de-

312

manded the girl.

"In your eyes, because they're the windows of the mind, Ad," replied Speedy. "You're seeing those faces as you speak of them, and, therefore, I can see them, too. Not as clearly as you do, of course."

"What might they look like to you?" asked the girl, gaping still wider as she heard more of this insight into the mysterious science.

"I can see the chief man of all, the one that the others look toward. He's not very tall. His shoulders are wide. He has a round face, like the face of a frog. . . ."

"The saints forgive us all!" gasped the girl. "It's enough to take and make a body religious, is what it is, to hear you talk."

"There's another man," said Speedy, "who's very tall with buck teeth and a smile on his mouth, but none in his eyes." Of course, Speedy knew if Dupray was there, Bones was reasonably sure to be with him.

"Oh, my poor heart," said the girl. "It's pretty near cracking, it's so excited. I never was so scared in my life, just seeing the spooky way that you look through things. When you look into my mind, don't you see the big greaser with the great big chin, though?"

Speedy started. Then he peered into the stupid, frightened eyes of the girl again.

Mexican? A big Mexican with a heavy chin. Then, very clearly, the image of the great Bardillo recurred to his mind. Bardillo, joined with Dupray. The world could hardly have furnished two more perfect devils to work in conjunction against him.

"Yes, of course, I see him," said Speedy. "I see his wide shoulders and his narrow hips."

"Oh, save me!" cried the girl. "It ain't to be believed. You can look inside of the minds of folks, just as easy as nothing at all. I seen you do it, and I can swear to it, now. I've seen, and I know." She broke out again: "D'you see the older Mexican with the tall man?"

Speedy could guess at that figure easily enough. If Bardillo was there, accompanied by an older Mexican, it must be none other than that grave and wise counselor of villainy, the great Marañon.

"The man with the gray beard?" Speedy pronounced calmly. "Yes, I can see his face, too, and even the purple pouches under his eyes. I see him quite clearly, now that you begin to concentrate your own seeing on his face."

Ad shook her head violently from side to side for a long moment. "I ain't one to believe no foolishness," she said solemnly,

314

"and I ain't one to pay out money on fortune-tellers. But if you was a fortune-teller, I wouldn't dare not do what you told me to do. I wouldn't dare. That's certain! But ain't you gonna do nothin' but stand there and wait for 'em to come?" she asked after a moment's silence.

"I'll do something at the right time," replied Speedy.

A footfall sounded on the floor.

"They're comin' now," moaned the girl, flying into a panic. "They'll think that I been telling you and warning you. They'll never know that you been warning yourself. Tell me what to do. Oh, they'll murder me, too!"

"I won't let 'em touch you," Speedy assured her calmly. "There's only one man coming. Get back there, so that when the door opens, you'll be behind it."

She obeyed, in terror, turning her face to the wall, and throwing up her arms against it, in order to press flatter.

A moment later, there came a soft knock on the door. Speedy, who had pulled off his boots, was sitting on the edge of the cot as the door opened and the full dignity of Pa Clive appeared against the velvet blackness of the hall.

315

X

"Hullo," said Pa Clive. "Turnin' in?"

Speedy nodded and smiled.

"Why," said Pa Clive, "we was just gonna have a taste of whiskey punch downstairs in the kitchen, and we sorter wanted to have you with us. It ain't a warm or a friendly thing to keep the guests away from the punch bowl on a night like this here." He stood smiling, a picture of benignity, rubbing and wringing his hands at the thought of the benefits that he was to bestow upon the stranger.

Speedy, considering the dignity of that hypocrite, smiled again and nodded. "I'll have my boots on again in a minute," he said, "and then I'll be down with you. Thanks a lot."

"No thanks, no thanks at all," said Pa Clive. "Wancha to be happy is all I wancha to be in this here hotel. We'll be expectin' you down right smart, then?" He paused in the door, turning sidewise, smiling and nodding at Speedy in the most inviting manner.

"I'll be with you before long," Speedy said, picking up a boot.

"That's it, that's it," said Pa Clive. "Come right on down."

He closed the door behind him, very, very

gently, and then his footfall went slowly down the hall and his voice rose in a booming bass, as he sang "Tenting Tonight."

Even the icy terror of Ad was dissolved by this. She turned to Speedy, gasping: "And them waitin' down there to murder you, and him singin' for joy because he's already countin' the murder money in his palm. Oh, what a snake and a sneak he is. You ain't gonna go down, are you?"

"I'm going down," said Speedy. "I told him that I'd be down there before long, and I'm going."

She retreated to the door. "Whacha gonna do to 'em?" she breathed, all her fears for this mysterious man dissolving as she faced the perfect calm of Speedy.

"I haven't quite made up my mind, yet," replied Speedy. "But I know that I'll have to go down. Ideas will come to me after I'm there, perhaps?"

She opened the door. "The saints be good to you," she muttered, "or the devil, because it's more like that it's him that helps the likes of you." And she went hastily off down the hallway.

Speedy moved quickly the instant the door shut after her. The window was already open, and now he stepped to it and leaned out. He could survey the side of the kitchen, in this manner, the drawn, yellow shade made brilliant by the lamp that was shining inside the room. There was no one outside that he could see.

He slipped through the window, and, hanging from the sill by his hands, he began to swing his body back and forth in a slow oscillation, whose arc became wider and wider with every movement. He had gained a sufficient impetus presently, but he waited for a few more seconds, until a fresh uproar of wind struck the house and set it trembling and rattling. Then he loosed himself and shot through the air toward the edge of the kitchen roof. In his stockinged feet he landed lightly upon it and clung there, balancing with some difficulty as the force of the wind struck against him. From the eaves, he dropped again, without sound, to the ground and stepped to the window.

There were half a dozen small rents in the shade, and through those gaps he peered until he had seen every corner of the kitchen. It was a deathtrap, well prepared for him.

Facing the door through which he was expected to enter, stood the great Charles Dupray, his hands empty, but how quickly they would both be garnished with weapons, the instant that there was need.

To his left and ready fo.
was Marañon, holding a do.
sawed-off shotgun. He alone woul.
ficient engine to sweep away half a.
lives, if men tried to crowd toward him.

At the central table was Pa Clive, with a
cup of coffee actually before him, from
which he sipped. But he sipped with the
cup held in the left hand, and in his lap was
a big Colt.

His son stood back against the wall, with
a naked revolver in his ample grasp, and the
great Bardillo was beside him. All five were
in readiness to blast the life from the body
of that kindly invited guest.

Speedy smiled faintly. But he missed the
cadaverous frame of Bones. Where could
that giant be?

Speedy stepped to the corner of the
kitchen wall and, just outside the kitchen
door, he saw his man. They had posted
Bones as the rear guard, in case Speedy
should manage to rush through the converg-
ing lines of fire and get out the doorway.

Speedy shook his head. There was a subtle
and unbelievable compliment in the impli-
cation that, in spite of the deathtrap's
completeness, they had decided that it
might be possible for him to live through it
and escape through the doorway.

iament was prepared
nst a man who had

ly posted in reach the
lk with.

ble down behind the lofty
ed behind him, and, reach-
ward, caught the butt of the
riot g... hich Bones was armed, and
quickly snat... d it away from him.

There was not a sound. Bones, wheeling
about and grasping at air, found the terrible
twin muzzles planted against his breast and
the slender form of Speedy behind them.

With his head, Speedy gestured to the
side. "Move," he said.

Bones, turning a little, stalked in the
indicated direction, across a wind-swept,
space and into the shelter of the wall of the
woodshed.

"We can talk here," said Speedy. And
Bones, halting, faced back toward the other.

"Well," said Speedy, "it was a good idea,
and pretty well worked up, but they'll have
to wait a while for me, those fellows in the
kitchen."

"How d'you find out?" demanded Bones.

"How do you think, Bones?" Speedy said.

"Some fools would say it was your mind-
reading," admitted Bones. "But I ain't a fool

of that kind. Whacha gonna do with me?"

"Mind-reading was the trick, nevertheless, Bones. Oh, it's just a trick, but it works as well as though it were a real power, most of the time. Now, Bones, I want to talk to you a little. I haven't much time . . . they may get impatient in yonder . . . but I've brought you a message."

"Yeah?" said Bones.

"This is the way of it," Speedy explained. "You have a relative in the East. A cousin. He's dying of heart disease and wondering if he'll live long enough to hear that you've been located. For you're to be his heir, Bones. His name is Littleton, and there's a lawyer named Raymond, Henry Raymond, who'll give you all the details of where you're to go and what you're to do. The law wants you, and so you'll have to move with a good deal of care. But there's a fortune waiting for you."

"Hold on," said Bones.

"I'm telling you the truth," said Speedy.

"You mean," said Bones slowly, "that you come up here and waded through this bit of hell, tonight, just for the sake of bringing me good news?"

"I'll be honest with you, Bones," Speedy stated. "It's not entirely for your own sake that I've done it. It's rather for the sake of that fellow Littleton, who's gasping his life out, waiting to get in touch with you. I'd like to know that that poor devil had some comfort before the end."

Bones made no answer.

"I'll tell you," said Speedy, "that I can't waste time talking, Bones. I've got to be on my way again. The message had to come to you. Luckily Dupray seems to have guessed that I was on my way. Raymond is a crook of the first water and must have kept in touch with him all the time. But I've found you, and you know the news. The only thing that's left is the address of Raymond in. . . ."

"I know him," Bones said in a deep, husky voice. "And I know that the whole job is a plant."

XI

"A plant? The whole job?"

"Yes, Speedy, a plant. But look here. Somehow, it kind of flabbergasts me . . . I mean, you coming up here through hellfire for the sake of bringing the yarn to me. That's what I can't get over. Maybe not so much for me, but for Littleton. What's Littleton to you?"

"Why, he's a sick man, Bones. That's all."

"He ain't even alive . . . he ain't nothing

to you, anyhow. You know what you come into . . . you know them that are in the kitchen?"

"I've just finished looking at 'em," Speedy said.

"Hand-picked, except old man Clive," said Bones. "The choice of the world, when it comes to murder and such, and you run the risk of all that, because you get your sympathies worked up for a sick man, do you?"

"Heart trouble is no joke," said Speedy.

"Neither is Dupray and Bardillo a joke," said Bones. "Why, Speedy, I aimed to cut your throat myself, is what I aimed to do."

"Who planned it?"

"I think it was mostly Bardillo's idea. I heard him and Dupray talkin' it over."

"What did they say," Speedy asked.

"The whole picture was that you'd have to be tempted into doing a job that looked dangerous," replied Bones. "And the meanest, most dangerous job that they could think of was to line you up to take a message right to Dupray. Him that would be waiting to kill you. So they picked me out, and said that I was the heir of Littleton. Then they hired Raymond, the crooked lawyer, to advertise for you, and offer rewards to anybody that would get word to you that he wanted to see you. That's all there was to the game. And it worked. What a fool you were, Speedy, to be took in that way by those skunks."

"Yes, I was," agreed Speedy, but without bitterness. "One of these days, I'll be a fool just once too often. This time I was pretty close to it."

"Speedy!" Bones suddenly exclaimed in a low voice.

He made a sudden gesture; Speedy whirled, crouching to the side as he did so. No human being could have moved more swiftly, more adroitly. But the gun butt was already suspended over the head of Speedy and crashing down. It struck him as he dodged, only a glancing stroke from the mighty hand of young Alf Clive, but, had it landed fully and squarely, it would have shattered his skull like a shell. Even as it was, it knocked him into a pit of darkness.

When he came to, he was sitting in a chair in the kitchen of the Clives, hand and foot, leg and arm, head and shoulder lashed with many weavings of small twine to the chair in which he sat.

He lifted his head and saw Pa Clive facing him.

The older man nodded and smiled on

him. "There you be, Speedy," he said. "There you be, out of the dark and back with us once more, and all of us mighty glad to look at you." He laughed as he said this, and stroked his reverend beard.

"That'll do from you," snapped Dupray.

"All right," said Clive. "I ain't one to talk out of my turn. But there's Speedy . . . many a man has hunted him . . . many a man has tried to get at him . . . and how many ever had him cornered before this? Tell me that. But my Alf, he went out and got him with his two hands, is how he went and got him."

Alf smiled and lifted those two immense hands as they were mentioned, examined them with his own eyes, and then looked proudly around the room.

"He did a mighty good job," said Dupray. "One that I won't forget."

Bardillo waved a hand impatiently toward the host. "We'd better finish off this business right away," he said.

"It's all right, Bardillo," said Speedy. "Don't be in such a hurry. I won't talk, because I know he wouldn't believe me even if I told him."

"Wouldn't believe what?" Dupray asked, scowling.

"Nothing," said Speedy. "It's all right."

"Sure it's all right," said Dupray.

"We're losing time," broke in Bardillo. "You've got him. Let's put an end to him and get on."

"What's the hurry?" asked Dupray. "He ain't done much to you, Bardillo. But he's done plenty to me. He's blocked me, checked me, and made a fool of me. And now I want to enjoy this for a minute or two. I don't want to be hurried about it. He's going to die, and I want to taste his death. I want to linger over it. It's meat and drink to me, Bardillo."

"I hate him," Bardillo said deliberately, "as much as one human being can hate another, but he's dangerous, and we had better use the good moment to put him out of the way."

Dupray did not even glance at the speaker, but feasted his eyes on Speedy.

"I gotta have my way about it," he said. "I've waited and prayed for this day to come. Now I'm going to use it. I'm going to gorge. Speedy is here in front of me . . . he's helpless. Give me time, Bardillo, because I have to have it."

XII

Bardillo seemed no more contented after the remarks of Dupray, but he prepared to submit, as to the inevitable. He merely said to Marañon: "It's a bad business. Every drop of blood in me is against it."

"But look," said Dupray. "Here he is, tied so that, even if he were a snake, he could not wriggle loose. He has no friends near him. Every one of us has a reason for getting rid of him. How could he possibly get away, Bardillo?"

"There might be twenty men closing in around the house for him," suggested Marañon.

Dupray shrugged his shoulders and smiled. "You don't know him as we do," he said. "He works alone. He plays a lone hand. Sometimes he may ride with one other man, but that's all. Bones, what happened to you out there?"

"Why," said Bones, "the idea was that I was to guard the door against anything from the inside, not the outside. I was watching the door, not the whole forest around me. And pretty soon comes a tug from behind and I turn around and my gun's in the hands of Speedy, and pointed at my chest. He fetched me off to the woodshed."

"They were talkin' plumb agreeable when I come up," put in Alf. "I dunno what the hunch was that made me turn and go out there. It was the long wait for Speedy that made me sort of think that he might be up to something, I guess. So I went out, sneakin', and seen the two of 'em beside the woodshed."

"What were you talking about, Bones?" said the chief.

He looked with a cold eye upon the big man, and Bones answered: "What would we be talkin' about, anyway? What would anybody be talkin' about that was on your trail?"

"Didn't he tell you about the sick man and the millions?" asked the other.

"Sure he did," said Bones. "But he wanted a big return for that. He seemed to think that I might have some idea where your money was cached away. That's what he was talkin' about so fast. I'm to get the Littleton coin, and I'm to tip him off where he thinks that your cache might be. Kind of weak-witted, ain't he, to think that the money would still be in the cache . . . if I knowed where it was?"

"Even if you knew," put in Speedy as though anxious to defend his reputation against this attack, "even if you knew where it is, you'd be afraid to touch it, on account of Dupray. Don't talk bigger than you are, Bones."

"I'd be afraid to touch it?" said Bones. "I gotta mind to go and bash you in the face!" He stepped closer and balled up his big fist as he spoke. A sympathetic smile appeared upon the face of Alf, for one, but Dupray raised a warning hand.

"Back up, Bones," he said. "There's plenty of time for all of that. Speedy, you started out after my cache, did you? I mean, what people call my cache. You really, think that I've got money buried away, do you?"

Speedy shrugged his shoulders. "Everybody knows that you have a fortune and a big one laid away, Dupray," he said. "There's no doubt about that. You've taken money by the hundreds of thousands, and jewels, solid gold, and all that. Now, you never spend a penny, so the stuff must be somewhere. It won't evaporate. Eh, Bardillo?"

The Mexican started. "Why do you ask me?" he said.

"All right," replied Speedy. "There's no use talking about it, I suppose. Only. . . ." He shrugged his expressive shoulders again.

"I don't follow this," remarked Dupray, frowning at Speedy, and then at Bardillo.

"Bardillo's a hard fellow to follow," admitted Speedy. "When it comes to that, he's a damned hard fellow to follow, I'd say." He smiled and nodded at Bardillo.

"I don't know what he's talking about," Bardillo declared, frowning.

"Of course, you don't," agreed Speedy. "Oh, I'm not going to try to talk about it, Bardillo. But I know the Mexican craft even better than Dupray knows it, I suppose."

Alf Clive put in: "There's some more money to be paid down. You've got your man, Dupray. I guess that I get the other half of that coin now?"

Dupray turned to Bardillo. "I've paid in my half," said Dupray. "You can pay your share now, partner."

Bardillo nodded, but he made a grimace as he did so. "Fifteen hundred dollars, eh?" he said. "That's half of three thousand."

There was a howl of protest instantly from Pa Clive. "It was five thousand!" he shouted. "Half of five is twenty-five hundred. I'll have twenty-five hundred, Bardillo."

"Will you?" said the Mexican softly and dangerously.

Dupray grinned broadly.

Pa Clive turned to the American bandit with appeal. "You know, Dupray, that it's twenty-five hundred comin' to me. I ain't

gonna be robbed. Not in my own house."
He stood up, irritated, still striving to clothe
himself with dignity, trembling with the apprehension of loss.

"Oh, it's all right," said Alf, "you'll get
enough, Pa. You didn't do nothin'. Me, I
done all the work. I got him, didn't I? I
turned him in, when he'd've got clean away.
It was me, wasn't it?" He jabbed a thumb at
his great chest as he said this and rolled his
little eyes around the room to collect ap-
plause that he felt was due him.

Dupray answered: "You did a good job,
Alf. You're going to do other jobs, and better ones, too. Better for the money that
you'll get out of 'em. I have my eye on you,
young man. I'm going to take care of your
future all right." He spoke this quietly, but
with a certain savage feeling, looking not at
Alf Clive, but at Speedy.

"Now, *Señor* Bardillo," said Pa Clive, "I
know that you ain't gonna back out of the
bargain. I know that you're gonna be a man
of your word."

"Your son has been paid," said Bardillo.
"When it comes to you, why here's fifteen
hundred, and that's enough."

The emotions of Pa Clive became so great
that he almost stifled, trying to shout out a
protest.

Speedy remarked: "Well, you ought to be a little more generous, Bardillo, considering everything. You know how much coin you'll soon have in your hands."

Bardillo scowled at the prisoner. "What money?" he said.

"Come, come," said Speedy. "I don't have to tell you that, I hope."

Bardillo laid down a small sheaf of bills upon the kitchen table. "There you are, *Señor* Clive," he said. "Not a penny more out of me. It's more than you deserve."

Pa Clive extended his hands to the entire universe, that it might take note of the injustice that was being visited upon him. "It ain't right!" he exclaimed finally. "It ain't honest. Alf, look! He's only give me fifteen hundred for my half. And I give my house to 'em for a trap. If it wasn't for my house, they wouldn't have Speedy. Alf, ain't you gonna do nothing about it? Your own father, your own flesh and blood!"

"Aw, shut up, will you?" Alf said genially.

"Yes, be quiet," commanded the great Dupray.

Old Pa Clive sadly gathered up the money and stuffed it into his coat pocket. "We've been cheated out of a thousand dollars this here day," he said. His eyes reddened as they turned upon the others. "All that I hope," he said savagely, "is that you don't have no good luck, no more . . . and that Speedy gets away, and that he cuts you up, every dog-gone' one of you. I been cheated. And a time'll come, gents, when you'll find out what it means to rob a Clive in his own house."

"That's enough out of you," said Dupray. "Fifteen hundred is too much, anyway. The other thousand, Bardillo, the other thousand can go to Alf here."

"Good!" exclaimed Alf.

"What other thousand?" demanded Bardillo, scowling blackly.

"The other thousand that goes to make up your half," Dupray explained quietly and coldly. "I've paid twenty-five hundred for my share. D'you think that your own share is going to be any less?"

"He's ridden a long way," put in Speedy.

Dupray turned to the prisoner. "You've gotta be talkin' still, don't you?" he remarked.

"It's true," said Bardillo. "I've ridden a long distance. I contributed the idea, also, that brought about his capture. You have a hundred reasons for wanting him out of the way. To me, he did only one injury. You must be just, *amigo.*"

Dupray nodded, as he listened. "I kinder

like to hear you," he said. "I kinder like to hear the way you try to slide out from under, but it won't work, Bardillo."

"It won't work, Bardillo," said Speedy. "No matter how you feel about it . . . and, of course, you're right . . . he'll make you pay."

"Make me?" said Bardillo, starting as though he had been struck.

"Come, Bardillo," Dupray said, still perfect master of himself. "You see how it is? Speedy is trying to make bad blood between us. That's his idea of a way to get free. We're to quarrel, and he comes off scotfree." He chuckled and stared at Speedy. "That's the idea, Speedy, I suppose?"

"Oh, no, Dupray," said Speedy. "Bardillo won't fight. He could stand to you, if he wanted to. He's as fast with a gun as you are, and a straighter shot, too. But he won't fight. Not yet."

"What d'you mean by that?" Dupray demanded sharply. "You talk as though you and Bardillo were in cahoots. You talk as though you knew something about him . . . you've talked that way ever since you were fetched in here."

Speedy stared at him and shrugged his shoulders.

"Go on and answer, Speedy," said Dupray.

"It won't cost you anything."

"It's no good," Speedy said. "If you're too blind to see for yourself, why should I tell you?"

"Too blind to see what?"

"Why, you old fool," exclaimed Speedy, as though his patience were exhausted, "d'you think that it's just an accident that Bardillo and I are here together? Is that a chance that's likely to happen, I ask you?"

"Now, what's he driving at, Bardillo?" asked Dupray.

"How shall I tell?" Bardillo answered, still with a clouded face because of the last words that had been spoken about him.

"Bardillo is really wonderful. Look at him, Dupray," said Speedy. "He keeps his face . . . no, not entirely. No, he begins to redden a little. But, on the whole, he keeps his face wonderfully. That's the sign of a good conscience, I suppose, in the eyes of the world."

"What are you getting red about, Bardillo?" asked Dupray.

"I?" Bardillo asked, growing hotter than ever and crimsoning to the eyes. "I ask you, what does this badgering mean, Dupray?"

"That's not so well done," Speedy said, tilting his head critically to one side. "Not nearly so well done. You shouldn't try to

335

bluster with a fellow like Dupray, Bardillo. Dupray isn't the sort to be talked out of face."

Dupray turned on Speedy. "Speedy," he said, "what the devil are you driving at with all of this?"

Speedy shrugged his shoulders and relaxed in the chair that held him. "If you're so blind that you can't see that Bardillo and I were to play the game together," he said, "why should I tell you about it?"

XIII

The wind chose this moment to leap on the house and shake it as a cat shakes a rat and the voice of the storm wailed down the chimney. A puff of smoke and ashes sifted through the cracks of the stove and hung in the air as thin clouds.

It seemed that the stroke of the wind was strangely appropriate, considering the sudden tension that had been placed upon the nerves of all the people in the room.

Even Pa Clive had stopped moaning about his losses.

"What game, Speedy?" Dupray asked in the most coaxing of voices.

"What game?" echoed Speedy. "What game d'you think? The game of getting at your hard cash, the stuff you've put away."

"There's no stuff put away," Dupray exclaimed, turning literally gray-green with excitement. "You mean that Bardillo had a deal with you to hunt."

"It's a lie," said Bardillo.

"Of course," said Speedy. "You've won, Bardillo. It was a pretty double-cross that you worked."

"Scoundrel!" shouted Bardillo, half maddened by the cunning series of lies in which he was being involved. He suited his action to his word by snatching out a revolver and covering the prisoner.

"Don't shoot," Dupray ordered.

Bardillo, turning his head, saw that the revolver of Charles Dupray was leveled on him. Big Alf had drawn a weapon, also, and Bones was turning the double muzzles of his riot gun toward the Mexican.

Only Marañon had remained cool and collected. He spoke now almost for the first time. "Friends," he said in a voice so calm that it was almost dull and lifeless, "we are not all children. It's simple enough . . . what is in the mind of *Señor* Speedy. He is cornered. He has no hope. Therefore, he tries to make great and sudden trouble between old friends. *Señor* Dupray, you will believe me, if you think for a minute."

"Of course, I'll believe you," said Dupray. "Of course, we're friends . . . only, I want to hear a little more from Speedy before he gets what's coming to him."

"Don't ask me," said Speedy. "I've talked too much already. I never hoped to convince you, Dupray. You're too bull-headed. You've made up your mind that this Bardillo will play fair with you, and nothing that I could say would ever change you."

Dupray wagged his frog face slowly from side to side. "What would you try to convince me of, Speedy?" he asked.

"I'm through arguing. I never wanted to argue from the first," Speedy replied. "You've got me, Dupray. Go ahead and finish me, or let Bardillo do the trick. He's anxious enough to, for fear I should talk some more about him."

"Dupray," gasped Bardillo, "I must kill him. I cannot stand here and listen. My breath leaves me. I choke."

"Sure. And so do I," Dupray said. "He's going to die, and he knows it. But before we bump him off, let him talk a little. Put up the gun, Bardillo, will you?"

Bardillo, after a moment of silent struggle with himself, put away the weapon and turned his back sharply upon the others. He muttered something about being unable

338

to watch.

Speedy remarked: "That's a good stroke, Bardillo. If you can't keep your face, it's always better for a fellow to turn his back."

"What's that about a double-cross that Bardillo has worked on you?" demanded Dupray.

"Why," Speedy said, "I suppose he thought that it would be better to keep all the money in his own hands. Marañon, there, would never ask for a full share. He's simply an old retainer. When Bardillo gets his chance to work the game that he knows so well how to work . . . why, he won't need my help. It was only to get you flattened in the first place that made him suggest the deal to me."

"Are you going to listen to that barking dog?" exclaimed Bardillo, but still without turning to face them.

"Yeah, I'm going to listen," said Dupray. "It's sort of amusing to hear him lie, eh? Go on, Speedy."

"Oh, go to the devil," Speedy said, apparently growing weary. "Why should I talk to you? I only wish him all the more luck. I hope, when he has you stretched out, that he takes off your skin an inch at a time and burns it in front of your face."

"Thanks," said Dupray.

"That will make you talk fast enough," Speedy continued.

"Talk about what?" asked Dupray.

"Why, what do you suppose? About the place where you've hidden your stuff."

"I was to be caught and flayed alive till I told where I'm supposed to have cached my savings, eh?" Dupray murmured. "That's it, is it?"

"Ten thousand devils!" exclaimed the Mexican, whirling at last.

"It hurts when your ideas are put out in plain view like that, Bardillo, doesn't it?" Speedy stated cheerfully. "But tell me, old fellow, why you didn't go through with the original scheme with me? We could have worked it, easily enough. I was ready. You were ready. Dupray was suspecting nothing. He only thought that the hunt was for me . . . he never dreamed that he was the choice."

Dupray lowered his head and thrust it forward as he stared at Bardillo. "That's it, Bardillo," he said. "Why didn't you go through with the first idea, the main idea?"

Bardillo caught a breath. "Dupray," he pleaded, "is it possible that you'll believe this devil?"

"I don't know," Dupray answered. "I'm just thinking about it."

"You ought to keep your back to us," said Speedy. "Your face shows too much, and Dupray isn't blind."

In fact, the face of Bardillo was crimson and pale in blotches, so wildly had his temper risen. But the contorted features might have been the expression of any one of half a dozen evil emotions.

"It's not so pretty," Dupray said. "Damn it, Bardillo, I'm thinking that there's something in what Speedy says."

Marañon broke in: "Gentlemen, you're not going to be foolish? You're not going to be talked into trouble that will give Speedy his chance? Finish him now . . . this minute! Then, you'll see that his lies are as thin as air."

"Of course," Speedy said, nodding and perfectly at ease. "Finish me off, and then I won't be able to show you what they're made of, Dupray. It's a pretty Mexican game that they've been playing."

"Bardillo!" exclaimed Dupray.

Bardillo did not answer. His heavy lower jaw was beginning to thrust forward slowly.

"Bardillo," said Dupray, "I have more than half an idea that Speedy has told me the truth."

"Have you?" Bardillo hissed through his teeth.

"Turn your back, Bardillo," urged Speedy. "You're losing control of your face altogether. Turn your back and talk over your shoulder, you double-crossing cur. If you'd gone through with the first plan, we could have been rich, all of us. We could have roasted the information out of Dupray. But I'd rather die and rot than have worked with you as a partner, now that I see what you are."

As this speech burst from him, the hand of Bardillo flashed again for a gun. There would be no stopping him this time, and Dupray merely cried out in a high, barking voice: "Take it, then!" And snapped out his own gun.

Bones, with a shout at the same moment, leveled his gun, but he tripped in making a step forward; both barrels of the heavy riot gun roared in the air, and, as the revolvers began to boom, the explosions blew out the light of the lamp. The flame leaped twice in the chimney and died like a ghost.

Someone shrieked; bodies fell heavily. Men cursed. The red tongue of fire licked and darted like the red of blood from the muzzles of the guns.

Speedy found himself picked up, chair and all, and carried swiftly forward. A door crashed open under the weight of that charge, and, looking up by the dim light of the smoking lamp in the parlor, he saw that Bones was carrying him.

He was thrown down, helpless, to the floor. Then two slashes with a knife freed him; the great hands of Bones jerked him to his feet, and the voice of Bones was gasping: "Now, get out of it! I gotta go with you. My name's mud with Dupray, after this."

"Get out of it? No, no, I'll get back into it," said Speedy. "I'll thank you later, Bones." He turned toward the kitchen door, as he spoke.

Feet trampled furiously across the floor of the room; one voice was monotonously screaming on one note; the back door slammed. From the upper part of the house the voices of the women began, pitched high and small with the distance.

"It's too late for the best part of the fun," said Speedy, changing his mind.

He went back deliberately and picked up the lamp from the table. "We'll have a little look inside," he said.

Bones, amazed, agape, followed him like a child, a vastly overgrown child. He merely muttered: "It's a bad chance to take, Speedy. There's no good will come out of it."

"Maybe not," Speedy replied. "But I've got to see who's down and who's up." He carried the lamp to the door, and, holding it high above his head, he let the light stream into the kitchen. What he saw was the last of a wild confusion.

The table was down. Broken chairs littered the floor. The rear door had been kicked open and still hung upon one hinge. In the far corner lay big Bardillo, crumpled against the wall, with Marañon kneeling beside his chief. Old Pa Clive, his hands stretched above his head, was still screeching like a madman. He ran blindly, staggering, toward the light.

XIV

Pa Clive ran on as Speedy drew back from before his blind charge. He collided with the farther door, in his effort to get into the hall; he tore the door open; he dashed out and up the stairs, and all the while that meaningless yelling was dinning through the air.

Then Speedy advanced into the kitchen, Bones with him. The lamp was placed on the table, and Bones relighted the lamp that had been put out when the riot gun was accidentally discharged from his hands.

The great Bardillo was not the only man who had been wounded. Other bloodstains led toward the door. But Bardillo was dying from a dreadful wound in the breast, and he kept one hand vainly covering the place, while the blood streamed out. He retained his perfect calm. Recognition was in his eye as Speedy stood before him, saying: "What can I do, Bardillo?"

"There was a flask of whiskey on the table," said Bardillo. "It's fallen somewhere on the floor now. If it's not broken, I'd like to have a swallow of the stuff."

"Certainly," said Speedy.

Bones had already found the flask, unbroken, and was bringing it. He uncorked and placed it at the lips of the dying man, who took a deep swallow.

Then he closed his eyes for a moment, breathing rapidly. The bleeding increased perceptibly at the same time.

"We can make him more comfortable, Marañon," said Speedy.

Marañon turned a face that was pale with hatred toward Speedy, and said nothing.

"I'm very well where I am," answered Bardillo. "I've only a minute or two before the light goes out for me. Don't move me. Marañon, I'm sorry to be leaving you, but I've had all I could ask for out of living."

Marañon grasped in both of his the hand that his master reached toward him.

Bardillo looked toward Speedy. "Tell me," he said, "how you knew that Marañon and I were hoping to get at the money that Dupray has hidden?"

"Everybody who comes near Dupray hopes the same thing," said Speedy. "That's not a novelty. I linked you up with me, in the lies I told him, so that he'd come closer to losing his temper. Finally he lost it. But I'm not so happy to see you lying here, Bardillo, as I would be to see him. I'm sorry for you. I've an idea that I've done you a good deal more harm than you've ever done me."

Bardillo smiled. His eyes dimmed. "I would have cut out your heart and carved it for dinner," he said, "with the greatest pleasure in the world. Don't speak of being sorry. Dupray turned on me, as I would have turned on him. There's nothing to regret, except that I got what I would have given to others . . . what I've given to others a good many times before this. Still, I must talk with you, Speedy."

"I will listen to you, Bardillo," Speedy said, "with all my heart. I tell you again, I'm sorry that this had to happen."

"I know that you're sorry," said Bardillo. "I've loved blood for its own sake all of my days, but danger is the thing that you've hunted. Murder has never been your way.

346

You've made Dupray a tool to kill me, and you've made me a tool to wound Dupray. I think he may die of that wound, too. I don't know, but I pray that he may. Hell would be an empty place for me, unless I could find Dupray there when I arrive. Speedy, I want to talk to you about yourself."

"Go ahead," said Speedy. He drew closer and dropped on one knee.

Once again Marañon turned a look of hate toward the young American. Bardillo saw it and murmured: "Don't hate him, Marañon. He was beyond my reach, and, therefore, he'll be a thousand light years beyond yours. Let him go his way. It's not for the wolves and the coyotes to bother the mountain lions, Marañon. Leave Speedy alone. Go back to El Rey. You can keep a few of the men together who used to follow me. Keep them until you've gathered as much of the money as you can. Then sell everything. You know where it is all kept. Sell out. Go to France. Go to the Riviera. You'll be safer there than in Spain. Stolen money keeps half the people who live there already. You'll be welcome among 'em. Settle down. Let me think of you as living in some old castle, surrounded with comfort, drinking my health, while I burn in the fire and cultivate a long, long thirst. And now, Speedy."

He turned his head toward the American, who leaned still closer, so as to catch every whisper.

Bones, also, fascinated by this mysterious scene that was like a reconciliation, leaned closer, also, gaping horribly above them.

"Speedy," said the dying man, "I've wasted too much time. I'm going faster than I thought. But I want to give you my last warning. You've come to the end of your tether. You've ridden your last chase, and hunted down your last man. Let the devil burn colder in you, Speedy, or soon there'll be nothing left to burn. Your luck has been as wonderful as you are. But now, I warn you. I can see it with the eye of my mind. I can feel it with my blood and bones. Be careful. Leave the man trail, Speedy. Settle down quietly, if you can. Find a wife. Leave. . . ." He choked. His head jeered back. A tremor went through his body.

"*¡Señor!*" cried Marañon suddenly in a shockingly loud voice.

"Hush, Marañon," said Speedy. "He cannot hear you." He reached forward with delicate fingertips, and drew down the eyelids of Bardillo over eyes that were still bright in death. Then he stood up, but Marañon had flung himself down on the bloody

348

floor beside his master and lay shuddering there.

Speedy beckoned to Bones, and the pair of them went quietly out into the night.

"That old Marañon," muttered Bones, "he seemed to sorter like Bardillo, after all. But it beats me, Speedy. Why would Bardillo want to give you a warning like that . . . just to throw a bluff? He can't know anything real, and he just wants to throw a chill into you?"

"Not that," Speedy said. "He was talking out of the bottom of his heart. They say that men can see through clouds and time, when they come close to death. And Bardillo was seeing something about me. Perhaps about Marañon, also." Speedy laid a hand on Bones. "I've been close to death before," he said, "but never as close as this. And you got me out of it."

"No," said Bones, "you talked yourself out. I just loaned a hand at the finish. But you'd done the main work all before. If I'd been any kind of a man, I'd've stopped big Alf when he knocked you down and started draggin' you back to the house. But I'll tell you how it was . . . I didn't exactly realize then what sort of a gent you was, Speedy, and how you was giving my life back to me and trying to tell me news that was good

349

for me, at the very time that I was layin' low to murder you."

Speedy felt the tremor that ran through the body of the man beside him, and Bones went on: "It wasn't till you sat there in the kitchen, with the wolves all gathered around you, settin' on their haunches, their eyes shining at you, they was so hungry for your blood . . . it wasn't till just then, that I looked and seen the kind of a man that you was. All man, all steel, and nothin' weak about you. When you talked, I didn't realize, for a long time, what you was up to, and how you was laying Dupray ag'in' Bardillo. I didn't, till just before the gun play begun. When I realized it, I said to myself that brains like you had couldn't be put out with bullets. A second later the guns were roaring, and I grabbed you and carried you out. That was all. I just seen, in a flash, that it wasn't the right time for a man like you to die."

He ended this speech very simply, but a sort of wonder had come over Speedy.

After a moment, he said: "Let's get farther away from the place. A lot farther away. I can't stand the noise that the women are making."

They moved on toward the barn.

"Does it seem to you," asked Speedy,

"that the game's worthwhile, Bones?"

"What game? The crooked game?"

"Yes."

"I dunno," answered Bones. "It's the only thing that I pretty near ever turned my hand to."

"What was it that started you?" asked Speedy.

"Oh, I was a kid, fifteen or so. And I thought that I was smart enough to play crooked cards, and I got called in the middle of a deal. So I tried a gun play, and I dropped the wise guy, all right. I thought I'd killed him and rode for it, got away, and before I heard that he wasn't dead, I'd done too much ever to go back inside the law ag'in."

Speedy nodded in the darkness. "How do you feel about it . . . the crooked game, Bones?"

"Why," replied Bones, "it ain't any shame for me to tell you the truth, Speedy. I'll tell you that I feel kinder sick and cold around the heart most of the time, when I think of what's to come. But I don't let myself think much. Not a dog-gone' lot, anyways."

"Suppose you chuck it, Bones?" said Speedy.

"Chuck it?" said Bones. "What else would I do? Where'd I go? No decent man would

351

have nothin' to do with me."

"Do you know where John Wilson lives?" asked Speedy.

"Sure I know! Didn't the whole gang of us try to get you there?"

"Then go back to Wilson," Speedy advised. "Tell him that I sent you, will you? Tell him that he's to put you up for a while, and he'll do that."

"I would've cut his throat, once," said Bones.

"That makes no difference," said Speedy. "He'll do what I ask him to do. Will you go there? I'll come back when I can. And then we'll try to arrange something for you. Any man who's sick of a wrong life ought to have a chance to lead a right one."

"What'll become of you? Where are you going now?" asked Bones.

"Dupray," said Speedy. "I've made a vow in my heart to get him, this time, and get him I shall, if I have to spend my life on the trail."

"Hold on," murmured Bones.

"Well?"

"Ain't you forgetting," said Bones, "the last thing that Bardillo said to you?"

"I'm not forgetting," replied Speedy solemnly.

"He said," went on Bones, "that you were

at the end of your rope. He said it almost like he had a way of knowing."

"Perhaps he knew," agreed Speedy. "I can tell that. But the fact is that I have to take the trail myself."

"Well," said Bones, "I know that if Bardillo couldn't budge you, I can't say nothing that will."

"I've got to go," said Speedy. "There was never a devil in the world that's worked as much mischief as Dupray. He'll do it again, too. I can't leave his trail. It may be the end for me, or for him, or for both of us."

Bones sighed. Then he said: "What can I do? You won't take me with you on the trail, Speedy?"

"No," answered Speedy. "I can't do that. You were his man. You worked under him."

"That's true," answered Bones. "I'm best pleased to be away from the business. But I'm wishing you luck."

XV

The sun was out of the zenith and beginning to go westerly, and the heavy shadows of the pine trees were growing longer when Alf Clive rode up the trail with a rifle balanced before him, the mustang between his legs looking hardly larger than a big dog, such was the bulk of the rider. When he came to the top of the hill, he turned the head of the mustang and looked back across the heads of the trees toward the rolling ground beyond. Then he shrugged his broad shoulders and made a gesture of surrender with one hand.

"Hello, Alf," said a voice behind him.

"Speedy!" cried Alf. He whirled in the saddle and raised his rifle. But it was some seconds after this that he saw the other behind the thick, high shrubbery along the road. Behind the man he could gradually make out the silhouette of a horse.

He was half a mind to send a bullet at the two figures, but second thought bewildered him, because it was plain that, if there had been mischief in the mind of Speedy, he had had plenty of time to shoot his quarry full of holes.

So Alf delayed the bullet and, while he was in the quandary, Speedy calmly led his horse out onto the road and mounted it.

"How are things with you, Alf?" he asked.

"What brung you here, and whacha want with me?" asked Alf sharply, adding: "I got you covered, Speedy, and don't you try none of your dog-gone' tricks, neither." He tried to speak as fiercely as possible, but there was a great awe in his voice and face as he considered the other.

"Why, Alf," said Speedy, "I have nothing against you."

"Me that nearly got you murdered?" said Alf. "You ain't got nothing ag'in' me?"

"Not a thing," Speedy said. "It wasn't you that nearly got me murdered. It was the five thousand dollars that Dupray and Bardillo offered. That was all. You did your job to get the money, and you did it very well, too. You got the money and that ends the business, so far as you and I are concerned. I have a bump on the head for change . . . that's all."

"You're jokin'," declared Alf.

"I mean what I say," answered Speedy. "I have nothing against you, and I'm not on your trail."

Alf drew a great breath. "They say that your word's better than anybody else's oath," he remarked.

"You can trust it now," said Speedy.

"Who you after, then?"

"Dupray."

"I was with him, and he up and left me," said Alf. "Went off, and said he'd be back. I've waited half a day, and he ain't come. He slipped away, after I'd been pretty useful to him, too. I was gonna work for him, but I ain't gonna be treated like a hound

355

dog by no man, not even a Dupray."

"That's the right spirit," said Speedy. "You lost him where?"

The eyes of the big fellow narrowed, but suddenly he broke out: "Well, why shouldn't I tell you? He done me dirt, runnin' off like that. And you could've popped me full of lead from behind that bush, yonder. Well . . . I left him back yonder, where the woods peg out, and there's only a few big trees dotted around on the hills. Back there is where I left him. How'd you manage to trail us this far?"

"I used my eyes, and guessed a little now and then," Speedy answered.

"Used your eyes?" murmured the other. "But look here, Speedy, it's three whole days that we been riding."

"That's true."

"We laid about a hundred trail problems that would've puzzled the devil himself. But . . . well, that was what Dupray said, that you'd find the way through in spite of anything that we did. You got me beat, Speedy."

"Not at all, Alf," replied Speedy. "I simply kept on casting ahead, and I had luck in finding the trail again."

"Luck don't come a hundred times in a row," Alf said, shaking his head and staring with a brutal wonder and envy. "I wish I knew how you done it." He added suddenly: "How's things back there at home?"

"Not very good for you, Alf," said Speedy. "If I were you, I'd keep away from your father and mother, for a time. They seem to blame you for getting the twenty-five hundred, while they collected only fifteen hundred. I think your father and mother don't deny that you may have had something to do with the killing of Bardillo."

"I didn't do no shooting at Bardillo," Alf stated. "I was only shooting . . . in the dark . . . at . . . at. . . ."

"At me," Speedy said, smiling a little.

"Well," blurted out Alf. "I was scared what you might do to me, if you got away. You guessed that even in the dark, did you? You knew that I was shootin' at you?"

Speedy passed over the absurd question easily. "I found blood here and there, Alf, along the trail. Was Dupray badly hurt?"

"Yeah, in the body, somewheres," said Alf. "I dunno just where. He didn't ask me for no help. He didn't say as it was hurting him much, neither. He just rode along and kept his mouth shut."

"He has courage," Speedy said, nodding his head. "But how did he look?"

"Why, just the same kind of frozen frog

face that he always has," said Alf.

"Ate well?"

"He didn't eat much. He don't never eat much."

"Hold up through each day's riding?"

"He held up, all right. He's an Injun. He never gets tired on the back of a horse. Only this morning, he laid in his blankets kind of late. He didn't want no breakfast but coffee, and he went off finally, and told me he'd ride back in an hour. He didn't come. He went and give me the slip."

"Thanks," said Speedy. "That's all I want to know."

"And what do you make out of that, Speedy?" asked Alf.

"Nothing, except what I guess," answered Speedy.

"What's that?"

"Why," answered Speedy, "that, if I were you, I'd put that twenty-five hundred dollars in some good ranch, take a mortgage on the rest, and try to settle down."

"Hey!" exclaimed Alf. "You can read minds, can't you? How'd you know I was thinkin' of that?"

"Only a guess," replied Speedy.

"When I seen you and Dupray and Bardillo at one another," said Alf, "though you was only usin' words, I begun to see that I

358

could never rise to the top in that kind of a game. I'm just as glad that Dupray turned me off. So long, Speedy."

"So long," Speedy replied, and rode his horse down the slope up which Alf had just come.

XVI

He rode on for two hours into the midst of that rolling country, tree-dotted, beyond the edge of the woods, which he found exactly as Alf had described it.

There he camped. It was almost useless for him to search in detail, because the whole face of the country was covered with grass two and three feet high, and there were thickets here and there sufficient to have hidden regiments.

But there he camped, and ate hardtack, drank from the canteen, and watched the sky from time to time with the patience of an Indian, who is quiet because Nature is a book in which he is reading.

So Speedy was reading, and in the evening he noted with much interest two or three buzzards up in the zenith.

That night he slept long and awoke in the rose of the morning. His face was wet with dew. He went down the hill to a brook, undressed, bathed, rubbed himself dry, dressed again, shaved, returned to his camp, and ventured on a very small fire to make coffee. That and a bit of hardtack out of his saddlebag were his only food. For food bothered him on the march hardly more than it bothers a migrating bird.

At length, he resumed his survey of the skies.

There were more buzzards, now, and they were circling quite a bit lower down, above one particular hill, he thought, more than the others.

He waited until the sun was at 9 a.m. More and more buzzards were flying now in their grim circles, a dozen birds in all, the lowest of them very near to the ground.

Then he started, rode straight across country, abandoned the horse at the bottom of the hill that the birds seemed to have selected, and went up through the grass as noiselessly as a snake.

The grass cleared away a little toward the top of the hill, for here stood three immense trees, left from the primeval forest. Speedy did not know their names, but their heads were as rounded as the heads of beech trees.

Here the cattle that grazed on the range took shelter from the sun about noon, and the grass was eaten down gradually until the top of the hill was quite bald.

As Speedy emerged from the tall grass, facing the three great trees, he noticed that half of the middle one had fallen. The remnants of the vast log were stretched along the ground in a mound of decay with the grass already closing over it. The great, broad stump of the ruined trunk rose a dozen feet from the ground.

It was beyond this tree that a horse was grazing and, seated on the ground with his back against the stump and just his shoulder visible was Dupray. As his head turned, Speedy saw enough to recognize that unforgettable mask of a face.

He left the screen of grass and stole forward. That horse, yonder, might warn his master. If Dupray turned — well, Speedy, as usual, carried no gun.

So he stepped on the ground as a shadow falls, smoothly drifting forward. He saw a buzzard sail down to the ground and light on the fallen log, its horrible, naked red head thrust out. It peered at Dupray, whose weary voice said: "Not yet, sister. Not yet!"

Speedy stepped around the side of the great tree trunk and, with a flick of his toe, kicked away the gun belt that Dupray had unbuckled and laid to the side.

Dupray looked up and scrutinized his face

with eyes that turned green with hate.

"I knew you'd come, Speedy," he remarked in the calmest of voices.

"I had to come, Charley," replied Speedy. "This had to be the last trail, either for you or for me. It seems that it will be the last one for you, though."

Dupray regarded him silently for a moment, utter devastation stirring slowly in his face. Then he said: "You win, Speedy. You won from the first fall of the cards. And to think that I've had you spread out, helpless, tied. All you needed was one push of a knife. To think that I had you like that."

"Nothing but luck. You can't beat such luck, Charley," said Speedy.

"Not luck, but your damned brain, like the brain of a rat and a fox rolled together."

"Don't be too rough, Charley," pleaded Speedy. "No matter what you feel about me, you might remember that I'm the friend of Al."

"The damned cur," said the robber. "He's throwed me over, his own flesh and blood, to herd with you."

"Rough talk, brother, rough talk," commented Speedy. "But tell me why you picked out this spot to come and die in."

"How did you find me?" asked Dupray with a snarl.

"I watched the buzzards gather. When Alf told me that you'd lain late in the blankets this morning, I could guess that the wound was making you pretty sick."

"Reading the minds of birds now, are you?" asked Dupray.

"I'd rather read your mind, man," replied Speedy. "I'd rather find out why you've come here to die."

"I come as far as I could crawl," said the other. "That's all. Speedy, if you're a decent man, you'll scratch a hole and bury me away from the buzzards."

"This is the heart of your range, partner," Speedy commented. "Oh, I'll bury you, well enough. Don't worry."

"Just hoist me up . . . it's no great trick, if you get me onto a horse first. Then dump me down inside the hollow of that trunk, there."

"How d'you know it's hollow?" asked Speedy.

"How? Why, they're always hollow when they've stood as long as that," answered Dupray.

"Not always. Not by a long shot," replied Speedy. "You have been here before, Dupray. Wanting to die in that hollow stump like a sick owl . . . is it because you've got your stuff cached inside . . . the gold, the

363

diamonds, and the sheafs of hard cash, Dupray? Is that the place?"

Dupray looked at him and smiled. "D'you think I'm fool enough to use that sort of a hiding place, when I've got every hole in the mountains to use if I want it?"

Speedy nodded. "Why not?" he asked. "The cattle tramp around here . . . they'd cover up the sign you'd make in coming and going. Not many people would suspect you of hiding it away in an open hole like that. Yet a good wrapping with a tarpaulin would be enough to see it through the weather."

Dupray suddenly choked. His mouth opened. He bit at the air like a dog in agony. The spasm passed, and, with his head hanging over on his shoulder and his body slumped down to the ground, he gasped: "Speedy!"

The tramp leaned over him. "Dupray," he said solemnly, "I thought I hated you like a snake, but I can't help being sorry for you when I see you here. If you've got any word to leave for Al, tell me, and I'll surely carry it to him."

"Yes . . . for Al . . . closer," said the dying man.

Speedy dropped to one knee and put his ear close to the lips of Dupray. "What is it, Charley? Louder."

"This," Dupray said, and suddenly struck upward with a long-bladed hunting knife that he had managed to get into his hand from the inside of his coat. He could have driven it straight through the heart of Speedy, but savage venom made him try for the throat, and, in his blindness, the crook of his arm struck under the elbow of Speedy.

The blow had failed, and Speedy was away like a shadow.

"Damn you!" breathed Dupray. "I'll get you yet and. . . ." In his frenzy he got to his feet, scooped up a revolver from the fallen belt, and fired. His bullet went wild, hitting the ground, as he pitched forward on his face. He was dead when Speedy reached him. Like a wild beast, he had used his death agony to maintain the fight.

In the deep pit of the hollow tree trunk, as he had requested, Dupray was buried, wrapped in thick folds of tarpaulins that Speedy had found inside and that covered many securely wrapped parcels, exactly as he had imagined. But the contents of those parcels now filled the saddlebags of two horses, and made, in addition, a staggeringly heavy pack that he lashed over the saddles. The money and the jewels were the main items, but the weight of the burden was the massive gold, the gold that Dupray had loved to fondle and stroke like a cat beside a family hearth.

Then Speedy took his way down the slope. The evening was coming on, for he had been long in the hollow of the trunk. A fortune for a dozen men was weighting down the horses he led, but there was no content in his mind. It was blood money, won by crime, hoarded for no good end. To him, it would be of no use.

There must be another trail, still, beyond this, perhaps another beyond that, always another, to the end of his days. And those days, according to the dying Bardillo, would not be long. But somber moods could not last long with him. Plucking at his small guitar, he began to sing as he led the horses over the next hill and straight into the gold and crimson of the west.

ABOUT THE AUTHOR

Max Brand® is the best-known pen name of Frederick Faust, creator of Dr. Kildare, Destry, and many other fictional characters popular with readers and viewers worldwide. Faust wrote for a variety of audiences in many genres. His enormous output, totaling approximately 30,000,000 words or the equivalent of 530 ordinary books, covered nearly every field: crime, fantasy, historical romance, espionage, Westerns, science fiction, adventure, animal stories, love, war, and fashionable society, big business and big medicine. Eighty motion pictures have been based on his work along with many radio and television programs. For good measure he also published four volumes of poetry. Perhaps no other author has reached more people in more different ways.

Born in Seattle in 1892, orphaned early, Faust grew up in the rural San Joaquin Valley of California. At Berkeley he became a student rebel and one-man literary movement, contributing prodigiously to all campus publications. Denied a degree because of unconventional conduct, he embarked on a series of adventures culminating in New York City where, after a period of near starvation, he received simultaneous recognition as a serious poet and successful author of fiction. Later, he traveled widely, making his home in New York, then in Florence, and finally in Los Angeles.

Once the United States entered the Second World War, Faust abandoned his lucrative writing career and his work as a screenwriter to serve as a war correspondent with the infantry in Italy, despite his fifty-one years and a bad heart. He was killed during a night attack on a hilltop village held by the German army. New books based on magazine serials or unpublished manuscripts or restored versions continue to appear so that, alive or dead, he has averaged a new book every four months for seventy-five years. Beyond this, some work by him is newly reprinted every week of every year in one or another format somewhere in the world. A great deal more about this author and his work can be found in *The Max Brand Companion* (Greenwood Press, 1997) edited by Jon Tuska and Vicki Piekarski.

The employees of Thorndike Press hope you have enjoyed this Large Print book. All our Thorndike, Wheeler, and Kennebec Large Print titles are designed for easy reading, and all our books are made to last. Other Thorndike Press Large Print books are available at your library, through selected bookstores, or directly from us.

For information about titles, please call:
(800) 223-1244

or visit our Web site at:
http://gale.cengage.com/thorndike

To share your comments, please write:
Publisher
Thorndike Press
10 Water St., Suite 310
Waterville, ME 04901